3 9082

MW00873469

Presented to the

In honor of

Lily B. May

by

Chris & Dianne May

The Fire Dragon Storm

Anne Cameron

GREENWILLOW BOOKS
An Imprint of HarperCollins*Publishers*

This book is a work of fiction. References to real people, events, establishments, organizations, or locales are intended only to provide a sense of authenticity, and are used to advance the fictional narrative. All other characters, and all incidents and dialogue, are drawn from the author's imagination and are not to be construed as real.

 Printed in the United States of America. For information address HarperCollins Children's Books, a division of HarperCollins Publishers, 195 Broadway, New York, NY 10007.
www.harpercollinschildrens.com

Black-and-white illustrations by Victoria Jamieson

The text of this book is set in 12-point Times New Roman.
Book design by Paul Zakris

Library of Congress Cataloging-in-Publication Data is available.
Cameron, Anne.
The fire dragon storm / by Anne Cameron.
pages cm.—(Lightning catcher ; [4])

ISBN 978-0-06-211286-6 (hardback)

16 17 18 19 CG/RRDH 10 9 8 7 6 5 4 3 2 1
First Edition

To Michael and Catherine.

And to Paul, for the floodles.

PROLOGUE

ANGUS McFANGUS RIP

If you are a regular reader of the *Weekly Weathervane*, you will know that any article the magazine prints with a large red warning symbol should only be read with extreme caution, while wearing a pair of flame-retardant gloves. You will also know that any features in the most recent edition, concerning a dreadful tragedy at the Canadian Exploratorium for Extremely Chilly Weather, should be hidden away inside a locked drawer, along with the *Weathervane*'s dangerous recipes for spicy chicken custard, and only read by a fully qualified lightning catcher.

Reports of the calamity at the Canadian Exploratorium

had reached one lightning catcher, Principal Delphinia Dark-Angel, several days before the article had appeared. But she studied the *Weekly Weathervane* now, as she sat at a table in the Frog's Bottom Bakery.

Glacier Cave Collapse Causes Chaos in Canada
A series of ancient glacier caves, discovered over fifty years ago in a rare blue-ice glacier, have collapsed without warning. The caves, situated close to the Canadian Exploratorium, had recently passed a series of rigorous pickax safety checks and meltwater tests and were being used at the time for emergency cold weather survival training.

Delphinia Dark-Angel stared at the dreadful pictures that accompanied the article. A deep open wound snaked its way through the glacier, showing where the caves had once stood. The chasm was now filled instead with enormous slabs of cracked ice that looked thick enough to slice through solid rock. The line underneath the photos, however, contained the most alarming news of all.

▲ ▲ ▲

Three second-year lightning cubs, who were visiting the Exploratorium during their Christmas break, were tragically killed in the incident. Their identities have since been confirmed as Angus McFangus, Dougal Dewsnap, and Indigo Midnight.

Dark-Angel sighed heavily inside the long black coat she was wearing, feeling a sudden flare of anger. All her careful plans for the McFangus boy had now come to nothing. Every hour she'd spent arranging his future, every effort she'd made to ensure that he was being steered along the correct path, had been a total waste of her valuable time. He had carelessly lost his life on a ridiculous jaunt through the hollowed-out entrails of a dangerous glacier, and now, the future looked very grim indeed.

She snapped the magazine shut, pulled her hood down over her closely cropped white hair—hiding a mole on her left cheek—and hurried out the door of the bakery. She headed straight across the cobbled square toward Crevice and Sons, the fine-bone merchants, thankful that the day was dull and miserable and the square almost deserted.

The shop did nothing to lift her spirits. Dank and dreary,

it was filled with jars of powdered bone and an assortment of rare animal skeletons. The smell of ancient dust made her nostrils tingle unpleasantly as she finally reached the shop counter. Mr. Crevice, one of the owners, stood behind it. White haired and skeletonlike, he was waiting for her with a sour expression on his sunken face.

"Mr. Crevice," Dark-Angel began tartly. "I have warned you repeatedly not to call me into your shop during daylight hours. It is far too risky. If anyone from Perilous should see us talking . . ."

"This won't take long," Crevice said in a curt manner. "Dankhart wants to know if the story about the Canadian Exploratorium is true." He nodded toward his own copy of the *Weathervane* lying open on the counter.

The principal frowned. "Why on earth wouldn't it be true?"

"It's easy enough to fake an accident," Crevice said. "Dankhart wants proof that those lightning cubs are dead. He had big plans involving his niece and the McFangus boy, and now, if what the *Weathervane* says is true, those plans will have to change."

"I am not a magician, Mr. Crevice. I cannot simply

produce evidence out of thin air just because Scabious Dankhart wants it. Besides, it happened in Canada."

"Dankhart doesn't care where it happened." Crevice leaned across the counter and pressed his withered face close to Dark-Angel's. "He says if you're unwilling to hand over some proof, I'm to remind you of the *special* arrangement you have with him."

Dark-Angel hesitated for several moments, glaring at the bone merchant. Then, with some reluctance, she took a trampled pair of small round glasses from her pocket, along with the remains of what looked like a silver lightning moth. She laid them carefully on the counter.

"These belonged to Dougal Dewsnap. They were recovered from the scene of the accident and sent to Perilous late last night so I could return them to his father, Aloysius."

Crevice picked up the glasses and inspected them carefully. "What about McFangus and the Midnight girl? Where's the proof that they're dead?"

Dark-Angel shivered, but she placed a badly scuffed belt buckle shaped like a bolt of lightning tarantulatis, and a battered copy of *The Dankhart Handbook* next to the other objects. Indigo's name was scribbled on the inside page of the book. "If Dankhart requires further proof that the accident was real, he should consult the Canadian newspapers. Aloysius Dewsnap and the Midnights have been informed of events, naturally. It goes without saying that they are beyond consoling." Dark-Angel paused for several seconds, swallowing hard. "I was on my way to return these personal items to them when I received your note."

"Aloysius and the Midnights will have to wait. Scabious will want to see these things for himself." Crevice reached out a bony hand to scoop up the evidence laid out on the counter, but Dark-Angel was too quick for him.

"Not so fast, Mr. Crevice." She grabbed him by his scrawny wrist and held it tightly. "There is the small matter of my payment first. I have heard nothing from Dankhart since I delivered the fire dragon scales. Please tell him that if he requires any further help from me, we must discuss the promises he made first. Until then, these items will remain with me."

"Have it your own way." Crevice yanked his wrist free.

"But you'll be paid when Dankhart's ready. At the moment he's got more important things to think about than what he owes you."

With one last bad-tempered glance, Crevice turned and shuffled his way into a small office behind the counter, closing the door with a snap.

Dark-Angel left the shop swiftly. She hurried back across the cobbled square with the battered belt buckle, the pair of smashed glasses, the remnants of a lightning moth, and a handbook weighing extremely heavily in her pockets.

1
CHRISTOW'S

Several hours later, Angus McFangus, who definitely *wasn't* dead, hurried across the same cobbled square with his uncle Maximilian Fidget and his two best friends, Dougal Dewsnap and Indigo Midnight. They gave the bone merchant a wide berth, sneaking instead past the Horrible Endings Bookshop and down a small dingy side street, stopping only when they reached the cover of Christow's All-Weather Supplies shop.

Uncle Max shuffled everyone swiftly inside. He closed the door and locked it securely behind them. Before anyone could speak, there were sounds of a sudden scuffle in the darkness.

"Oh no!" Angus wailed. "Not again!"

A light flicked on overhead. Angus stared down at a tiny, mechanical, squidlike creature that had crawled up the inside of his coat sleeve and attached itself to his wrist, its tentacles flailing wildly.

"Get this thing off me!" he said, trying to shake it loose, but the strange creature held fast.

"Stop struggling. It'll only grip tighter." Indigo pushed Dougal aside and attempted to pry the squid loose with her fingernails.

"Ow! Watch it, will you? That's my skin you're trying to peel off!"

"Sorry. But it—just—won't—let go." Indigo gritted her teeth, pushed her hair—the color of horse chestnuts—out of her face, and gave it one last tug. "Got it!"

The creature released its grip suddenly. It slipped through Indigo's fingers, soared gracefully through the air . . . and landed on top of Dougal's head.

"Argh! I've got a tentacle up my nose!" Dougal shrieked. "It's trying to suck my brains out!"

"If you will allow me?" Uncle Max swooped in front of Indigo, took a firm hold of the squid by its tentacles, twisted clockwise, and then pulled hard.

Squelch!

Dougal staggered away, breathing heavily.

"Is everyone all right?" Uncle Max asked, inspecting the tentacle burns on Angus's wrist and the nasty red welts that were already appearing on Dougal's nose.

"Yeah, absolutely fantastic," Dougal mumbled angrily. "I always like to finish off the afternoon with a tiny squid stuck up my nostril."

"Perhaps everyone should check their coats and personal possessions before we go any farther. If any more squids have stowed away inside our clothing, it might be best to deal with them now," Uncle Max said, sounding excited. And then he plunged his hands into his pockets without a single ounce of concern.

Angus checked his own coat more carefully, almost jumping out of his skin when his fingers brushed against a smooth pebble he had in his pocket. The spring-loaded, self-propelling, stick-o-squids, Uncle Max's latest invention, had escaped from his uncle's workshop at the Windmill in Budleigh Otterstone three days after Christmas. Shaped like tiny octopi, they were capable of launching themselves through the fiercest of storms and sticking to any surface with the aid of their suction cups. There, they could monitor even the worst weather without slipping, sliding, or losing their grip. Unfortunately, the squids seemed to prefer attaching themselves to lightbulbs, doorknobs, and the remote control for the television. For three whole days it had been impossible to leave any room in the Windmill without suffering several painful tentacle burns. Angus had accidentally trodden on an infestation of the stick-o-squids in his slippers, which had caused his feet to swell to the size of melons.

The dangers caused by the squids, however, were nothing compared to the hazards Angus, Dougal, and Indigo had faced at the Perilous Exploratorium for Violent Weather and Vicious Storms, where they were training to become lightning catchers. They were extremely lucky, in fact, to have made it halfway through their second year following some dramatic encounters with scarlet sleeping snow, rancid rain, and murderous stinging fog, which had almost squashed the life out of Angus. The chances of their completing the rest of their training without serious lightning burns or whirlwind whiplash scars were extremely slim, especially since Angus was a storm prophet. His talents had already brought him dangerously close to some extremely odd and aggressive weather. But there was nowhere else on the entire planet that he would rather be, and he couldn't wait to return.

Dougal, who was a dedicated bookworm, was far less keen on some of the more risky aspects of life at Perilous. With short black hair, round glasses, and a rather pudgy build, he was much happier surrounded by books, apart from the ones that contained vicious booby traps. He also had a talent for solving very tricky word puzzles and weather mysteries and had recently won third prize in Cradget's famous Tri-Hard Puzzle Competition.

Indigo, on the other hand, thrived on danger. She had already saved Angus from a number of hazards, including falling coconuts, an exploding Farew's qube, and some treacherous icebergs. But she had shown the most courage of all when she'd finally come face-to-face with her villainous uncle, Scabious Dankhart. Indigo had refused to crumble under his kidnapping threats or the glare of his sinister black diamond eye. Unfortunately, she had also made the horrible discovery that she bore the distinctive mark of the Dankharts on her hand. There was nothing she could do to rid herself of the telltale pattern and she kept the bleckles covered up beneath the sleeves of her coats and sweaters as often as she could.

It was far too stuffy in Christow's All-Weather Supplies shop, however, to keep bundled up inside their thick winter coats for long. And once Angus was sure there were no squids hiding in his hood, he unbuttoned his coat and glanced around the shop for the first time.

It was much smaller than any other shop he'd visited in Little Frog's Bottom, and it appeared to contain twice as many goods. Every available inch of floor, wall, and ceiling space had been filled with wet-weather clothing, camping equipment, and protective lunar goggles, leaving only a narrow path for them to walk on.

"What are we doing in here?" Angus asked, trailing behind his uncle, who had now set off through the tightly packed shelves.

"As an old friend of Gabriela Christow, I have my own set of keys, which I am free to use at any time to collect supplies."

"So we're here to buy something?" Angus asked. "But I

thought we were supposed to head back to Perilous."

He stared at a massive display of rubber boots as they hurried past it. The boots came in sickly pink, luminous green, tartan, rainbow, and lightning. Did his uncle need to stock up on winter boots and woolens? Or had he brought them here to find a tub of storm repellent to help protect the bushy halo of white hair that sprouted from his head, his eyebrows, and both his nostrils?

"Fear not, my dear nephew. You shall return to the Exploratorium before the day is done," his uncle said cheerfully. "I must warn you, however, that Christow's is one of the most dangerous shops in the whole of Little Frog's Bottom, and I would advise extreme caution as we make our way through the shelves."

"All the shops in Little Frog's Bottom are dangerous," Dougal said, lowering the hood on his long coat.

"Ah, but Christow's is the only place where you are at great risk of being struck by mechanical forecasting flies," Uncle Max said.

Dougal's face fell. He inched closer to Angus and Indigo for safety, searching the ceiling for any buzzing swarms as they walked in single file through a long thin corridor lined with wobbling, sun reflector mirrors.

Angus smiled at his own bizarre reflection, distorted by the surface of the reflectors. His pale gray eyes had both shrunk to the size of peas. His head had gone to a point, forcing his mop of brown hair into a tufted peak. The lobes of his small bear-shaped ears had stretched and were now dragging along the floor behind him like an extra pair of stringy arms.

"Nice," Dougal said, standing beside him. "We should ask if we could have one of these in the lightning cubs' living quarters. It might make Percival Vellum look less like a gargoyle."

Angus smiled. It was a relief to finally return to Imbur Island and Little Frog's Bottom. They had arrived too late in the day to visit Cradget's, which sold dangerous self-destructing puzzles, or to stop for a quick prune and cuttlefish pie at the Frog's Bottom Bakery, although he wasn't sure his digestive system could cope with any more experimental cooking. Uncle Max had made several batches of chewy curry-flavored toffee over the holidays, and Angus was still picking it out of his teeth.

The holidays had been surprisingly normal, considering

the dangers the whole of Perilous was now facing. Angus, Dougal, and Indigo had spent the entire first week discussing the dramatic appearance of an enormous lightning tower above Castle Dankhart at the end of the previous term. They'd also stayed up long into the early hours of the morning whispering about Principal Delphinia Dark-Angel's treachery and the fact that she had betrayed every single lightning catcher and cub on the planet, by stealing some golden fire dragon scales and handing them over to Scabious Dankhart. It was a secret they had sworn to keep from everyone else until Jeremius McFangus, Angus's other uncle, could decide how to act. Dankhart and his monsoon mongrels now intended to combine these powerful scales with lightning storm particles, captured with the lightning tower, to produce storms of cataclysmic power. A dark cloud was literally hanging over the future of Perilous and every Exploratorium around the globe.

The weather in Devon throughout the last two weeks had been unusually calm, however, with nothing but some light drizzle and chilly easterly winds. Christmas, therefore, had gone ahead without interruption and with all the usual carol singing, tree decorating, and mince pie eating. Angus had found it extremely difficult to enjoy the festivities with thoughts of Dankhart, the lightning tower, and his parents suddenly creeping into his consciousness when he was eating Brussels sprouts or playing a game of charades. There had been no cards or presents from his mum and dad, as they were spending their second yuletide trapped in one of the dungeons at Castle Dankhart. And Angus had never feared for their lives more.

When the day to return to Perilous had finally arrived, Uncle Max had taken them to catch the early morning ferry. As soon as they'd reached the Isle of Imbur, he'd bundled them into long hooded coats and shepherded them onto an open-topped steam-powered coach that had dropped them off at the edge of the square in Little Frog's Bottom. He had then brought them straight to Christow's without a single word of explanation. And he was now hurrying them through the cramped shelves, checking his watch several times a minute.

"Come along, my dear Angus, there is no time to dawdle," Uncle Max said.

"Hang on a minute." Dougal stopped to look up at

the ceiling. "Why's it raining in here?"

A canopy of umbrellas popped open automatically above their heads, protecting them from the surprise downpour.

"We've just walked into an umbrella testing section," Indigo said, pointing to a notice.

Some of the umbrellas were triangular, and others were musical or had tiny fish swimming in water between layers of plastic. But some were leaking like sieves.

"Hey!" Dougal yelled, ducking swiftly as a furry yellow umbrella with fangs snapped shut just inches above his head. "Watch out for that one with molars. I think it might be carnivorous!"

It took a further fifteen minutes to battle their way past chaotic shelves filled with foghorns, snow scoopers, and an automatic snap-shut picnic basket that was, quite frankly, dangerous. When they finally climbed a set of dingy stairs at the back of the shop and emerged through a doorway at the top, Angus was surprised to find himself standing outside on a flat section of roof.

"Whoa!"

The whole of Little Frog's Bottom came into view before them, as they'd never seen it before. In the cold afternoon gloom it looked still and deserted. The statue of Philip Starling and Edgar Perilous peered straight over their heads toward the darkening horizon. In the distance, tall and impressive and sitting high above the town, was Perilous.

"Look." Angus nudged Indigo and then pointed.

He was extremely pleased to see that the Exploratorium had survived the holidays in one piece. There were no dangerous storms lingering above its towers or skulking close by. Lights were already twinkling through its many windows. He could just make out the glass-domed roof of the library and felt his heart leap inside his chest. Everything looked perfectly normal, as if they could saunter straight into one of Miss DeWinkle's spectacularly boring lessons on fog and pretend nothing had changed. But this term, Angus knew, life at Perilous would be very different. Dankhart and Dark-Angel had seen to that.

"Why has your uncle brought us up to the roof?" Indigo asked, shivering beside him in the wind.

Uncle Max was now watching the skies overhead with keen interest.

"You don't think he's spotted some of those mechanical forecasting flies, do you?" Dougal said. "Maybe we should go back inside and grab some insect repellent, just in case? Or some flyswatters?"

Angus was just about to question his uncle when he felt it. The roof beneath his feet began to tremble gently. At the exact same moment a peculiar, rhythmic throbbing reached them on the breeze.

"What's making that noise?" Dougal said, looking even more nervous.

It sounded remarkably like a storm vacuum sucking up giant hailstones, and Angus had heard the distinctive noise only once before.

He turned quickly and studied the horizon. The afternoon had remained overcast and dull, with a thick layer of gray clouds sitting over the whole island. One of the clouds, however, was now scudding its way across the rooftops of Little Frog's Bottom toward them in a very odd manner.

Angus felt his stomach lurch. It could mean only one thing: the dirigible weather station was approaching Christow's at top speed.

2
THE DARK TOWER

"What's going on?" Indigo yelled above the throbbing, which had now reached earsplitting volume.

The cloud screeched to an abrupt halt, directly above Christow's, and hovered. But before Angus could explain anything, the wisps of gray parted with a sudden breeze, and they each caught a glimpse of a huge ship, shaped like an old Spanish galleon, hidden inside. Impressive white sails billowed in the breeze. An anchor was just visible on the starboard bow and a large balloon floated above, keeping the whole vessel airborne.

"Your uncle Jeremius has come to take you the rest of the way," Uncle Max shouted over the deafening sound.

"But wouldn't it be easier just to catch a steam-powered coach?" Dougal asked, looking extremely apprehensive as the loading doors of the weather station opened above them and a wicker landing basket was lowered.

"Jeremius will explain everything once you are aboard," Uncle Max bellowed, holding onto his bushy white hair as it flapped around his face. "I must bid you and your friends a fond farewell for now, young Angus."

Only a minute later Angus, Dougal, and Indigo were being hoisted up into the large vessel. Dougal instantly turned pale; he kept his eyes firmly shut and clung to the ropes above his head as the landing basket swayed worryingly in the breeze.

Indigo peered over the side, waving as Uncle Max and Christow's shrank away beneath them. Angus fixed his gaze on the weather station, feeling extremely glad that it had now been five hours since they'd eaten lunch.

Clunk!

The loading doors closed beneath them, and the wind dropped away suddenly. The landing basket settled on the floor. Two seconds later Angus felt the whole weather station lurch forward. It was already on the move again.

"Welcome aboard!" a familiar voice said.

Angus clambered out of the basket and raced over to greet his other favorite uncle, Jeremius McFangus. Jeremius was tall, with broad shoulders, and a rugged, weather-beaten appearance that came from spending long hours in the underground snow chambers at the Canadian Exploratorium for Extremely Chilly Weather. He also enjoyed trekking across dangerous ice shelves and chasing rogue storms and monsoon mongrels around the globe. It felt like months since Angus had last seen his uncle's familiar gray eyes and small bear-shaped ears, features that never failed to remind him of his dad.

"I'm glad to see you've all survived Christmas at the Windmill." Jeremius pulled Angus into a brief hug. He smiled broadly at Dougal and Indigo.

"Yeah, no thanks to the squids," Dougal said, the color slowly returning to his cheeks.

"Why didn't you come to Devon for the holidays?" Angus asked, suddenly feeling impatient for answers.

Jeremius had promised to join them for the festivities. But a hastily scribbled card had turned up on Christmas

Eve, canceling his plans, and they'd heard nothing from him since.

"I'm afraid I had something important to arrange instead," Jeremius said, scratching the stubble on his chin.

Angus frowned. "So, why didn't you just meet us back at Perilous?"

"We're not heading back to Perilous. Look!" Indigo pointed out the nearest porthole as the weather station executed a slow turn and began moving away from the Exploratorium.

"What's going on?" Dougal stared anxiously at the changing view.

"Yeah, where are we going now?" Angus asked.

Jeremius shook his head and smiled. "I'd forgotten just how many questions you three like to ask. I'll need reinforcements if I'm going to explain this properly. You'd better come with me."

He turned and led them straight into a dark, narrow passageway. The ship's timbers creaked and groaned as the weather station continued to pick up speed. Angus peered through one of the portholes. He could see nothing but whiffs and puffs of thick gray cloud in the growing gloom. On the inside, the weather station seemed strangely deserted.

Jeremius took them down a short flight of stairs and into a small cozy cabin. It was brightly lit with cheerful brass lamps set around a large wooden table. It was also occupied.

"Ah, Angus, how nice it is to see you, Miss Midnight, and Mr. Dewsnap again." Aramanthus Rogwood smiled kindly at all three of them as they entered. "I trust you have spent your holidays wisely, eating far too many slices of your uncle's excellent Christmas icicle cake and engaging in some very noisy pillow fights?"

Angus smiled. Aramanthus Rogwood was one of his favorite lightning catchers in the whole of Perilous. His amber, owl-like eyes twinkled in the flicker of the lamps. His toffee-colored beard was braided down the middle to keep it out of his way.

Rogwood was not alone. Catcher Sparks stood beside him with a very steely expression. Her hair was pinned into a tight bun, and her arms were folded across her leather jerkin, which had been reinforced with several shiny new buckles and metal studs. Angus felt his smile slip slightly. Catcher Sparks was not the kind of lightning catcher to ask about pillow fights. She was far more likely, in fact, to send them off to clean something revolting, like swamp-filled rubber boots or snot-repelling handkerchiefs. She had never come to meet them as they returned for a new term at Perilous before, and he wondered what she was doing here now.

"Aramanthus, Amelia, and I have just come back from a series of high-level discussions at the London office," Jeremius explained, closing the door behind them. "We've been meeting with the most senior lightning catchers from around the globe."

"Is that why you couldn't come to the Windmill for Christmas?" Angus asked.

"It's one of the reasons, yes." Jeremius glanced briefly at Rogwood. "We've been debating how to deal with any storms that Dankhart might throw at us and drawing up some emergency plans. Two of our smallest Exploratoriums are already on high alert after some unusual cloud formations have been spotted in their skies. Dankhart hasn't struck yet, but it's only a matter of time."

"His ultimate aim, of course, is to destroy the lightning

catchers, our entire network of Exploratoriums, and everything we have fought to achieve over the last three hundred and fifty years," Rogwood said.

"With the lightning catchers out of the picture, there would be nothing to stop him from covering the planet in terrible storms and holding the rest of the world to ransom," Jeremius added.

Angus shivered and tried hard not to imagine it. Upon closer inspection, under the soft glow of the brass lamps, all three lightning catchers were showing definite signs of fatigue and strain, with dark circles under their eyes.

"Some of us believe, however, that we cannot simply wait for the worst to come," Rogwood said. "We have been discussing ideas of the best way to destroy the lightning tower."

"But what if the tower is too powerful?" Catcher Sparks asked sharply.

"As I was just about to explain, Amelia, before we stopped off at Christow's, Edgar Perilous and Philip Starling made detailed plans of the original lightning towers that were built in London prior to the Great Fire of London in 1666."

Rogwood took several sheets of ancient-looking parchment from a shelf under the table and unrolled each of them with great care. Angus, Dougal, and Indigo edged closer as he weighed the corners down with three empty mugs and a sugar bowl. The plans were obviously very old and fragile, and they had crumbled to dust in several places.

"Those aren't the original drawings, are they, sir?" Angus asked.

"Indeed they are, Angus. I have been allowed to borrow them from one of the artifact rooms in the Inner Sanctum of Secrets on the strict understanding that I will return them without stains or additional rips or tears."

Angus studied the parchment with interest. A series of technical-looking illustrations clearly showed the lightning tower design from every angle, giving detailed dimensions.

"I believe our best chance of success is to destroy the tower with a storm to rival that which started the Great Fire. We must force history to repeat itself," Rogwood said. "I have been studying these plans for almost two weeks now, and have identified a number of weak spots in their construction, which might be used to our advantage."

Jeremius nodded. "It won't be easy. As lightning catchers our expertise lies in defeating the weather, not producing deadly storms of our own. And Dankhart and Swarfe will have improved upon the design of these original towers. But Delphinia has already agreed that we must try to create our own storm and is keen to drive our plans forward as quickly as possible. She has put the entire Lightnarium, Valentine Vellum, and his team of experts at our disposal."

"Pr-principal Dark-Angel knows what you're planning?" Angus asked surprised. "Er . . ." he added, glancing pointedly at Catcher Sparks and wondering how much he should reveal in front of her.

"Ah, let me assure you, Angus, Catcher Sparks knows everything that we do about Dark-Angel's treachery," Rogwood explained calmly. "All lightning catchers have now heard that some fire dragon scales have been stolen from the tomb of Moray McFangus in the Perilous crypt. But the six of us in this room are the only ones who know the true identity of the thief."

"What about Felix Gudgeon?" Angus asked, wondering why the gruff lightning catcher wasn't on the weather station with them.

"Gudgeon likes to speak his mind," Jeremius said. "And as he also works directly for Delphinia, I believe he would find it more difficult than most to feign loyalty if he knew what she had done. We have decided to keep it between ourselves for the time being at least."

"Catcher Sparks showed no hesitation in joining us when Jeremius and I asked for her help," Rogwood added. "You may speak freely in front of her."

"Er, thanks, sir," Angus said, glancing warily at the stern lightning catcher all the same. "But won't Principal Dark-Angel just tell Dankhart everything she knows about your plans?"

"Yeah, wouldn't it be easier just to get rid of her instead?" Dougal asked.

"Now is not the time to try to convince everyone of Delphinia's treachery, especially as we have no solid evidence to back our claims," Jeremius said. "The last thing we need is to suddenly find ourselves in total disarray and without a leader. We'd be handing over Perilous on a plate to Dankhart. The lightning tower is a far more pressing concern."

Angus stared at his uncle, shocked. He'd half expected Rogwood and Jeremius to have a brilliant plan to remove Dark-Angel from Perilous before she caused even more damage. He also had some serious concerns about Valentine Vellum. Was he assisting Dark-Angel in her treachery? And if so, wasn't he the very worst person to help the lightning catchers create a storm to destroy the lightning tower?

The weather station banked hard to the left suddenly, causing mugs to slide across the table. Angus caught a brief glimpse of snowcapped mountains through one of the portholes.

"Are we heading toward Mount Maccrindell?" he asked, surprised.

Jeremius nodded. "We wanted to get a proper look at the lightning tower before returning to Perilous. We've been receiving daily reports and updates at the London office, of course, but things can change very quickly above Castle Dankhart. After that, we'll be taking you, Dougal, and Indigo straight to Perilous."

"None of the other cubs have returned yet," Catcher Sparks added. "The Exploratorium will be as empty as it's ever likely to be, give or take a dozen lightning catchers, giving us the ideal opportunity to get you three inside without being spotted."

Angus frowned. "Why does it matter if anyone sees us?"

Jeremius exchanged awkward looks with Rogwood. "There is another reason why I couldn't come back to the Windmill for Christmas," he said. "I had to return to the Canadian Exploratorium to organize something important."

"It might be easier just to show them, Jeremius," Rogwood said kindly. He took a rolled-up copy of the *Weekly Weathervane* from a deep pocket in his leather jerkin and placed it facedown on the table.

Jeremius hesitated for a second and then turned the magazine over. Angus looked at the front cover.

"There's been an accident at the Canadian Exploratorium?" he asked, shocked.

Jeremius nodded. "Read the feature on page five, and then I will explain everything."

Angus turned to page five and quickly scanned

the article, which spoke in detail of the glacier caves' collapse.

"Hang on a minute. What's this bit at the bottom?" Dougal said, tracing the words with his finger as he read the final passage out loud.

"'Three second-year lightning cubs . . . killed in the incident. Their identities have since been confirmed as . . . Angus McFangus, Dougal Dewsnap, and Indigo Midnight.'"

Angus gripped the edges of the table, suddenly feeling unsteady on his feet.

"But none of us have ever even been to the Canadian Exploratorium!" Indigo blurted out.

"Yeah, the *Weathervane* must have got its facts wrong," Dougal said, looking startled. "I mean, we're definitely not dead." He glanced down at his hands and feet, as if to confirm the fact.

"The *Weathervane* is only printing what it believes to be true," Jeremius said calmly. "After everything that happened with Dankhart in the bone merchant's, Rogwood and I felt it was only a matter of time before another attempt was made to kidnap any one of you, or worse."

"S-so you're trying to make everyone think we're *dead*?" Indigo said.

"And you made a whole set of ancient glacier caves collapse on purpose?" asked Angus, stunned by the news that his life had come to a dramatic, icy end.

"A minor accident in the underground snow chambers wouldn't have convinced anyone," Jeremius said. "It had to be something big and sensational, where lives could have been lost."

"Then we set about leaving a false trail of evidence behind as proof that it had actually occurred," Rogwood said. "Just as Dankhart did with the weather vortex when he was trying to hide the lightning tower."

"Before I left for Canada I managed to obtain an old pair of Dougal's glasses from Aloysius, and a belt buckle to match the one your parents gave you, Angus," Jeremius explained. "Catcher Sparks let herself into Indigo's room in the lightning cubs' living quarters and took a copy of *The Dankhart Handbook* with Indigo's name scribbled inside it."

"After the ice caves collapsed, Jeremius made sure these items were sent directly back to Delphinia with a detailed accident report, so she could be in no doubt that you three perished," Rogwood said.

Jeremius nodded again. "If Delphinia believes you're dead, it will be much easier to convince everyone else. And if she's still in league with Dankhart, this proof, or news of it, will reach him very quickly."

"But what about my mum and dad?" Indigo asked, her voice barely more than a whisper.

"I gained full consent for my plan from your parents before I journeyed to Canada," Jeremius reassured her quickly. "Needless to say, Aloysius was more than happy to play along," he added, turning to Dougal. "They know you are both safe and well. Sadly, it was too risky to get word to Alabone and Evangeline. It might seem cruel, but for the time being at least, it is better for them to believe the accident truly happened."

Angus swallowed down a sudden wave of nausea, which had nothing to do with the turbulence the weather station was now flying through. Had his mum and dad already heard the tragic news? Had Dankhart raced down to their dungeon with a copy of the *Weathervane*, to rub salt into their wounds?

"But if everyone thinks we're dead, how can we return to Perilous?" Angus asked.

Jeremius grinned. "Rogwood and I have a plan."

"Obviously, the fact that you have now perished will require some changes to your curriculum." Rogwood smiled at them through his beard. "Catcher Sparks will explain more when we reach Perilous. But I guarantee that you will not be bored."

All conversation was halted suddenly as the weather station flew into a bumpy patch of turbulence, which sent Dougal toppling sideways across the room. Angus held on to the edge of the table with one hand and his stomach with the other, hoping he wasn't about to vomit over the ancient lightning tower plans.

"We are approaching Castle Dankhart," Rogwood said, glancing out the nearest porthole as soon as the turbulence had passed. "I think you three would be more comfortable in the passenger observation lounge while we carry out our aerial inspections."

The passenger lounge was totally deserted. Angus, Dougal, and Indigo chose three seats at the front, which were firmly bolted to the floor. Great whirls of clouds rolled past the large viewing windows, which stretched all the way across the roof, giving the impression they were flying through a thick no-way-out fog.

As the weather station drew closer to Castle Dankhart, the weather took a serious turn for the worse. Terrible gusts of howling wind shook the timbers beneath their feet and rattled the windowpanes, trying to force their way inside. Angus fidgeted nervously in his seat as the weather station hit yet more pockets of unstable air, and he wondered if stories of their deaths might not have to be fake, after all.

For the next five minutes he was flung violently around in his seat, accidentally kicking Indigo in the shins, twice. "Sorry! Sorry!"

"I think I'm going to be cloud sick," Dougal moaned, turning an unnatural shade of green.

The weather station banked hard to the right . . . and then to the left . . . and to the right again, as if it was being put through its paces on a special airborne slalom course. And then suddenly, the shaking stopped.

"What's happening now?" Indigo asked, brushing her hair out of her face.

The clouds cleared, the wind dropped, and a range of snowy mountains came into view up ahead. Dark and foreboding, Castle Dankhart sat like a giant ugly spider in the middle.

"Look!" Angus stood up and pressed his face against the window, trying to see the stone building from every angle as the weather station flew closer and closer. He'd seen photos of the castle in the *Weathervane* and he'd spent hours poring over detailed floor plans in *The Dankhart Handbook*, but in real life, the castle was far larger and more brutish than any pictures could convey. Soot-black turrets pierced the sky; grimy windows stared blankly at them as they soared past; ugly gargoyles seemed to sneer at their presence. And looming over everything, so vast and frightening it made his stomach churn, was the lightning tower. Angus stared at the enormous skeletal structure as they flew past it. Metal struts and stairs ran through the heart of the pyramidal form.

"I don't believe it," Dougal said, suddenly pointing down to the very bottom of the rock upon which the castle sat. "Dad was right about the crocodiles in Dankhart's moat. I can see them swimming about."

Angus stared at the tiny specks floating in the glinting water and shivered. Everything about the castle was sinister and spooky, from the black, gnarled icicles that dangled over every doorway to the strong smell of sulfur that seemed to swirl in the air, seeping in through the viewing windows above their heads. Even the weak wintry sunshine was doing its best to avoid shining upon its walls and turrets.

"Do you think my uncle Scabious can see us?" asked Indigo, swallowing hard.

"Yeah, I bet he's watching us right now," Angus said. It was the closest he'd been to his parents in eighteen months. He stared hard at the castle windows, wondering if his mum and dad had already spotted the weather station. Or could they perhaps hear the powerful engines? He fought down a mad urge to open one of the viewing windows wider and yell his parents' names as loudly as his lungs would allow, or to send a scribbled message on a paper airplane sailing through one of the castle windows.

"We're going in for a closer look," Indigo said.

Angus held his breath as the weather station altered course and began to circle in slowly toward the upper reaches of the castle and the lightning tower. This tower bore little resemblance to the original drawings Rogwood had just shown them, or to the towers Angus had seen with his own eyes through the retrospectacles in London. It was much bigger and stronger, with thick metal supports and gleaming crossbeams. Indigo watched in silence as they flew around it again, looking sick at the very sight of it.

"The lightning catchers are never going to destroy that with a single lightning storm," Dougal said.

A swirling vortex of weather surrounded the top of the tower, with violent flashes of lightning, and storm clouds the color of pitch. The weather station nudged its way into the outer reaches of the eddy. The skies instantly darkened to an angry, thundery black.

"I don't believe it. We're heading inside the vortex," Dougal said.

Hailstones battered the windows as they drew closer and closer to the lightning tower, circling it for a third time.

"Why's the weather so much worse inside the vortex?" Angus asked, trying to take his mind off the churning inside his stomach.

"The lightning tower's pulling all the weather that's passing over the island toward itself and spinning it up into a dangerous whirl," Dougal explained. "It's forcing normal, ordinary storm particles to clash together and change, transforming them into something much more violent."

"I think we're picking up speed," Indigo said anxiously.

Angus could feel the center of gravity shifting beneath his feet as the weather station completed yet another rotation. He was also starting to feel dizzy. There was a sudden lurch to the right.

"Whoa!" Angus slipped sideways in his seat.

The weather station, caught by the vortex, was being dragged toward its core.

"We're too close! We'll never get out again!" Dougal yelled, staring around the observation lounge in a panic, as if hoping an emergency exit might suddenly appear.

"Hang on to something!" Angus shouted. The weather station creaked and groaned as it was flung around inside the whirling cloud. There was another violent pitch to the right. The passenger lounge began to roll, tilting sideways at a very precarious angle. Angus felt his whole body suddenly slide out of his seat. He grabbed wildly at anything that would stop him from plummeting through the air as the weather station turned all the way onto its back and came to a halt upside down.

"Is everyone all right?" he asked, his legs swinging uselessly beneath him as he clung to an armrest.

He glanced urgently to his left. Indigo had somehow managed to hook her feet under the edges of the bolted-down seat and was now hanging like a bat. He twisted round to the other seat beside him and felt his insides heave. Hanging on by one hand, his legs flailing wildly in midair, Dougal was now dangling directly above one of the large open viewing windows. If he fell, he would plunge straight through the opening, slide around the edge of the huge balloon, which was now hanging beneath them, and then tumble hundreds of feet to a very sudden death at the foot of Castle Dankhart.

"I c-c-can't hold on!" Dougal yelled. His glasses had

fallen off his nose and were now hooked around his left ear.

"Here, take my hand!" Angus said, trying to hold his own weight with his right hand while reaching out to grab his friend with the other.

"I can't reach! My fingers are slipping! I'm going to fall!"

"Hold on!" Indigo shrieked as the weather station gave another lurch. "I think it's going to right itself!"

The great airborne galleon rolled without warning. Dougal tumbled sideways with a strangled yell.

Angus felt his body fall back into his seat at a very awkward angle, his knees colliding with his ears.

"Ooof!"

Indigo was already clambering over his tangled arms and legs in an effort to reach Dougal, who was lying in a crumpled heap on the floor.

Bang!

The door at the back of the passenger lounge sprung open. Jeremius charged toward them, his clothes disheveled, as if he'd just sprinted through every section of a weather tunnel. Rogwood and Catcher Sparks were hard on his heels.

"Is everyone all right? Was anyone injured?" Jeremius asked urgently.

Dougal sat up and shook his head several times as the entire party reached him. He looked extremely pale and dazed.

"I've got a horrible feeling," he said with a gulp, "that pretending to be dead is going to be even more dangerous than being a lightning cub."

3
FOG MITE MYSTERY

Dougal sat wrapped in a blanket for the rest of the journey, sipping a hot mug of cocoa to calm his nerves, and by the time they finally reached Perilous, darkness had fallen. Docking lights twinkled on the roof as the weather station powered down its engines, released its landing ropes, and came to a gradual standstill. Jeremius and Catcher Sparks bundled Angus, Dougal, and Indigo quickly along the narrow passageways and out through a small door. They walked hastily across the roof before any other lightning catchers could spot them.

"Is it my imagination or do things look a bit *different* since the last time we were up here?" Angus said quietly.

All weather experiments, glass storm jars, and measuring equipment had been cleared to make way for dozens of storm vacuums, which had been turned to face Castle Dankhart. Several makeshift lightning shelters, which looked like tiny circus tents, had been put up. There were cloud-busting rocket launchers and mountains of large steel storm nets piled on top of one another like giant stacks of holey pancakes. Angus swallowed hard. Perilous was getting ready to defend itself. He took a fleeting look at an enormous machine with extendable ladders and grappling hooks as they hurried past it.

"What do the lightning catchers need grappling hooks for, miss?" Dougal asked Catcher Sparks.

"That's none of your business, Dewsnap. And watch where you're walking!" she added as Dougal almost tripped over the end of the weather cannon. "We're trying to keep your arrival quiet, not announce it to the whole of Perilous with a spectacular explosion of red sparks."

And before they could see what else had been moved up to the roof, she rushed them through a trapdoor and down a set of gleaming metal stairs.

"Catcher Sparks will take you from here," Jeremius said

when they reached the bottom. "I'll come and see you as often as I can. But if you three could at least *try* to stay out of trouble in the meantime, it would make my life a lot easier."

"Er, we'll try," Angus said, deciding not to make any promises he might be forced to break.

"There's one more thing before I go." Jeremius pulled Angus to one side. "Rogwood and I have discussed it at length, and we both agree it's far too risky to continue with your storm prophet lessons at the moment."

"Oh," Angus said, suddenly feeling disappointed.

He'd spent much of the previous term in the Inner Sanctum of Perplexing Mysteries and Secrets, learning about the very first storm prophets. After visiting their impressive, dragon-shaped tombs in the crypt and watching some highly illuminating projectograms, he'd made the startling discovery that storm prophets not only could predict when dangerous weather was about to strike but could also control any storm.

There had been times when Angus would have been relieved if his fire dragon had simply melted away in his sleep, leaving him as normal as every other lightning cub at Perilous. But the threat of the cataclysmic lightning storms that the lightning tower could produce had made things much more complicated. And now that he'd seen the monstrous structure with his own eyes, he was more sure than ever that he should try to use his storm prophet talents to help defeat Dankhart, to rescue his mum and dad, or even save his friends from deadly danger. Dark-Angel was extremely keen for him to develop his talents. And for once, Angus agreed with her.

"There will be plenty of time to improve your skills in the future," Jeremius said, choosing his words carefully. "Besides, Evangeline would have me marooned on a desert island if I let anything else happen to you," he added, with a sheepish smile. "I'll be in enough trouble as it is when she finds out you've been clambering over icebergs in the Rotundra and fighting off monsoon mongrels."

Angus felt his breath catch in his chest at the mention of his mum's name. Clearly, Jeremius believed they would both see her again one day. He spent several happy moments imagining his fearless uncle cowering before her scolding.

As soon as Jeremius had gone they followed Catcher

Sparks through the familiar stone corridors and passageways. But Perilous was eerily quiet and deserted.

"This is giving me goose bumps," Indigo said as they passed the empty kitchens, where the stone fireplaces stood cold and uninviting.

Instead of taking them down to the lightning cubs' living quarters, Catcher Sparks rushed them straight to the library.

"What are we doing here, miss?" Angus asked as they stopped outside the library's doors.

"As you can see, McFangus, the library has been closed and declared out of bounds due to an unfortunate infestation of fog mites."

The doors had been sealed shut with a huge padlock. A dozen large red signs warned everyone to "Keep Out!" There was also a lengthy notice explaining the complicated de-infestation procedures that were taking place inside, and an eye-watering description of symptoms, which could occur if anyone had been exposed to the mites, including itching, stinging, and a painful burning skin rash.

"Er, if there are fog mites in the library, shouldn't we

be heading in the opposite direction?" Dougal said, looking thoroughly alarmed and automatically scratching his ear, which had once been bitten in a fog mite attack.

"Calm down, Dewsnap. There are no fog mites. Rogwood has convinced everyone at Perilous, including Principal Dark-Angel, that there has been a genuine infestation. The library has been declared out of bounds for the next four months. Not even Miss Vulpine is allowed to enter. It is, therefore, the perfect place to conceal three lightning cubs. No one will disturb you in there."

"I don't care what Sparks says. If I see anything buzzing through this library, I'm making a run for it," Dougal whispered as the lightning catcher unlocked the doors and shuffled them inside.

The library at Perilous was large and rambling, with a splendid spiral staircase leading up to a balcony. Cold winter moonlight flooded in through an impressive glass-domed ceiling at the top. Normally, the library was filled with the comforting sounds of rustling pages; of lightning cubs whispering, sniggering, sneezing, and gossiping. And with the booming voice of Miss Vulpine, the school librarian, shouting at anyone who accidentally smeared melted chocolate across the pages of her precious books. But now . . . Angus stopped and stared around as Catcher Sparks locked the door behind them. Dust particles drifted through the musty-smelling air. There was an unnerving atmosphere of deep silence, as if every living thing inside the library, including the mice and the book fleas, had sensed some kind of danger and fled.

Catcher Sparks headed straight up to the reference section on the balcony and came to a halt in front of a solid wall of technical tomes on storm science.

She grabbed the spine of the largest book and gave it two small tugs.

Clunk!

Angus stumbled backward as a door-shaped section of shelf swung open, revealing a narrow set of wooden steps.

"You will be staying in Miss Vulpine's living quarters, which she has also been forced to vacate due to the fog mites," Catcher Sparks said, leading the way up the first flight of stairs, which then turned sharply to the right and continued to ascend. At the top they came to another door, beyond which was a cramped landing.

"McFangus, Dewsnap, you will be sleeping in here." Catcher Sparks opened the nearest of four closed doors. Angus caught a brief glimpse of a large room with two beds and a dusty-looking armchair. "Midnight, this is your room," Catcher Sparks said, flinging open a door on the opposite side of the landing, revealing a small room decorated with rose-printed wallpaper and frilly bedcovers. "There is also a bathroom and a sitting room." She pointed to the final two doors. "Try not to damage any of Miss Vulpine's personal possessions. Do not go poking about in the cupboards or rifling through things that don't belong to you. And do not go wandering around the library."

"But, miss, what if we want something to read?" Dougal said.

"Then you will restrict yourselves to the reading material on the balcony. After dark you will remain in your living quarters; we do not want anyone spotting mysterious lights or starting hysterical rumors about ghosts and haunted bookshelves. Your meals will be brought up to you by me, Rogwood, or your uncle Jeremius. There is a small private roof terrace, which you may use for the purposes of fresh air only. If I hear any reports of mysterious water bombs, snowballs, or Cradget's products being dropped from there, there will be trouble," she warned, fixing each of them with a stern glare. "The library will be kept locked at all times, to prevent any unwanted visitors. Now, I really must return to the experimental division."

And before they could ask any more questions she descended the stairs with the new buckles on her leather jerkin clinking. They heard her close the door at the bottom with a snap.

"Come on," Angus said, dumping his coat on a hook in the landing. "Let's have a proper look around."

Miss Vulpine's living quarters had a rather dreary feel. The boys' bedroom was decorated in various shades of unappealing brown, with faded lightning bolt wallpaper. Indigo's room was slightly more welcoming, with a patchwork quilt on the bed and ruffled lampshades. The bathroom had scratchy, threadbare towels and cold ceramic tiles. An assortment of lumpy, mismatched armchairs had been squashed into the small sitting room. The green carpet looked like an army of mice had nibbled on it.

"This must have been where your dear old uncle Scabby stayed when he was pretending to be Mr. Knurling, the librarian," Dougal said, carefully testing out the springs in one of the chairs.

Indigo turned pale and stared down at her feet. Angus tried not to imagine Indigo's uncle warming his hands by the fire, and failed. The disturbing image made Miss Vulpine's rooms even less appealing, and he suddenly wished they were all back in the Pigsty instead, the tiny cozy room that was wedged between his and Dougal's bedrooms in the lightning cubs' living quarters.

Thankfully, a hot dinner of beef stew and dumplings had already been left on a small table in the corner of the room.

"Can you believe the day we've just had?" Dougal said as they settled themselves before the fire to eat. His pet lightning moth, Norman, was doing circles above their heads, stretching its shiny metallic wings. "Although I suppose it could be worse," he added through a mouthful of dumpling. "At least we won't run out of books to read."

"And Rogwood said something about not letting us

get bored. So he must be planning some lessons for us," Indigo said.

Angus frowned, pushing a chunk of beef around his bowl. "But what if something happens with the lightning tower, or with my mum and dad? How are we supposed to help if we're locked inside the library and Jeremius and Rogwood won't even let me practice being a storm prophet?"

Dougal and Indigo exchanged worried-looking glances.

"Jeremius is only trying to keep us safe," Indigo said gently.

"Yeah, and let's face it, one fire dragon isn't going to be much use against Dankhart and the kind of lightning storms he's threatening to unleash, is it?" Dougal said. "You'd need loads of fire dragons to defeat them."

It was only several hours later, after discussing the dramatic events of the day in detail, that they finally went to bed.

Dougal dived straight under his covers. "Urgh! This mattress is really cold and lumpy."

Angus pummeled his pillows with his fists, trying to

make them more comfortable, and then stared up at the flaky paint on the ceiling, thinking over what Dougal had said earlier. He hated to admit it, but Dougal had a point. One fire dragon, belonging to a very inexperienced storm prophet, wasn't enough to defeat a monstrous storm created by the lightning tower. But Angus couldn't just give up, sit back, and wait for the worst to come. And he wasn't completely useless, either. He'd already managed to see off—with the help of an icicle shower—two monsoon mongrels in the bone merchant's shop. He'd also sent a cloud of rancid rain chasing after Percival Vellum in the storm hollow, even if it had been a total accident.

Strangely, his dreams had been entirely dragon free over Christmas, and he'd felt none of the familiar flames and stirrings inside his chest. But if he could just practice, improve his weather-wrangling skills, he might one day be as talented as the great Moray McFangus, who had once saved several lightning catchers from a storm cluster.

But practicing with any kind of weather wasn't going to be easy. He couldn't exactly stroll into the Lightnarium and ask Valentine Vellum to set a lightning storm loose. The weather tunnel was also out of the question;

he ran the risk of bumping into far too many lightning catchers or cubs. In the Rotundra he'd be spotted in an instant by Jeremius, who would march him straight back to the library and place a team of snarling snow wolves outside the doors, to make sure he never escaped again.

Angus sighed and continued to stare up at the ceiling, thinking hard.

What he needed was a place that was separate from all normal lightning catcher activities, a place where he wouldn't be seen, heard, or caught red-handed. But what chance did he have of finding anywhere to try out his skills, now that they'd been locked inside the library?

He woke up early the next morning, still puzzling over the tricky problem. He got dressed quietly, trying not to disturb Dougal, who was sleeping soundly, and crept across the landing into the sitting room. He closed the door softly behind him . . . and almost passed out with shock.

"All right, Angus?"

A tall figure with scruffy horse-chestnut-colored hair stepped out from behind one of the armchairs.

4

A YODELING OF YETIS

"G-Germ?" Angus tripped over the edge of the carpet and stumbled, collided with the stack of dirty bowls from last night's dinner, and sent them clattering across the floor.

The door flew open behind him almost instantly.

"What's going on?" Dougal staggered into the room, rubbing sleep out of his eyes.

Indigo was seconds behind him. She squeaked at the unexpected sight of her brother.

"Surprise!" Geronimo Midnight grinned. "All right, little sis? You should see the look on your face. It's like you've just discovered some piranha mist fish in your socks."

Indigo blinked at her brother. "What are you doing back at Perilous?"

"Old Doctor Fleagal wants to sterilize the sanatorium before everyone returns for the new term." Germ was training to be a doctor and spent most of his time sweeping up old scabs and flakes of crusty crumble fungus, as well as studying disgusting things like snow boot boils. "Plus, I'm starting a new phase of my training now that I've passed all my exams on spots, bumps, and hailstone bruises."

"But how did you know we were here?" Angus asked.

"I didn't." Germ shrugged. "I mean, I knew you three weren't really dead and everything. Mum told me a few days ago before news hit the *Weathervane*. But then I saw Catcher Sparks sneaking out of the library yesterday evening. All the other lightning catchers have been avoiding it like the plague, so I thought I'd come and see what she was up to."

"But weren't you worried about the fog mite infestation?" Angus asked, impressed at Germ's daring.

"Sparks didn't seem that fussed," Germ said. "So I thought I'd risk it."

Indigo frowned at her brother. "How did you find the secret doorway up to Miss Vulpine's living quarters?"

"Oh I figured that out eons ago," Germ said. "Can't say I think much of her taste in wallpaper," he added, making a face at the dreary, speckled gray all around them.

"This is brilliant!" Dougal perched himself on the arm of a chair. "Germ can be our man on the outside. Can you bring us some hot pastries from the kitchens next time you visit?"

"Never mind about the pastries. Germ can tell us exactly what's going on in the rest of Perilous," Angus said. "We'll never get anything useful out of Sparks."

"Oh yeah, I should have thought of that." Dougal grinned sheepishly.

"So, what *is* going on?" Angus asked. It already felt like days since they'd seen anyone else.

Germ thought for a second. "Dark-Angel came back to Perilous late last night. Doctor Fleagal says she's been to the London office. Valentine Vellum's been oozing about the place like a seeping boil, as usual. And everyone's talking about what happened to the Exploratorium in Iceland of course."

Indigo's brow puckered. "Why, what has happened to it?"

"Ah. I'm afraid you're not going to like it, little sis," Germ said, giving her a brotherly pat on the shoulder. "But our dear old uncle Scabby's just attacked it with a lightning storm."

Indigo clamped a hand over her mouth in horror, accidentally knocking Dougal off the arm of the chair with her elbow.

"When did it happen?" Angus asked.

"Late yesterday afternoon. I overheard Rogwood and Catcher Sparks talking about it last night when I went sneaking up to the kitchens for a midnight snack," Germ explained. "The London office issued an emergency evacuation order for the entire Exploratorium after a massive storm was spotted heading straight toward it. Some of the senior lightning catchers stayed behind to try to defend it. But the storm lasted for hours, according to Rogwood."

"Was anybody hurt?" Indigo asked quietly.

"It sounds like most of the lightning catchers got out in time," Germ said, sounding unusually serious. "Some have taken shelter in the Exploratorium in Nuuk; some are heading back to Perilous, but three lightning catchers are still missing."

A terrible silence suddenly filled the tiny room. Angus swallowed hard. This was exactly what Dankhart and his monsoon mongrels had been threatening to do since they'd built the lightning tower. And they wouldn't stop at destroying one tiny Exploratorium in Iceland. There were bound to be more attacks, more tragedies, and more bad news to come.

"Did the building survive?" Angus asked, already fearing what the answer would be.

Germ shook his head. "It was completely destroyed, along with all equipment, research materials, and a huge collection of antique storm globes."

"The Icelandic Exploratorium was really old. It was built not long after Perilous," Dougal said, looking sick to the stomach. "It had a brilliant collection of icicles, some of the oldest and longest in the world. There was a really ancient one that had formed in the shape of a grizzly bear. My dad showed me a picture once. He always said he'd take me to see it when I was old enough."

Dougal sighed sadly as a heavy silence fell once again.

"Well, as much as I'd like to stay and continue this jolly conversation, I should have been in the sanatorium five minutes ago," Germ said, heading for the door.

"Hang on a minute!" Angus grabbed Germ by the arm before he could leave. "How did you get into the library? The doors are supposed to be locked."

"Who says I came through the doors?" Germ said, his old grin returning. "There's more than one way into this library, if you know where to look."

Angus felt his spirits suddenly lift. "Will you show us? Jeremius is planning to keep us locked up in here until they destroy Dankhart's lightning tower."

"Only if you can get dressed in five seconds," Germ said, checking his weather watch. "I'm already supposed to be up to my earlobes in disinfectant."

Angus and Dougal raced back into their bedroom.

"We'll have to be careful," Dougal said, getting dressed at double speed. "If we're not back in Miss Vulpine's rooms before someone appears with our breakfast . . ."

Angus glanced at a dusty clock on the wall. It was still only a quarter to seven. They had plenty of time to go exploring. He pulled on some shoes and tried to tie his laces as they flew out the door. They followed Germ and Indigo down the narrow stairs and back into the library.

"What I'm about to show you is strictly top secret," Germ said, thoroughly enjoying himself now. "I discovered it when I was studying for my exams last term. I accidentally knocked a hot mug of onion soup over a pile of Miss Vulpine's most treasured books and needed to make a quick getaway before she had me vaporized. I was planning to sneak behind her desk and out through the main library doors when she wasn't looking. But then luckily, I tripped and fell against a bookshelf, and hey, presto!"

Germ stopped in front of a tall shelf stacked high with various weather dictionaries. He grabbed the spine of a thick book with a dull brown cover and tugged it. Indigo stumbled backward as a hidden door swung open. Beyond it a low, earthy tunnel disappeared into damp-smelling darkness.

"Are you sure this doesn't just lead down to the storm drains?" Dougal asked, wrinkling his nose in disgust.

"I'm insulted by the very notion," Germ said, pretending

to be offended. "This passage leads to your freedom, if you're brave enough to take it. Follow me and watch out for giant worms."

"G-giant worms?" Dougal said.

Germ grinned. "They're nothing much to worry about unless they slither down the back of your neck and drop straight into your underpants."

Dougal quickly tied a scarf around his neck, tucking both ends into his sweater.

Germ led the way, navigating the twists and turns inside the cramped passageway with ease. Angus tripped over his own feet several times in the darkness and banged his head painfully on something that felt like solid rock. Thankfully, there was no sign of any worms. But he was just beginning to wonder if Germ was leading them on a wild-goose chase when the tunnel began to wind its way uphill, and a few moments later, they were tumbling into a corridor outside the library. Angus blinked in the sudden light. He turned just in time to see a secret wooden panel sliding shut behind them in the wall.

"How do we get back into the library again?" Indigo asked, brushing dirt and cobwebs out of her hair.

"Simple, there's a lightning bolt carved into the corner of this panel." Germ pressed the lightning bolt with his thumb. They watched as the panel slid open and closed once again.

"Who else knows about the secret passageway?" Angus asked, staring along the corridor in both directions, double-checking that they were alone.

Germ shrugged. "Miss Vulpine definitely doesn't. Some of the other lightning catchers might, but I've never seen anyone else use it, and I've never told anyone it exists except for you three. So keep it under your hats," he said, thumbing the side of his nose.

"Yeah, we will, and thanks, Germ! This is brilliant!" Angus said as Indigo's brother disappeared down the corridor with a cheery wave.

"So, where shall we go?" Indigo asked, looking keen to escape the confines of the library.

"We could go down to the lightning cubs' living quarters and grab some stuff from our rooms," Dougal suggested. "Nobody else is back yet, so it should be deserted."

But Angus shook his head. He already knew exactly where he wanted to go. Germ's secret tunnel had suddenly reminded him of other tunnels he'd already visited with Gudgeon.

"I'm going down to the testing tunnels," he said, trying to sound braver than he felt.

Dougal frowned. "What on earth do you want to go down there for? Aren't they used by the experimental division for testing dangerous new devices?"

"Yeah, but it's also the perfect place for me to practice my storm prophet skills." He felt his pulse beginning to race at the possibilities they presented. "I've already been down there with Doctor Obsidian, and you heard what Germ said about the Exploratorium in Iceland. I mean, what if Dankhart sends a storm over to destroy Perilous next time? What if I can do something to help? If I train myself up a bit, I might be able to control the weather, or stop the storm. I don't know what I *can* do yet, but Jeremius and Rogwood won't even let me find out. I can't just hide in the library and wait until the whole thing is over."

"But how are you going to train yourself?" Indigo asked, sounding worried.

"By using Doctor Obsidian's projectograms," Angus

said. "It's a start, anyway. You don't have to come with me," he added, desperately hoping that they would.

"Of course we're coming with you. We'd never let you go on your own," Indigo said without hesitation.

Dougal, however, looked distinctly nervous.

Perilous was still eerily quiet as they made their way into the nearest tunnel. Angus took a familiar right turn and followed the path down at a steep angle into the labyrinth of stone veins and arteries running through the rock upon which Perilous sat.

"Weren't some of these tunnels sealed up hundreds of years ago?" Dougal's voice echoed around them in the darkness. "I mean, nobody knows what's inside them, do they? So, there could be a whole troupe of mutant fog phantoms just waiting for us to go blundering into their lair."

"As long as we stick to the route I took with Gudgeon, we'll be safe," Angus said, hoping it was true.

They continued downward for what felt like hours. Monstrous shadows followed their every step. Angus could feel the weight of rock pressing down on him from all sides. He was just wondering how much farther it could be when the tunnel leveled off and opened out into a roomy cavern. Several closed doors were set deep into the walls.

Angus sneaked into Doctor Obsidian's office—which, thankfully, stood dark and empty—and grabbed a set of keys from the back of the door. He then led Dougal and Indigo through another doorway that was almost opposite from the doctor's office, and into a narrow stone tunnel.

"Whoa." Dougal stopped and stared at a long line of steel safety doors stretching out ahead of them. "What's going on behind those doors?"

Several were bursting at the seams and looked ready to pop. Others were emitting a strange hissing sound, as if they were filled with a volatile gas that smelled like . . .

"Ew! Boiled cabbage," Dougal said, holding his sweater sleeve over his nose.

The next testing tunnel gave off a loud belching noise as they passed it, and Angus instantly felt a hot, sticky breeze waft past his ankles. Loud sloshing noises were coming from behind another door. It sounded like a party of lightning catchers holding a splashing competition.

They stopped outside the last door at the end of the

corridor. Angus took a deep breath, fitted a key into the lock, and turned it. The inside of the tunnel was just as vast as he remembered, with rough stone walls stretching far back into the shadows. There was a stale smell in the air, as if the tunnel hadn't been used for some time.

"This place is big enough for an underground skating lake," Dougal said, his voice echoing into the depths as Indigo closed the door behind them.

"This is the testing tunnel where the original storm prophets came to practice," Angus explained, repeating what Doctor Obsidian had told him some time ago. "There's a giant storm vacuum in case the weather gets out of hand."

Indigo stared up at the ceiling as Angus pointed out a battery of storm bellows, some air vents for releasing any overzealous winds, and a giant plug for dealing with sudden floods.

The projectogram box that Doctor Obsidian had used for Angus's training sessions lay abandoned at the side of the tunnel.

"So what do we do now?" Indigo asked, eager to get started.

"Um, I suppose I just pick a projectogram and see what happens," Angus said, suddenly feeling awkward. He'd never attempted to tackle any kind of training on his own before, or in front of Dougal and Indigo. What if he made an idiot of himself? Or worse still, failed to see his fire dragon at all?

He sorted slowly through the box of plates, trying to calm his nerves. Each one had been neatly labeled.

"This one looks like it could be thunderstorms," he said, holding it up to the light. "The label says something about lightning tarantulatis."

Dougal and Indigo hurried over to the side of the tunnel, giving him some space to tackle the lightning alone. Angus took a deep breath and slotted the plate into the back of the box.

Click!

He peered into the darkness. There was no sign anywhere of a thundercloud or spider-shaped lightning. Instead, the whole tunnel was suddenly filled with the pungent odor of wet dog.

"What's that horrible smell?" Indigo edged away from Dougal, holding her nose.

Dougal scowled. "Well, don't look at me. I had a bath last night before bed."

"Er, I think there's something in here with us," Angus said, staring into the shadowy tunnel. "I can hear some sort of snuffling noise." And a dozen pairs of strange green eyes blinked at him from the darkness. Dougal and Indigo joined Angus as something tall and hairy, with feet the size of trash can lids suddenly emerged. It was covered in a thick, shaggy pelt and looked like it hadn't touched a bar of soap in years. The smelly creature glared at them and then threw back its head and began to wail. The sound was appalling, like several high-pitched foghorns being mangled to death. Other wailing voices quickly joined in.

"I don't believe it. It's a yodeling of wild mountain fog yetis!" Dougal shouted above the dreadful noise as more yetis appeared from the darkness.

"Make it stop!" Indigo yelled, her hands clamped tightly over her ears.

Angus fumbled with the plate in the back of the projectogram box for several seconds before he finally managed to rip it out. The yetis disappeared and silence fell.

"This plate must have been mislabeled," he said, shoving it to one side so he wouldn't accidentally choose it again. He picked another one cautiously. It claimed to be a Swedish snowstorm.

Click!

They were standing on top of an enormous sand dune. Scorching desert stretched out before them in every direction. A long train of camels shimmered in a distant heat haze. A luxurious-looking hotel called the Mirage promised a chilled swimming pool, a palm tree retreat, and sand sculpture lessons.

"Er, I'm no expert," Dougal said, grinning, "but I don't think you're going to learn much about being a storm prophet from this projectogram."

Indigo snorted with giggles. Angus couldn't help smiling. He removed the plate before they got sunstroke.

At the back of the box were several unlabeled projectograms. He picked one at random.

"If this turns out to be a flower arranging festival in the middle of Little Frog's Bottom, I'm going back to the library," he said.

Click!

"Oh no! What now?" Dougal's voice suddenly sounded muffled.

A thick, foglike substance descended all around, making it almost impossible for Angus to see his own hand in front of his face. The walls of the tunnel had disappeared. He had the odd sensation that they were now standing outside.

"Maybe we're supposed to be out on the Imbur marshes," Indigo said.

Dougal waved his arms through the dense mist to try to see what lay beyond it, while Angus stared down at where his feet would be. They were standing on a narrow wooden platform that was barely big enough for the three of them. It was closed in on all sides by railings. Beyond the rails, faint lights blinked and flickered in the distance. Angus dropped to his knees and stared through a gap between the wooden boards as the foggy substance suddenly cleared, and he felt his head spin. Spread out beneath them, a long way down, was a flat roof littered with large storm jars and giant wooden rain funnels.

"Oh!" he said, surprised.

He was looking down on Perilous. Several lightning

catchers were scurrying across the roof, shouting urgently at one another, pointing toward the platform where he, Indigo, and Dougal now stood.

"What? What is it?" Dougal hovered anxiously as Angus clambered to his feet again.

"Don't panic, okay. But I think . . . I think we're standing on a weather viewing platform high above Perilous."

"We're what!" Dougal stared around wildly, a look of terror in his eyes. "Oh no, I'm a-a-a-absolutely p-p-p-petrified of heights!"

"But it isn't real," Indigo said. "You're still standing on the testing tunnel floor."

"It doesn't matter. My stomach can't tell the difference. Can't you just turn the projectogram off?" Dougal pleaded, clinging to the railings, his face now a bilious shade of green.

"Just give it a few more seconds, okay?" Angus said, peering toward the horizon. "I want to see what happens next."

"We already know what's going to happen." Dougal swallowed hard. "We've been through hundreds of storms since we came to Perilous, and every single one of them has dumped tons of snow, ice, and rain on top of us and soaked us down to our socks."

But Angus could now feel a charge of electricity in the air. There was a sudden streak of golden lightning to the west, followed quickly by a rumbling of thunder. A threatening cloud was hurrying across the sky and straight toward Perilous with unnatural speed. A moment later it came to rest directly above their heads and hovered there.

Whoosh!

All three of them ducked as something huge skimmed the base of the cloud.

"What was that?" Indigo said, searching the skies warily.

Angus spun around just in time to see a flash of fire, like a comet shooting through the sky.

Whoosh!

They ducked again as another enormous object flew overhead. It soared so low this time that Angus felt his hair part down the middle of his head. A fiery tail flicked and disappeared into the cloud, and he suddenly understood.

"They're fire dragons!" he yelled above the wind, which was howling around them and making the platform sway.

"Then how come I can see them?" Dougal said loudly next to him.

"Because it's just a projectogram." Indigo was breathless with excitement. "Right now, we can see the dragons because they aren't real."

Angus watched, transfixed, as lightning lashed out, illuminating several more fire dragons inside the cloud above. They swooped and dived, twisting endlessly through strands of storm with long streaks of flame.

"What are they doing?" Indigo yelled.

"I think . . . I think they're trying to control the lightning," Angus said, without taking his eyes off the magnificent creatures. "I saw them doing the same thing in 1666, through the retrospectacles."

But there was something different this time, Angus realized. The dragons weren't just attempting to drag the storm away from the Exploratorium and disperse it. They were also fighting with one another. Fire dragon plunged after fire dragon with talons drawn and tails swishing wildly as they chased across the skies. The heat from their flames was incredible.

"Watch out!" Indigo warned as one fiery creature fell,

tumbling through the clouds. It narrowly missed the platform, scorching the wood around their feet.

"Are you absolutely positive this isn't real?" Dougal yelled.

Angus watched, mesmerized, as yet more dragons joined the fray. Several creatures looked larger and more vicious than the others. They barreled into the smaller fire dragons with ferocious speed and force, knocking them through every inch of sky and cloud.

"Look out!" Dougal was pointing directly overhead to where two scaly creatures were now locked in battle, plummeting through the sky in a tangle of burning flames.

Angus dived and grabbed the projectogram from the back of the box. Real or not, he had no desire to know what it felt like to be incinerated by the fighting dragons. The tunnel was suddenly dark, quiet, and empty once again. He could hear nothing but the beating of his own heart and several stray hiccups coming from Dougal's direction. He was just about to suggest retreating back to the library when—

"Would somebody care to explain to me why you three aren't dead?" a stern voice said.

Indigo turned sharply on her heels and gasped. Angus dropped the projectogram with a *bang*, which echoed loudly round the walls.

Principal Delphinia Dark-Angel had just walked into the testing tunnel behind them.

5
LOST PROPERTY

"Explain yourselves!" Dark-Angel marched into the tunnel, her usual stony expression replaced by a strange mixture of anger and surprise. Angus took several steps backward as she came to an abrupt halt, towering over them.

"Dewsnap, tell me what is going on this instant or I will see to it that you, McFangus, and Midnight spend the next month draining swamp water from the marshes."

"I, um, I . . ." Dougal faltered.

Dark-Angel turned to Indigo instead. "Quickly, girl, tell me— Do any of your parents know that you did not perish in an accident at the Canadian Exploratorium?"

Indigo hesitated for a second and then nodded.

Dark-Angel let out a long sigh before continuing. "I assume that Jeremius is at the bottom of this elaborate charade?"

Angus glanced sideways at Dougal and Indigo. There was little point in lying now. "Yes, miss."

"He faked an accident at the Canadian Exploratorium, to protect you from Dankhart and his monsoon mongrels?"

Angus nodded, trying hard not to say any more than was absolutely necessary.

"Jeremius has more brains than I give him credit for," Dark-Angel said, studying them shrewdly. "I am a little surprised, however, that he did not inform me of his intentions."

"He couldn't, miss," Angus said hurriedly. "He said if *you* believed we were really dead, then it would be easier to convince everyone else."

"Did he indeed?" Dark-Angel raised an eyebrow at him. "And where has Jeremius been concealing you now that you have returned to Perilous?"

"W-we're staying in the library, miss," Indigo said. "In Miss Vulpine's living quarters."

"Ah yes, of course. That explains the sudden infestation of fog mites. No one will disturb you in there; you will be safe enough for the time being."

Angus quickly swallowed down a mad urge to ask Dark-Angel if they would be safe from *her*. Now that she knew they were still alive, would she pass the information straight on to Dankhart? And what would Indigo's uncle do when he found out?

"I really should congratulate Jeremius on his highly inventive plan. It's a shame he felt it necessary to destroy some very old and important glacier caves in the process," Dark-Angel continued. "But I was indeed convinced that you, Miss Midnight, and Mr. Dewsnap had perished. I am very pleased to see you have not," she said, almost smiling. "All three of you have shown quite some promise as lightning cubs."

Angus stared at the principal, flabbergasted. She had never said anything so complimentary before.

"I am curious to know, however, why you are loitering in this testing tunnel."

"Er," Angus said, not really sure how to answer. Telling Dark-Angel he was hoping to practice his storm prophet skills had never been part of the plan. Before he could think of another explanation, however, Dark-Angel's eyes fixed on the projectogram plate that he'd dropped on the floor.

Her eyebrows shot up in surprise. "Jeremius is allowing you to continue with your storm prophet training?"

"Er," Angus said again.

Dark-Angel understood instantly. "So, you are here without his consent? You have decided to take matters into your own hands."

Angus tried to keep his face impassive. Dark-Angel already knew too much.

"I am impressed, McFangus," the principal said, studying him closely. "I have always believed that your skills could prove crucial to us here at Perilous. I would not normally agree to any training without strict supervision, but these are not normal times. Unlike Rogwood and your uncle, I have never been afraid to steer you toward your rightful destiny as a storm prophet."

She folded her arms with a thoughtful expression. "Very well, McFangus. I will pretend I haven't seen you or your friends here today."

Angus frowned. "I—I don't understand, miss." This was not the response he'd been expecting.

"It is quite simple: I will go along with the story that you and your friends perished. I will also ensure that this room is made accessible to you at any time. I will instruct Doctor Obsidian to lay out a range of tools that may assist with your training. If you foolishly allow yourselves to get caught, however, I will deny ever having this conversation," she warned. "This will be our secret, possibly the first of several that could benefit us all greatly. I must have your solemn promise that you will tell no one about our arrangement, including Jeremius."

"Er," Angus said, taken aback. The fact that Dark-Angel now knew they were alive would almost certainly cause a swift change in his uncle's plans. Jeremius would whisk all three of them straight back to the Windmill at Budleigh Otterstone, where they would be absolutely no help to anyone. Whatever the cost, Angus couldn't let that happen.

"Well, McFangus?" Dark-Angel was still staring at him with pinpoint focus. "Do you agree to my terms?"

Angus glanced at Dougal and Indigo. "W-we promise

not to tell anyone, miss," he said quickly, before he could think better of it. Dougal and Indigo both nodded in silent agreement.

"Then it is settled." A small, calculated smile crossed the principal's lips. "Please make sure you lock the door after you leave the testing tunnel. And, McFangus," she added, "welcome back to Perilous."

And without another word she turned and marched straight out of the door, closing it behind her.

"Whoa!" Dougal sagged with relief as soon as the coast was clear. "That was scarier than coming face-to-face with a cloud full of murderous stinging fog!"

"Of all the lightning catchers who could have found us in here . . ." Indigo said, looking almost as shocked as Angus felt. "We've got to find Jeremius and tell him what's happened."

Dougal nodded eagerly. "Yeah, with any luck, he'll put us straight back on the weather station and we'll be on our way to a secret, cozy, lightning-proof bunker somewhere before you can say 'lying, cheating, principal–lightning catcher.'"

But Angus shook his head slowly. "We can't go

anywhere. We've got to stay at Perilous, and we've got to keep our promise to Dark-Angel."

There was a short stunned silence, then . . . "Have you completely lost your marbles?" Dougal shrieked. "Now that Dark-Angel knows we're still alive, she's bound to go skipping off to Indigo's dear old uncle Scabby. We're not safe at Perilous anymore."

"But it's the only place I can improve my storm prophet skills," Angus said carefully, trying to explain. "And if Dark-Angel's willing to let me use the testing tunnels . . ."

"You don't actually think she's going to keep her end of the bargain, do you?" Dougal looked extremely miffed.

"Dougal's right," Indigo said quietly. "For all we know, she's planning to let you train yourself up so she can hand you over to my uncle Scabious, just like she handed over the dragon scales."

Angus thought about the possibility that Dougal and Indigo might be right and then instantly decided he didn't care. Dankhart was planning to do terrible things, whether Dark-Angel handed Angus over to him or not. He, Angus, had to be ready to face the worst storms imaginable. Staying at Perilous was his only hope.

It felt extremely strange, however, promising to keep a secret from his uncle with the very person who had betrayed them all.

Angus replayed the conversation with Dark-Angel over and over inside his head as they retraced their steps slowly through the tunnels, hoping he hadn't just made the most reckless and dangerous decision of his entire life. Thankfully, they reached the sliding panel outside the library without meeting anyone else. They hurried down the secret tunnel and emerged beside the shelf full of weather dictionaries several minutes later, feeling hot and out of breath. Angus checked his weather watch. They'd been gone for almost two hours.

It was obvious that Catcher Sparks had beaten them to it when they finally entered Miss Vulpine's rooms through the doorway at the top of the secret stairs. Their breakfast, which had gone cold, had been left with a stern note telling them to meet her beside the librarian's desk at nine o'clock.

"That gives us precisely five minutes to gulp down some toast and get changed into our uniforms," Dougal said, already looking worn out. "We'll never make it to the end of the day if it carries on like this."

Twenty minutes later, after Dougal had ransacked the bedroom looking for his sweater and Indigo had eventually found it stuffed behind a cushion in the sitting room, they raced back down to the library. Catcher Sparks was already waiting, her nostrils flaring dangerously.

"Where on earth have you three been?" she demanded angrily as Angus tucked his shirt into his trousers and attempted to knot his yellow tie. "And why weren't you upstairs when I delivered your breakfast?"

"N-none of us could sleep, miss," Indigo said, thinking quickly. "We've been exploring the fiction section of the library, and we lost track of time."

"Well, make sure that it does not happen again, Midnight. I am extremely busy in the experimental division. I cannot simply stand around waiting for you three to turn up for lightning cub duties whenever you feel like it."

"Duties?" Dougal frowned. "But, miss, we're supposed to be dead!"

"That's no excuse, Dewsnap," Catcher Sparks snapped. "You will continue your training as lightning cubs in as normal a manner as possible. Now, comc with me. We've wasted enough time as it is."

They followed in silence as Catcher Sparks turned straight toward the main library doors, the new buckles on her leather jerkin clinking once again.

"She's not taking us out into the Exploratorium, is she?" Angus whispered.

At the last second, however, Catcher Sparks veered off to the left and led them straight past the doors and beyond several narrow aisles of books until they reached a roomy cupboard. Catcher Sparks shuffled them inside. It was stocked with plentiful supplies of pencils, book-binding materials, and several Cradget's products that had clearly been confiscated from their unlucky owners. They came to a halt in front of a tall pyramid of shiny metal buckets. Angus was just wondering if they were about to spend the day mopping the library floors when Catcher Sparks reached inside one of the buckets at the bottom of the stack. She plucked out a key, slotted it into a tiny lock hidden between the rusting handles of the buckets, and turned it. The whole pyramid swung open, revealing a doorway behind it.

"I don't believe it," Dougal whispered. "This place has got more secret passageways than a castle in a fairy tale."

Angus had a strong feeling, however, that the fairy tale was about to come to an end. At the bottom of a set of stairs, another door led to a long, dimly lit corridor that reminded him of a dungeon. Hard cobbles covered the floor. A few faint light fissures flickered along the walls, giving the impression they could fail at any moment. The corridor was lined with a large number of closed wooden doors.

"This is the lost property department," Catcher Sparks announced, her voice echoing around the walls. "In the early years at Perilous, most lost items were disposed of if they weren't claimed by their owners in a matter of months. But one of our earliest librarians, Mr. Rintoul, saw that over time, this collection of lost property could form a valuable historical record of our everyday life here at Perilous, and an archive of unclaimed articles was formed."

Angus stared at the closed doors, trying to imagine what lay behind them. Abandoned rubber boots perhaps, or piles of old storm schedules from the Rotundra?

"In more recent years the archive has fallen into disarray. Mrs. Roach, the librarian here for many years, had an arthritic hip and couldn't manage the stairs, and then there was Mr. Knurling."

Angus and Dougal both glanced at Indigo, who stared straight ahead, her cheeks glowing fiery red.

"Miss Vulpine has done her best to bring some order to the chaos, but she has been kept extremely busy by current events, so it will be up to you three to sort through it and catalog every item." She pointed to a large book lying open on a desk outside one of the doors where someone with very neat handwriting had clearly made a start on the job.

"Um, catalog what exactly, miss?" Angus asked, still puzzled.

Without another word, Catcher Sparks set off down the corridor, passing rooms that had clearly been set aside for items found in the research department, the sanatorium, the kitchens, the living quarters, and the roof. There were also rooms for stuff discovered in the cloud gardens, the gravity railway carriage, the stone tunnels and passageways, the weather tunnel, the entrance hall, the Rotundra, and the testing tunnels. Catcher Sparks stopped at the far end of the corridor, in front of a door marked "Lost Property: Experimental Division."

"I'm not going in there," Dougal whispered as she disappeared inside the room, clearly expecting them to follow. "There's bound to be something with hooks or suction pipes lurking about in the shadows."

Luckily, however, the room was stacked high with nothing but row upon row of neatly arranged shelves. Some of the lost property had been placed in boxes. Other items had been vacuum-packed to stop them from rotting.

"The most recent articles of lost property have been placed at the front of the room, closest to the door. The oldest ones are at the back," Catcher Sparks said, leading them to the darkest corner, where most of the shelves were covered in thick layers of cobwebs, dust, and mold. The air smelled damp, with a strong hint of things that were slowly decaying.

"But, miss, this has got nothing to do with the weather," Dougal said.

"I am aware of that, Dewsnap, but I will not have you three twiddling your thumbs in the library, getting bored and causing trouble. Besides, this is the only place I can guarantee you will not run into any of your fellow lightning cubs. You will set aside anything that is broken, putrid, or disintegrating." She pointed to some garbage bags on the floor. "This is a list of various items lost by current lightning catchers." She took a sheet of paper from her pocket and handed it to Indigo. "It details the year each item was lost, and the name of the lightning catcher now searching for it. If you come across any of these items, they should be set aside, and I will reunite them with their owners. In particular, I would like you to look out for a pair of canary-yellow rubber boots decorated with green jumping frogs."

Dougal chuckled quietly beside Angus. "I wouldn't be caught dead wearing those. I wonder who they belong to."

"They belong to me, Dewsnap." Catcher Sparks folded her arms across her chest angrily. "And I will thank you not to snigger at my personal belongings."

Dougal's ears turned a violent shade of pink.

"This is not an excuse to sit around gossiping. I will expect to see the beginnings of a neatly written catalog by lunchtime. You may begin."

Catcher Sparks left the room without another word and closed the door behind her.

"We'd better get started." Angus approached the first set of shelves with a heavy feeling in his stomach. Sorting through piles of lost property was the last thing he felt like doing after his conversation with Dark-Angel.

"This place is like a rabbits' warren. How are we supposed to find anything in here?" Dougal said.

"Maybe that's the real reason it's called the lost property department." Angus picked up an odd glowing glass tube and inspected it. "Because once something's been brought down here, there's no hope of it ever being found again."

He pulled a box onto the floor that, according to the label on the front, held the contents of a storm vacuum that had gone berserk in the experimental division just the day before.

"I knew it." Dougal inched away from the box. "I said there'd be suction pipes!"

Angus emptied the contents onto the floor. "Everything's covered in fluff and dirt."

There were torn maps and wall charts, broken feathered quills, chewed pencils, and what looked like the remains of a fancy fairy costume, complete with sparkly wand

and wings, both now ripped to shreds by the force of the powerful vacuum.

"Who'd be crazy enough to wear fairy wings in the experimental division?" Angus said, surprised. Indigo picked a copy of the very latest *Weathervane* out of the debris and tried to flatten out the pages, which had been twisted and crumpled.

"I don't believe it. Cradget's is holding a massive sale." Dougal pointed despondently to a full-page ad. "All their timer puzzles are half price. And we're stuck in the stupid lost property department."

"Did we miss anything else?" Angus asked, untangling a pair of blunt scissors from a ball of frayed string.

"There's an in-depth weather forecast for Isle of Imbur," Indigo said, scanning the magazine quickly. "It says the weather over the next week is going to be unpredictable, with the likelihood of some hail, snow, frost, sunshine, rain, and gales."

"That's really helpful, that is," Dougal said, rolling his eyes.

"And . . ." Indigo turned a page and stopped reading abruptly.

"What?" Angus asked.

"I don't believe it. There's something in here about us!"

Angus abandoned the box and hurried over. Beneath a recipe for toasted turnip sandwiches was a somber-looking article in bold black letters.

"'Tributes to Angus McFangus, Dougal Dewsnap, and Indigo Midnight pour in after tragic accident at Canadian Exploratorium,'" Indigo read the headline, turning pale.

"Who are the tributes from?" Angus asked, staring over her shoulder.

"There's one here from Catcher Grimble," Indigo said, reading it aloud. "'Agnes Munchfungus, Douglas Drainpipe, and India Mildew were three of the finest lightning cubs I've ever had the pleasure to teach in the research department. They will be sorely missed.'"

"Typical." Dougal shook his head in disbelief. "Even when we're dead he gets our names wrong."

"What does Nicholas Grubb say about us?" Angus asked, seeing the familiar name underneath Catcher Grimble's.

"'I reckon Dark-Angel's not telling us the truth about what really happened in Canada. I was one of the last people who spoke to Angus on the ferry when we broke up for Christmas, and he said he was spending the holidays in Devon.'"

"If everybody else reads that, we're in big trouble," Dougal said.

There were heartfelt tributes from Jonathon Hake, Nigel Ridgely, and Violet Quinn, all fellow second-year lightning cubs. Winnie Wrascal, the lightning catcher who had supervised their duties in the forecasting department the previous term, was too distraught to speak.

"It's really odd reading what other people thought of us now that we're supposed to be dead," Angus said with a shiver.

"It's a good thing nobody asked any of the Vellums to say a few words," Dougal said. "They would have been unprintable."

Angus stared at the quotes, wondering what the same people would say once they discovered he, Dougal, and Indigo were still very much alive. Indigo turned to the front cover of the *Weathervane*, still trying to flatten the pages, when a sudden look of dismay crossed her face.

"What's wrong now?" Angus asked.

Indigo placed the magazine on one of the lower shelves

with trembling fingers, so they could all see it. Angus stared at the cover, wondering why the *Weathervane* had printed a photo of some crumbling old ruins surrounded by large heaps of rubble. It took him several seconds to realize that the dreadful image showed all that was now left of the Icelandic Exploratorium.

Indigo shook her head. “It’s just so terrible.”

“Dankhart must be testing his storms out on one of the smallest Exploratoriums first, to see if they’re strong enough to destroy it,” Angus said, forcing himself to study the pictures in detail.

“Are there any pictures of the actual storm?” asked Dougal. “Germ said the London office had issued an evacuation warning, so they must have seen it coming.”

Angus flicked through the remaining pages but found nothing except a long-winded article about submersible storm detectors.

“I wonder how big the storm was,” he said. “I mean, did it look any different from a normal thundercloud?”

“If Indigo’s dear old uncle Scabby had anything to do with it, it probably had luminous green lightning and screaming thunderbolts.”

"Oh please, don't!" Indigo burst out suddenly, making Angus and Dougal flinch.

Her shoulders began to shake with great, heaving sobs.

"Um, is everything all right?" Angus asked, wishing he could think of a less stupid question.

"No!" Tears were streaming down Indigo's anguished face. Dougal took a clean handkerchief from his pocket and handed it to her cautiously, at arm's length. "Why does my uncle Scabious have to hate the lightning catchers so much? Why does he have to try to destroy everything?"

"Um, that's an easy one. Because he's a complete maniac," Dougal said, looking confused.

"But he wasn't always like that." Indigo dabbed at her eyes, taking great gulps of air in an effort to control her tears. "I mean, Mum . . . says he used to be a good brother. . . . He had no interest in the weather when he was younger. She said he wanted to leave Imbur . . . and travel the world."

Angus could clearly recall a highly confusing photo Indigo had once found of her mum as a young girl. It had shown Etheldra Dankhart, sitting on a trunk, laughing with her older brother, Scabious, a boy with short hair and an innocent smile. His resemblance to Indigo had been striking.

Angus patted Indigo's arm awkwardly as she blew her nose.

"Mum says everything was different after my grandparents died," Indigo continued. "She says that's when Uncle Scabious changed."

"Yeah, changed into a total weather lunatic, just like all the other Dankharts before him," Dougal said.

Indigo's face crumpled once again. "I just wish I understood why."

The rest of the day passed very slowly indeed. The work was incredibly dull, and they were soon covered in a fine layer of dust. The highlight of the morning came when Indigo discovered a tiny collapsing skeleton that could then rebuild its own body, bone by bone.

"I'm definitely taking this back up to Miss Vulpine's rooms," Dougal said, swiftly putting it into his pocket.

Indigo frowned. "But it doesn't belong to us."

"Who cares? Nobody's coming back for it now, are they?"

At lunchtime Catcher Sparks returned briefly to inspect

the entries they'd made in the catalog and left them with a large plate of egg sandwiches. As soon as Dougal had eaten the last one, they discussed their encounter with Dark-Angel in the testing tunnels.

"I still think we should consider telling someone about Dark-Angel," Indigo said quietly.

"Yeah." Dougal nodded. "This isn't like playing a stupid trick on Percival Vellum. We could get ourselves killed."

"And what did Principal Dark-Angel mean about this being the *first* of several secrets?" Indigo said, biting her lip.

Angus avoided Indigo's gaze, pretending to coil a length of copper wire. Dark-Angel's words had been deeply disconcerting. He had no idea what her real plans involved. Or how dangerous life inside Perilous was about to become.

"We'll just have to be really careful," he eventually said.

"How is that going to stop Dankhart from destroying the library with a gigantic storm?" Dougal hissed.

They left the lost property department at the end of the day feeling hot, tired, and glad to be back in Miss Vulpine's rooms. Dinner had already been laid out on the table in the sitting room. Angus tucked hungrily into the plate of goulash. After having second helpings of chocolate sponge cake and pink custard, they spent the rest of the evening discussing the fire dragon battle that had raged above their heads in the testing tunnels.

"I didn't even know fire dragons could fight one another," Indigo said, sitting with her legs curled up underneath her.

"Rogwood told me about two storm prophets who had a weather duel in the Inner Sanctum once, but it was just a stupid argument." Angus remembered the room Rogwood had taken him to where the huge fossilized imprint of the battle had been left behind. "He never said anything about fire dragon fights over Perilous."

By the time Angus went to bed, his head was spinning. His dreams were instantly filled with a confusing jumble of images. He was standing in the testing tunnels with a group of fog yetis that were yodeling a medley of Christmas carols. Fire dragons swooped overhead, locked in yet another fierce tussle. Angus could suddenly feel a familiar burning sensation deep inside his chest.

Bang!

His own fire dragon finally appeared. It was a magnificent creature with molten fire dripping from its outstretched wings. Angus felt extremely glad to see it. He watched as it darted up to join the skirmish that was still raging about the tunnel. But the other creatures were bigger, ten times more dangerous and powerful. They turned instantly on his fire dragon. Talons ripped through its flames with a searing pain that Angus could feel, as if his own body had been struck. His fire dragon was suddenly falling. Weak and wounded, the fire dragon plunged into a deadly tailspin that could have only one possible outcome.

"No!"

Angus woke with a start, sitting bolt upright, half expecting to find the fire dragon still plummeting through the air above him. But the room was dark and quiet. Dougal was snoring gently in the other bed.

Angus lay back against his lumpy pillows, breathing heavily, rubbing the spot in his chest where just moments before a great fire had almost burned a hole through his rib cage. There was nothing there now, except the loud hammering of his heart.

He was woken again a few hours later by an odd noise, which sounded like two gigantic rocks being ground together. He stared sleepily around the room. Dougal's bed was already empty. He got dressed quickly and wandered into the sitting room, where he was met by a cold blast of icy air. The doors that lead out on to the roof terrace had been flung wide open. Angus grabbed his coat from the landing and followed the strange grinding noise outside.

The terrace was roughly the same size as the sitting room. It was also sadly neglected, with two moldy garden chairs, a rickety table, and rusting metal railings around the sides. The views across the island, however, were breathtaking. Little Frog's Bottom sat wintry-looking and cold, with smoke rising from its many crooked chimneys. In the distance Angus could clearly see the treacherous mountains they'd flown through in the weather station. He took a deep breath, filling his lungs with fresh air for the first time since they'd returned to Perilous.

Dougal and Indigo were wrapped up warmly in coats, scarves, and woolen hats. They were taking turns peering through what looked like a telescope, which was pointing over the side of the railing and straight down at a near vertical angle.

"What's going on? Why didn't you come and wake me

up?" Angus asked, rubbing sleep out of his eyes as he blinked in the bright morning light.

"We were just about to," Indigo said. "But then we discovered the telescope and— Oh, you'd better come and see for yourself!"

Dougal stepped to one side, beaming, as Angus bent over the telescope and stared down through the eyepiece. It took a second for his eyes to focus properly.

"Whoa!" He took a step backward in surprise. "I can see straight down into the gravity railway carriage." And he suddenly understood that the strange noise had been created by the carriage traveling up and down the rock upon which Perilous sat. The rest of the lightning cubs were finally returning.

He peered through the telescope again. Several third years were sniggering at Edmund Croxley, who had obviously got dressed in a hurry and had accidentally tucked his sweater into a pair of bright orange underpants. Theodore Twill and Nicholas Grubb appeared to be arguing over the last empty seat in the carriage and were shoving each other away from it. Clifford Fugg looked like he was about to be sick, clutching his stomach as the carriage shot upward at an alarming speed. Angus could feel his own stomach lurch in sympathy. When the carriage reached the top, lightning cubs spilled out into the courtyard. Angus felt a sudden pang of envy as they headed inside for some hot buttered toast in the kitchens, where they would undoubtedly receive a lecture from Catcher Sparks about rowdy behavior. It was the first time ever that he, Dougal, and Indigo had not been a part of the happy throng, although he definitely didn't miss seeing Pixie and Percival Vellum.

Angus watched as the thuggish twins barged through the rest of the crowd, elbowing two first years out of the way. Their gorillalike looks were magnified grotesquely by the telescope.

"Do you reckon Miss Vulpine uses this telescope for stargazing?" Dougal asked as Angus stepped to one side and allowed his friend to take another turn at the eyepiece.

Angus grinned. "Either that, or for glaring at anyone who hasn't returned their library books on time."

"Hey, if I turn it all the way around to the left, I can see straight through the roof of the Rotundra," Dougal said, swinging the telescope. "There're snowstorms and orange tents and igloos. It's just a pity we can't spy on Percival Vellum in the lightning cubs' living quarters. We could watch him picking his toenails."

"Ew! Don't!" Indigo wrinkled her nose in disgust. "Why on earth would we want to see that?"

Dougal stepped aside so she could take another turn looking through the lens.

"I can see all the way to Little Frog's Bottom," Indigo said, moving the telescope to a new position and adjusting the eyepiece. "There's Brabazon Botanicals and the statue of Philip Starling and Edgar Perilous."

"Can you see inside Crevice and Sons?" Angus asked, wondering if they could use the telescope to find out if the bone merchant had any more visits from Dark-Angel.

But Indigo gave a sudden yelp and leaped away from the lens.

"What is it?" Angus asked, wondering if she'd jabbed herself in the eye.

"Th-there's a storm." Indigo pointed toward the horizon. "It's coming across the town and heading straight for us. We've got to get inside!"

Dougal was already backing away in a panic. Angus, however, raced to the edge of the roof terrace and stared into the distance. There was no need for the telescope now. The storm was large and threatening. It was obvious by the way it was hurtling across the sky at an unnatural speed that it wasn't part of any normal weather pattern. It must have been sent straight from Castle Dankhart.

The tempest had closed the gap between Little Frog's Bottom and Perilous in a matter of seconds. It was bigger than any storm Angus had ever seen, filling the skies above the Exploratorium and beyond with a churning, menacing gloom. He stared at the pitch-black center, half expecting to catch a glimpse of fire and a flash of golden tail.

Crash! Crash! Crash!

Fifty lightning bolts suddenly struck out from the cloud, making all three of them cringe away from the blinding flare.

"Well, that's definitely not normal!" Dougal shouted above the rippling whipcracks of thunder that followed.

Crash! Crash! Crash!

Countless more lightning bolts burst out of the cloud,

as if a hundred storms had settled above Perilous at once. Each lightning bolt fractured as it hit its mark, sending dozens of smaller bolts in every direction like out-of-control firecrackers. Lightning struck out at the Rotundra, the weather bubbles, and the storm vacuums on the roof.

"Quickly! Back inside and close the doors!" Indigo yelled above the terrible noise of the storm. Dougal was already sprinting for the safety of the sitting room. Angus turned and ran, his foot catching on one of the chairs. He tripped.

"Ooof!"

He fell hard, scraping both his knees painfully. Indigo grabbed him by the coat and hauled him back onto his feet, shoving him through the doors before he could catch his breath. Dougal slammed it behind them and turned the key in the lock, as if it could somehow keep out the storm.

Crash! Crash! Crash!

Lightning struck the balcony, the telescope, and the very spot where they'd been standing just seconds before. Each bolt fractured and sent dozens more deadly fizzles of flame in every direction.

Smash!

The doors to the terrace were suddenly blown off their hinges. A fracture of lightning bolts forced their way inside.

"Take cover!" Angus yelled.

He dived behind the nearest armchair, where Dougal was already sheltering with his hands over his head. Indigo scrambled under the table where last night's dinner plates were still stacked in a neat pile.

Light fissures and picture frames were instantly incinerated as the lightning flashed in every direction, leaving long smoldering burns across the walls and carpet, which faded seconds later, filling the room with an acrid smell of smoke.

"Arghhh!" Dougal shrieked as yet more lightning struck the chair he and Angus were cowering behind. "If you want to improve your storm prophet skills, this would be an excellent time to practice!"

Angus stared at Dougal, shocked, suddenly wondering why his fire dragon hadn't already appeared. Why hadn't it burst out of his chest at the first hint of lightning trouble? He closed his eyes and tried to concentrate, searching for the familiar feeling of burning flames inside his rib cage.

But the hollow of his chest felt cold and empty.

"Nothing's happening!" He opened his eyes again as fresh flashes of lightning bounced around the room. "I can't even feel my fire dragon!"

"But you're a storm prophet! Can't you do *something*?" Dougal pleaded.

Angus grabbed Dougal's arm, dragged him to his feet, and made a daring dash across the room.

"Indigo! Run!"

He dived for the open doorway that led into the landing. Indigo shot out from under the table and followed, grabbing a mirror off the wall and using it as a shield to protect herself against a last crackle of dangerous lightning.

Flash!

Indigo dropped the shimmering mirror as it exploded. A hundred cutthroat shards flashed around the room and shattered the clock on the opposite wall as the storm finally began to fizzle, fade, and die.

6

THE SILVER LIGHTNING CLOUD

B*ang!*

They heard the door that led back to the library burst open. Jeremius came charging up the stairs toward them a second later, taking two steps at a time.

"Is everyone all right?" he asked urgently, stumbling through the open door at the top. "Was anyone hit by lightning?"

"We were on the roof terrace when the storm struck, but we managed to get inside," Angus explained quickly.

Indigo shuddered. "So did the lightning."

They took Jeremius into the sitting room. The lightning had burned almost everything to a blackened shell.

Luckily, a brief, intense rainstorm, which had clearly followed the fracture lightning through the open doors, had now quenched the worst of the fires.

Jeremius shook his head as the last of the raindrops fell and the cloud fizzled away to nothing. "I'm sorry. We had very little warning. There was no time to come up here and make sure you three were safe. We were lucky, this time. The storm wasn't fierce enough to cause anything other than some superficial damage," he said, stamping out some of the burns on the carpet that were still smoldering. "Dankhart isn't ready to destroy Perilous *yet.* He was simply trying to scare us, to show us that he means business."

"Well, we definitely got the message," Dougal said, shivering violently.

"We weren't expecting Dankhart and Swarfe to combine the dragon scales and the storm particles again so quickly after they destroyed the Icelandic Exploratorium. But now that they've perfected their technique, they won't hold back." Jeremius ran a hand over his anxious-looking face. "I'm afraid we can expect things to get much worse."

"That settles it," Dougal said as soon as Jeremius left

fifteen minutes later. "We've got to tell someone what happened in the testing tunnels. First, we bump into Dark-Angel, and twenty-four hours later your dear old uncle Scabby's trying to finish us off with some fracture lightning."

Angus stared around the devastated room and nudged a pile of ashes with his foot. Up until an hour ago it had been a lampstand. The lightning storm had lashed out at the very room where they were supposed to be safe. Could it really have been nothing more than a coincidence?

"But it doesn't make any sense." Indigo smeared a long streak of blackened soot across her forehead as she pushed her hair out of her eyes. "If my uncle Scabious wants Angus for his storm prophet skills, why would he try to kill him?"

"Because he's a total maniac!" Dougal said, exasperated. "Jeremius needs to know what's really going on before Dankhart turns up on that roof terrace in the middle of the night with a bag of storm globes. And what happened to your fire dragon?" he added, suddenly turning to face Angus with wide, anxious eyes. "That storm could have incinerated all three of us!"

"I-I'm sorry." Angus stared at his friends, feeling worse by the second. "I don't know why it didn't appear."

It wasn't the first time it had failed to show up lately either, he suddenly realized. When they'd seen the projectogram in the testing tunnels, with fire dragons swooping above his head, his own fire dragon had remained dormant and still, almost as if it were sleeping. The only time he'd even felt its presence recently, in fact, had been in his dreams. But his dreams couldn't help anybody.

News of the damage the storm had caused filtered slowly up to Miss Vulpine's rooms over the next twenty-four hours. Catcher Sparks told them, after some badgering, that the cloud gardens had been set alight and reduced to ashes.

Jeremius came back with Rogwood early the next morning to repair the smashed doors that led out on to the roof terrace and to replace the furniture that had been burned to a crisp. Thankfully, the damage to the rest of the room was much more superficial than it had first appeared, and after sweeping up the piles of ash, cutting out singed portions of carpet, and sponging the worst of the soot off the walls, it was habitable once again. It now had a rather charred appearance, however, making it even drearier than before.

"Dankhart and Swarfe aren't the only ones who've been creating their own weather," Jeremius told them when the job had finally been completed. "We've already started work in the Lightnarium on a storm to destroy the lightning tower."

"But how are you going to make a storm that's powerful enough?" Angus asked as Dougal tested out the springs in one of the well-worn replacement armchairs.

"We started off by experimenting with storm globes," Jeremius said, "but it soon became obvious they wouldn't be big enough."

"So, we are now exploring the possibilities of generating our own storms in the Lightnarium," Rogwood explained. "Catcher Sparks and her team in the experimental division have also got some interesting ideas about using weather crystals."

Jeremius nodded. "We're having a few teething problems. The storms tend to fizzle out far too quickly, but it's a start."

"But when will the storm be ready? I mean, Dankhart's

already destroyed the Exploratorium in Iceland," Angus said, feeling his anxiety rise. "What if he decides to attack the ones in Alaska or Norway next?"

Rogwood tried to hide the worry on his face with a weary smile. "We're working as hard as we can, Angus. In fact, Valentine Vellum and his lightning experts are testing a new batch of storms later today."

It was only when Germ arrived unexpectedly at dinnertime the following evening that they heard more details of the fracture lightning attack.

"Everyone's watching the skies, waiting for the next storm to hit," he said, finishing off a roasted potato that Indigo had left on her plate. "No one's allowed outside. Dark-Angel's yelling at anyone who even glances at a window."

"But did the lightning cause much damage?" Indigo asked anxiously.

"It caused havoc up on the roof, some of the windows in the lightning cubs' living quarters were blown out, and a water pipe burst in the experimental division. Some of the lightning got into the Octagon and burned down the door to the Inner Sanctum."

"You're kidding?" Dougal paused with a slice of chicken pie halfway to his mouth.

"Nothing got through the inner safety door, according to Doctor Fleagal, but Dark-Angel's not taking any chances. She's got a party of lightning catchers fitting a second door on the inside. The whole Exploratorium's crawling with lightning catchers day and night, so you three had better watch it if you're planning to sneak out of the library," Germ warned, licking cold gravy off his fingers. "I almost got caught by Miss Vulpine coming in here this evening. She was gazing at her books through the library doors, looking all forlorn. I had to duck under a study desk before she saw me."

"I hate hiding up here and just waiting for news," Angus said as soon as Germ had gone. "And what am I supposed to do about storm prophet practice now?"

"Germ's right," Indigo said, looking worried. "It's far too risky for another training session in the testing tunnels."

"But I can't just sit and wait in the library while Dankhart plans his next move."

Indigo stared down at the bleckles on her hand. Since her recent outburst she had looked even more uncomfortable and upset than usual when anyone mentioned her uncle's name. "And what if Jeremius is wrong and your uncle decides to destroy Perilous next time?" Angus asked, feeling an anxious knot tighten in his chest. "We've got to do something."

"I reckon there might be some stuff in the library about fracture lightning and storm prophets," Dougal said, looking much happier at the thought of doing some research. He had agreed for the time being not to tell anyone about their encounter with Dark-Angel. "We could go down and check it out now if you want."

Angus nodded gratefully. He grabbed his sweater and followed Dougal, who was already heading through the door at the top of the stairs.

"And there might be something useful in the lost property department we could use for storm prophet training," Indigo suggested, trailing behind them.

But they found nothing in lost property except some temperamental howling hurricane chimes and a bag of moldering storm sponges that smelled like the Imbur marshes.

The following afternoon brought another surprise. Catcher Sparks delivered their lunch with the news that they would be taking part in special lessons conducted by Gudgeon.

"But won't somebody recognize us, miss?" Angus asked, shocked.

"Fortunately for you, McFangus, Gudgeon is taking all first, second, third, fourth, fifth, and sixth years for lessons at the same time. Nobody will notice the presence of three extra lightning cubs, especially as these particular lessons require everyone to wear full wet-weather clothing. It is also an ideal opportunity to get you, Dewsnap, and Midnight out of the library before you take matters into your own hands and start creeping about Perilous at night, looking for trouble."

Angus tried hard not to catch Dougal's eye, hoping Catcher Sparks wouldn't see the guilty look on his face.

They emerged from the library half an hour later dressed in long yellow coats and matching hats pulled well down to cover as much of their faces as possible. Catcher Sparks marched them through the corridors without stopping to acknowledge anyone. They raced past the kitchens, where Angus caught a brief glimpse of Catcher Trollworthy, Catcher Greasley, and doddery old Catcher Grimble, who was swilling his false teeth around in a mug of hot tea. Dougal hid beneath his hat as they passed perilously close to Mrs. Stobbs carrying a tray of tea and some hot buttered toast in the direction of Dark-Angel's office. Moments later they climbed the familiar stone steps to the Octagon and were suddenly met by the sound of chattering voices. Up ahead, Angus could see Nicholas Grubb laughing with his friends, Kelvin Strumble and Joshua Follifoot. Juliana Jessop and a crowd of older girls were sitting in a large circle in the middle of the floor. Edmund Croxley was trying to organize a group of worried-looking first years into an orderly line.

Angus thrust his hands deep into his pockets, resisting the urge to wave. It felt extremely comforting to be standing among the other lightning cubs at last.

"It took me some time to convince Rogwood and Jeremius that this was a good idea," Catcher Sparks said, turning on them sternly as they joined the others. "So, do not let me down. Don't talk to anyone, and stay out of trouble, understand?"

"Yes, miss," Indigo said quietly.

They watched Catcher Sparks weave her way through

the center of the crowd and disappear into the experimental division on the far side of the Octagon.

"This is one of the strangest things we've ever done," Dougal said.

For several minutes they hovered silently, listening to Nicholas Grubb describe a heated argument he'd had with Clifford Fugg over a cactus that had suddenly appeared in his bed. Angus almost blew their cover when Gudgeon finally appeared in the Octagon. He was dressed in a battered leather jerkin that looked like it had been through several jagged razor rainstorms since they'd last seen him. A knitted hat covered his bald head. There were small flecks of something green stuck to the ends of his straggly gray beard.

Angus spent several moments toying with the idea of simply sneaking up to the gruff lightning catcher and telling him that he, Dougal, and Indigo were still very much alive and safe inside Perilous.

"You can't," Indigo whispered when he suggested the idea.

"Yeah, he'd have a fit right in front of everyone," Dougal said.

"And we've promised Jeremius and Rogwood," Indigo reminded him.

"But if Gudgeon knows about us, he could come and visit us in the library," Angus said quietly.

"I think it's a bad idea." Indigo shook her head firmly. "What if he confronts Dark-Angel and tells her everything?"

Before Angus could argue any further, Gudgeon had called for quiet, and silence fell across the gathered group.

"You all know why you're here," Gudgeon began abruptly. "You've all seen the pictures of the Icelandic Exploratorium in the *Weathervane*. There are storms coming out of Castle Dankhart that could destroy every Exploratorium on this planet, including Perilous, and there's no point pretending otherwise. You had a taste of what might happen the other day, and the chances are the storms will only get worse," he said, echoing what Jeremius had already told them. "Dankhart and his monsoon mongrels are threatening to obliterate the lightning catchers and everything we've worked to achieve. But they'll have to blast their way through three hundred and fifty years of weather knowledge and expertise first."

Angus wondered if the latest storm-testing session in the Lightnarium had been successful.

"There may come a time when every lightning cub has

to be evacuated to the emergency shelters in the stone tunnels and passageways beneath this Exploratorium, and you'll be doing drills to practice that soon."

A worried-sounding murmur swept around the Octagon.

"But in the meantime, Principal Dark-Angel thinks you need some extra training, and that's why I'm taking you into the Lightnarium."

The murmuring grew louder still.

"Before we go any farther, everyone needs to sign a declaration and hand it back to me," Gudgeon said.

"Why is there *always* a declaration?" Dougal moaned quietly as forms were passed through many pairs of hands from the front of the group to the back. "Why can't special lessons with Gudgeon involve something harmless for a change, like drawing pictures of fluffy snowflakes?"

Angus took his own form from a tall fifth year and read it quickly.

I, the undersigned, solemnly swear that I will never enter the Lightnarium without a fully qualified lightning catcher, and I understand that ignoring this safety instruction may result in sudden death. I promise never to stand outside in any lightning storm, or try to capture one in a storm net, storm jar, or storm vacuum, and I understand that doing so may also result in sudden, painful, irreversible death. Finally, I swear to follow all evacuation procedures in the event of a catastrophic attack on Perilous and not to go running off in a panic like an idiot.

Angus swallowed hard and scrawled an illegible signature at the bottom of his form. Of all the declarations he'd signed since first arriving at Perilous, this was by far the most frightening. He glanced at Dougal, who was swaying on his feet, looking dangerously faint. Angus gripped him tightly by the elbow, just in case. If Dougal passed out now and gave their presence away . . .

"First things first," Gudgeon said as soon as all the declarations had been collected. "Everyone needs one of these emergency lightning deflector suits and a pair of tinted safety goggles before we enter the Lightnarium." He pointed to a large crate sitting on the floor behind him. "From now on, these suits and goggles must be carried with you at all times, day and night. I know they're bulky," Gudgeon shouted above the sudden sound of loud groaning, "but there's no point complaining about it! If you get caught out in a lightning storm, they might just save your skin."

"What does he mean by *might*?" Dougal said with his eyebrows raised.

Angus grabbed a lightning deflector from the bottom of the pile. It was enormous and extremely difficult to hold on to, like trying to grapple with a slippery eel.

"These particular suits are bigger than the normal ones so they can be dragged on straight over coats, hats, and rubber boots," Gudgeon said. "And you lot need to practice getting them on in under thirty seconds."

"Thirty seconds!" Nicholas Grubb protested loudly. "But, sir, that's impossible."

"Impossible or not, that's all the warning we got the last time Dankhart sent a fracture lightning storm over Perilous, so you'd better put in some serious training. And seeing as how none of you is going anywhere near the Lightnarium until you're wearing your suits, that training will start right here. Get ready," Gudgeon said, staring at his weather watch. "Lightning deflector suits on in three, two, one, go!"

A frenzy of activity broke out all around. Edmund

Croxley ripped his suit within seconds and had to stand aside until another one could be found.

"Get out of the way, Follifoot! You're causing a pileup!" Clifford Fugg yelled as he went hopping past Angus with one foot thrust down an armhole.

Angus managed to get the tricky suit on over his head without any problems, but it then got stuck around his midriff like a life preserver that refused to budge, no matter how hard he tugged at it. Dougal had shoved both legs down the same opening and was jumping about like a competitor in a sack race.

"Stop!" Gudgeon yelled above the chaos. "Your thirty seconds are up. Stay exactly where you are so I can see who's got the hang of it and who needs extra lessons."

Keeping his head down, Angus nudged his way gently into the center of a group of fourth years as Gudgeon wandered past.

"Next time, try unzipping it before you pull it on over your fat head, Twill," Gudgeon said, rescuing the boy from the slippery folds of material.

More than one lightning cub had somehow managed to pull their deflector suits on inside out and back to front.

A tall fourth-year girl had to be cut free from a tangle of cuffs and pockets.

"Not bad for a first try," Gudgeon said, returning to the front of the group as Angus helped Dougal hop out of his own suit. Only Indigo had managed to get hers on correctly in the time allowed. "But everyone needs to practice this drill at least twice a day. Right, get your safety goggles on, stay close to me, and don't go wandering off."

Gudgeon opened the door to the Lightnarium and led the way down a narrow, badly lit corridor. A long line of lightning cubs filed in slowly behind him. Angus, Dougal, and Indigo lingered at the back of the group, pretending to fiddle with zips and buttons. Angus glanced at the faded fire dragon on the door as he closed it behind him, and felt a sudden quiver of anticipation. It had been in the Lightnarium where he'd first discovered his talent for predicting when lightning would strike. Would a return to the dangerous department encourage his fire dragon finally to reappear? He followed Dougal and Indigo down the narrow corridor and through the open safety doorway at the end and felt his head spin.

The Lightnarium was vast and cavernlike, with sheer

walls of rugged stone and an impressive collection of stalactites hanging from the domed ceiling. A strong smell of sulfur lingered in the air, making his eyes sting.

Gudgeon hurried them to the far end of the cavern, past a number of enormous storm generators, which were already humming with life. Fifty feet tall with thick metal coils, the generators loomed over the entire Lightnarium in a very sinister fashion.

"I'd forgotten how scary this place is," Dougal said quietly as Gudgeon shuffled them behind a protective safety shield and went to talk to Valentine Vellum.

"At least that's one good thing about being shut up inside the library," Angus mumbled. "We don't have to look at Vellum's ugly face."

Pixie and Percival's resemblance to the lightning catcher was obvious. They each had the same low, thuggish brow line. But Vellum's pin-sharp eyes were as cold and unfriendly as a winter icicle storm. The sight of them gave Angus an uneasy feeling. With a question mark still hanging over his loyalty, could Vellum really be trusted to help Rogwood and Jeremius develop a storm to destroy the lightning tower? Was Vellum in league with Dark-Angel and Dankhart as he, Dougal, and Indigo still feared? And if so, how would he and his friends convince anyone else?

"Do you remember the last time we were in the Lightnarium?"

Angus froze. Somewhere close behind him he could hear the familiar voice of Georgina Fox.

"Angus saved Indigo from that horrible ball lightning," Georgina said. "He pushed her out of the way and let it strike his arm instead."

"I still can't believe Angus, Dougal, and Indigo are dead. It's just so awful," Violet Quinn said quietly in reply.

Angus stared down at his feet, his face burning under his hat.

"I don't know why you're sniffing, Quinn," Percival Vellum said with a sneer in his voice. "Perilous is much better without Munchfungus and his pathetic little friends sniveling about all over the place."

Georgina gasped. "But that's a terrible thing to say!"

"So?" Percival's voice was belligerent. "It's not like Munchfungus can hear now that he's got himself buried under some ice caves, is it? I'm glad he's gone."

"Yeah, me, too." Pixie sniggered beside her brother.

"But Angus saved you from that fognado on the Imbur marshes." Jonathon Hake suddenly barged past Angus, Dougal, and Indigo and joined the conversation.

"You don't know what you're talking about, Hake. Munchfungus was trying to save his own skin," Percival said.

"That's not what I've heard." Jonathon sounded indignant. "It would have killed you if Angus hadn't seen it coming and knocked you to the ground."

"Yeah, and don't you ever forget it, you ungrateful toad," Dougal snapped, his voice rising clearly above the others.

Violet shrieked and swung around. Vellum spun on his heels with a startled expression.

"Who said that?" He stared at the lightning cubs gathered around them as Dougal hurriedly sank behind a tight cluster of sixth years.

"It sounded just like Dougal!" Violet's voice was quivering with fright.

"Maybe his ghost has come back to haunt us," Georgina suggested.

"This whole Lightnarium could be haunted," Violet whispered dramatically, clinging to Georgina's arm.

"Catcher Wrascal says she saw the ghost of an old lightning catcher in the storm archive once. It chased her with a jar full of contagious fog and threatened to tip it over her head."

"Yeah, you'd better watch your step, Vellum." Nicholas Grubb suddenly turned around and leaned over Jonathan Hake's shoulder to glare at the twin. "Your head's twice the size of Catcher Wrascal's, so you're an easy target for any ghost."

Indigo pulled Dougal and Angus away from the group as Violet, Georgina, and Jonathon continued discussing haunted parts of Perilous in an anxious huddle.

"Sorry," Dougal murmured when they were safely out of earshot. "But I couldn't help it. As soon as we're officially alive again, I'm telling everyone exactly what a stinking pile of boiled turnips Vellum is."

Angus grinned. The startled look on the twin's face had been the best thing that had happened since they'd returned to Perilous.

"We've got to be more careful," Indigo whispered. "Catcher Sparks won't let us come to any more lessons if we start rumors about ghosts in the Lightnarium."

All smiles came to an abrupt halt a few minutes later when Gudgeon returned to the group and started their lesson in earnest.

"Most of you have already seen different types of lightning in this Lightnarium. You've learned that lightning is unpredictable, dangerous, and difficult to understand. But for those of you who didn't quite grasp the basics the first time around, we'll go over them again now. Grubb, tell everyone how normal lightning is formed."

"Um, right, sir. Lightning," Nicholas began. "A single bolt of lightning contains approximately one million volts of electricity."

"One *billion* volts, Grubb, get it right."

"Yes, sir, that's what I meant to say, one billion volts of electricity. Lightning is formed inside a cloud when lots of bits of ice bump into one another, creating an electric charge."

"Go on, boy, what happens next?" Gudgeon urged after Nicholas paused.

"Um, eventually, the cloud fills up with electric charges. The lighter, positive charges form at the bottom of the cloud, and the heavier, negative charges form at the top."

"You've got it the wrong way around, Grubb," Gudgeon said, with a shake of his head. "The negative charges form at the bottom of the cloud, which causes a positive charge to build up on the ground beneath it, especially around things like trees, buildings, and lightning cubs who should know better than to stand outside in a thunderstorm," he barked. Violet Quinn and Nigel Ridgely flinched away from him. "The charge coming up from these objects on the ground, and the charge coming down from the cloud, eventually connect with each other, and that's when you'll see some serious lightning."

"That's just what I was going to say, sir," Nicholas said, making his friends snigger.

"Dankhart has developed a new kind of fracture lightning for the specific purpose of destroying Exploratoriums," Gudgeon continued in an extremely serious voice. "It doesn't form like normal lightning, which is one of the reasons it's so deadly."

"How does it form, sir?" Georgina Fox asked in a quiet voice.

"Lightning storms are gathered by the tower sitting over Castle Dankhart and sent straight down into some storm nurseries in the experimental chambers beneath. There, they are fed with even more highly charged storm particles." Gudgeon paused for a long second. "And other dangerous materials."

Angus glanced sideways at Dougal and Indigo. Gudgeon was talking about the fire dragon scales stolen from the coffin of Moray McFangus.

"The storms are then forced to grow rapidly to an unnatural size and are stuffed full of lightning. As soon as an individual storm is ready, it is released from Castle Dankhart. When it reaches its destination, lightning bursts out in every direction and fractures as it hits its target. Imagine a storm vacuum that's just sucked up several monsoons, three hurricanes, and a blizzard cluster. It would be bulging at the seams, overstuffed, waiting to explode, and when it does . . . "

Angus swallowed hard. He, Dougal, and Indigo had already seen the result at close quarters.

"The fracture lightning storm that occurred over Perilous wasn't as dangerous as it could have been, but it still melted two of the cloud-busting rocket launchers up on the roof. You lot need to know what to do if there's another attack. Your first defense against it is to take cover. Get inside if you can. Put on your lightning deflector suits and wait it out. *Never* go looking for it, understand?" he barked again, making Millicent Nichols yelp.

Nigel Ridgely put his hand up. "Sir, what happens if we can't get under cover?"

"You'll be learning all about that in your next lesson. Today, you're going to see exactly what the fracture lightning can do and the best place for you to observe it is right here in this Lightnarium."

An anxious murmur echoed around the cavernous walls.

"Catcher Vellum and his team of lightning experts have been working on one of the samples that was gathered from the recent storm. They've managed to take some of the sting out of it by lowering the voltage of the lightning it contains."

Angus glanced up at the angry-looking cloud that was already forming above their heads. It definitely didn't look like the low-voltage kind.

"As an extra precaution, just to ensure none of you leaves this lesson with your earlobes fried, we'll be using silver lightning moths to keep the lightning inside the cloud, so that none of it ever strikes the ground."

Angus heard Dougal take a swift intake of breath and saw his hand shoot to his pocket where Norm, his own pet lightning moth, was safely resting.

"Croxley, explain how silver lightning moths work," Gudgeon said.

Edmund stepped forward, drawing himself up to his full height. "The lightning moths are self-winding, they can see in the dark, and they're attracted toward movement. They are used to draw out lightning strikes on purpose, so the strength of a storm can be calculated. They are also capable of wrecking any room in less than five minutes." Edmund glared over his shoulder at Theodore Twill, whose own pet lightning moth had ripped Croxley's room to shreds some time ago.

"Catcher Vellum is a trained moth handler, and he'll be releasing the moths for this demonstration," Gudgeon said. Valentine Vellum brushed past him and placed a wooden crate on the floor. "Everyone should remain still until the moths have reached cloud level," Gudgeon added. "Since they're attracted toward movement they won't hesitate to charge at anyone who is waving their arms about in the air and acting the fool, Fugg!"

All heads turned in the direction of Clifford Fugg, who had been gesticulating wildly behind one of the fourth years.

A moment later Valentine Vellum opened the crate and gave it a quick shake. Dozens of silvery creatures rose up into the air, their wings flapping furiously and glinting in the light. They hovered at head height, just beyond the safety shield behind which the lightning cubs were gathered, and then shot up into the cloud above and disappeared.

For several minutes nothing happened. The cloud grew thicker and uglier overhead.

"I can see them. Look!" Nicholas Grubb pointed.

"Stop pointing, you idiot!" Gudgeon shouted. "Unless you want the moths to attack your arm."

"Oops. Sorry." Nicholas grinned shamefacedly.

All eyes had now turned to the cloud, where flashes of silver could be seen darting in and out of the gray, forming a silver lightning cloud. The moths were trying to draw the lightning out.

"What's wrong?" Angus whispered as Dougal suddenly started squirming beside him.

"It's Norm. He keeps trying to escape from my pocket. I think he can sense the presence of the other moths, or maybe even the storm. But I can't let him out. I mean, what if he gets struck by lightning?"

Dougal finally managed to calm Norman down, and Angus turned his attention back to the other lightning moths. It was the first time he'd ever seen them in action. They flitted through the cloud with great precision and agility.

He caught a sudden flicker of movement from the corner of his eye. There was a tiny flash of silver and a fluttering of six razor-sharp wings. Norm had broken free. Dougal darted out beyond the safety shield before Angus could grab him.

"Stop that boy!" Gudgeon yelled, making a desperate lunge for Dougal, but it was already too late. "Turn off those storm generators now, Vellum!"

Thunder was beginning to rumble deep inside the clouds. The rest of the moths, drawn by the sudden movement below, turned as one sleek, silver wing and began to dive on Dougal at breakneck speed, their wings flashing ominously.

Angus elbowed his way through to the front of the shield, but a burly fifth year pulled him back.

"That's my friend, you idiot! Let me go!" Angus said, struggling.

Indigo had somehow managed to wriggle through a tiny gap and shot straight out across the Lightnarium before anyone could stop her. She flung herself at Dougal, who was still frantically trying to catch Norm, and tackled him to the ground.

Swoosh!

The silver moths swooped low, missing Dougal's head by millimeters. They sped across to the far side of the Lightnarium, pulled out of their steep dive before they hit the rocky wall, and turned. Angus watched in horror as several long streaks of lightning lashed out at the moths.

Crash! Crash! Crash!

The lightning fractured as it hit the ground and danced across the cavernous room, showering Dougal and Indigo in a deadly cascade of angry sparks and fizzles.

7
THE LAST SECRET

For several terrible moments Angus could see nothing but a confusion of people racing about the Lightnarium. Five lightning catchers rushed forward and expertly caught the remaining moths in what looked like large, toughened butterfly nets. The storm swiftly began to fade and die. Angus held his breath. He still had no idea if his friends were lying injured on the floor or if Dougal and Indigo were even alive.

The way before him suddenly cleared and . . . Dougal was sitting upright, rubbing the side of his head. Indigo was kneeling on the floor beside him; at least it looked like Indigo. In their lightning deflector suits even Angus found it hard to tell them apart. He felt his limbs turn to Jell-O with relief.

Gudgeon was already hurrying across to the spot where the fracture lightning had struck.

"Sir!" A voice suddenly called from behind. "Millicent Nichols has just fainted, sir, and she looks really pale and ill."

Gudgeon stopped dead and stared back over his shoulder toward the shield, where a group had already gathered around the unconscious lightning cub. Dougal, on the other hand, was now showing speedy signs of recovery as Indigo helped him to his feet.

"Right, you two, stay put and don't move a muscle, whoever you are," Gudgeon warned, pointing a finger at Dougal and Indigo. "I'll be having serious words with you and your master lightning catcher about your reckless behavior. The rest of you, follow Edmund Croxley back to the Octagon while I deal with Miss Nichols."

"You heard what Gudgeon said." Edmund Croxley moved to the front of the group. "Everyone out of this Lightnarium, now! Move along there, Vellums. You're blocking the way."

Angus pushed through the crowd of lightning cubs and ran straight across to where Dougal was now pulling his hat down over his face as far as it would go.

"Are you all right?" he asked, breathless with worry. But apart from a small tear in Dougal's lightning deflector suit and a graze on his hand where Indigo had pushed him to the ground, he was completely unharmed. The same thing, however, could not be said for Norm. The silver moth had been struck by the lightning and was now lying in dozens of mangled pieces across the floor. A long streak of oil was leaking from what was left of its body.

"Come on," Indigo said as Angus helped Dougal scoop up the remains. "We've got to get out of here. Catcher Sparks will have a meltdown if Gudgeon comes over and finds out we're still alive."

Angus led the way as they hurried back across the Lightnarium after the last of the other lightning cubs, who were already disappearing through the steel door and back toward the Octagon. A wave of pure noise hit them as they reached the safety of the domed hall. Several of the smallest lightning cubs were now in tears. Others were discussing the incident loudly. Angus slipped quietly behind Nicholas Grubb and his friends and headed down the stairs before anyone could recognize them or stop Dougal to ask how he was feeling. They raced back to the library and hurried through the tunnel behind the secret panel. It wasn't until they emerged at the other end that they felt safe enough to speak again.

"I can't believe Norm's gone." Dougal took what was left of the lightning moth out of his pocket, and stared miserably at the shattered remains. "He was desperate to escape and join the other moths. I just couldn't stop him."

"It wasn't your fault," Indigo said.

"Norm was just following his instincts," Angus added kindly. "He was a great lightning moth."

Dougal nodded and sniffled loudly. "Yeah, he was one of the best."

"And he looked really happy before he, er, you know . . ." Angus said awkwardly.

"He did, didn't he?" Dougal wiped his nose on the back of his hand. "I'm sorry I rushed out after him like that. I just wasn't thinking straight."

"You would have been toast if Indigo hadn't gone hurtling after you," Angus said.

"Thanks, I really owe you one for that." Dougal smiled sadly at Indigo. "It could have been me lying mangled on the floor instead of Norm."

They made their way back up to Miss Vulpine's rooms in a respectful silence. Angus tried to shake off the horrifying thought that his best friend could have been killed in the Lightnarium. Dougal was only alive now thanks to Indigo's quick thinking and astonishing bravery, while he, Angus, had been no help whatsoever. In the middle of the Lightnarium, with a dangerous fracture lightning storm threatening to incinerate his best friend, his storm prophet skills had utterly failed him once again. Angus swallowed hard. Up until now, his biggest problem had been controlling the fiery creature, stopping it from appearing when he was upset or angry. But what if it had gone into some strange kind of hibernation, or worse still, had left him for good? What if he simply wasn't talented enough to keep it alive? Now would be the worst possible time to discover he was no longer a real storm prophet.

He was just wondering if Dougal and Indigo were up to a serious discussion on the subject when something flitted across the landing at the top of the stairs in front of them.

"What was that?" Angus said, taking the last few steps more slowly, just in case. "Did Germ say he was visiting today?"

Indigo shook her head.

Angus pushed the door to the sitting room open slowly and stuck his head inside. The stale smell of smoke still lingered in the air. A tall figure wearing robes of plain brown was waiting for them by the fireplace. He scowled at Angus with small beady eyes and a creased forehead.

"I don't believe it. What's Hartley Windspear doing here?" Dougal said, peering over Angus's shoulder.

Hartley Windspear was a holographic projectogram. Normally, he was kept locked up to stop him following lightning catchers around the Exploratorium, spouting useless facts about fog, Imbur Island, and the rare crest-fallen newt.

"Do you think he escaped from the Inner Sanctum?" Indigo asked, looking concerned.

"We could try asking him, I suppose," Angus suggested, without any real hope of getting a straight answer. Despite the fact that Hartley Windspear was a walking encyclopedia, it was sometimes extremely difficult to get anything useful out of him.

"Er, excuse me, Mr. Windspear," Angus started, taking off his lightning deflector suit and chucking it onto the same chair where Dougal and Indigo were also dumping theirs, "would you mind telling us what you're doing here?"

The projectogram stared at Angus and blinked.

"Does anybody know you've left the Inner Sanctum?" Indigo asked as Hartley Windspear wandered to the far side of the room, where he stood next to a window, his robes billowing in a holographic breeze.

Dougal sighed. "Hopeless. We'll get Catcher Sparks to take him back to the Inner Sanctum when she brings up our dinner."

"Catcher Amelia Sparks," the projectogram suddenly said, making them jump. "A fully qualified lightning catcher, an expert in experimental weather machines, and three times winner of the Imbur Island rubber boot-throwing championships."

"You're kidding," Dougal said, sounding slightly more cheerful. "Catcher Sparks is a boot-chucker?"

Angus grinned. He'd never be able to look at the lightning catcher in the same way again. "Do you think that's why she wanted us to find those canary-yellow boots in the lost property department?"

"Yeah, maybe those jumping frogs are supposed to be lucky or something."

"Hang on a minute," Indigo said. "Somebody's left a note on the table. It's addressed to all of us." She picked it up and showed them the envelope.

Angus recognized the precise handwriting even from a distance and felt his smile slip.

"It's from Dark-Angel," he said.

Dougal gulped. "I wonder what she wants."

Indigo opened the note carefully and read the contents out loud.

"This is Hartley Windspear, a holographic projectogram. I have sent him to your rooms with some extremely important information. Please say *snowdrops* to him, and he will reveal the purpose of his visit. Do not repeat anything that he tells you to anyone, including Rogwood and Jeremius. Please destroy this note once you've read it.

Principal Dark-Angel."

▲ ▲ ▲

Indigo folded the note and looked anxiously at them both. "She's asking us to keep another secret?"

"There's only one way to find out." Angus crossed the room and stood in front of Hartley Windspear, who was now gazing out the window. "Um, snowdrops," he said, feeling extremely self-conscious.

The projectogram turned to face him directly, suddenly looking alert and eager.

"Snowdrops," he began. "A password created by Principal Delphinia Dark-Angel to unlock crucial information regarding the last storm prophet secret. To be revealed to no one but Angus McFangus, Dougal Dewsnap, and Indigo Midnight."

"'The last storm prophet secret'?" Angus felt his insides squirm.

Before Hartley Windspear could say another word, however, they heard the unmistakable sound of a door closing. Someone was heading up the first flight of stairs toward Miss Vulpine's rooms.

"It's Catcher Sparks!" Indigo said, creeping quietly onto the landing. "I can hear the buckles on her leather jerkin clinking." She gently closed the door that sealed them off from the stairs.

"We've got to hide Hartley Windspear in one of the bedrooms," Angus said. "If Sparks catches him up here, she'll march him straight back to the Inner Sanctum and we'll never find out what the last secret is."

Hartley Windspear, however, stubbornly refused to budge an inch and stood firmly in the sitting room with his arms folded across his robes.

"Quickly, try fanning him with something," Dougal suggested as the footsteps drew closer still.

Angus stared desperately around the room. "Our lightning deflector suits!"

He grabbed a slippery suit and frantically flapped the projectogram onto the landing and through the open doorway into Indigo's bedroom. Indigo snapped the door shut just as Catcher Sparks reached the top of the stairs and yanked the other door open.

"Why are you three skulking about on the landing?" she asked, suspicion instantly crossing her face. "And why did I just hear doors slamming?"

"We, um . . . we heard you coming up the stairs, miss," Dougal said. "And we came out to meet you."

"Don't be ridiculous, Dewsnap. I do not need a

welcoming party, and you will keep all door slamming to a minimum," Catcher Sparks warned. "The last thing we need is for someone passing the library to hear you."

"Wh-what are you doing up here, miss?" Angus asked cautiously.

"I have just found Gudgeon searching for three lightning cubs who mysteriously disappeared after an extremely dangerous incident with a lightning moth in the Lightnarium." She glared down at all three of them. "Explain yourselves!"

"It was my fault, miss," Dougal said, still sounding upset and shaken. "My pet lightning moth escaped, and I— I tried to save him."

"You could have been killed, you foolish boy!" Catcher Sparks bellowed, her nostrils flaring dangerously. "The Lightnarium is no place to go running about like an idiot. And why, might I ask, did you have your own lightning moth in the first place? Lightning moths are dangerous pieces of weather equipment; they are not to be kept as pets."

Dougal shuffled his feet, his ears turning crimson.

"I assume that the lightning did not strike you?"

Catcher Sparks asked, sounding furious and concerned at the same time.

"No, miss."

"You have no injuries to report? You do not require any treatment for burns, lightning shock, or blinding flashes before your eyes?"

Dougal shook his head.

"Then you've had a very lucky escape, Dewsnap. But if you cannot control your behavior in the future, I will be forced to keep you, Midnight, and McFangus locked up in the library. Do I make myself clear?"

"Yes, miss," Angus mumbled.

Indigo nodded silently beside him. Dougal's shoulders slumped.

"I would also like to know how you got back inside this library when the doors are still locked."

Angus stared at the lightning catcher. They'd used the secret tunnel without thinking of the consequences.

"We, um, we . . ." he said.

"Rogwood let us in, miss," Indigo lied swiftly.

"Did he indeed?" Catcher Sparks scrutinized each of their faces for several seconds, but luckily, she asked no more questions. "Now, as you have already heard, Gudgeon is organizing some emergency evacuation drill practice for all lightning cubs," she said. "And as you three won't be able to take part without giving yourselves away, I have come to show you your own shelter, where you must proceed in the event of another attack on Perilous or whenever you hear the warning siren."

"Siren," a muffled voice repeated from behind Indigo's bedroom door. Angus had temporarily forgotten about Hartley Windspear, but it was obvious that the projectogram had been listening to every word of their conversation. Dougal quickly faked a loud coughing fit. Catcher Sparks glanced around the landing, confused.

"If you must cough, Dewsnap, kindly cover your mouth with your hand first," she said. "I did not come up here to catch your germs. Now, follow me."

"But can't it wait until tomorrow, miss?" Angus asked hopefully.

"It most certainly cannot. The safety of each lightning cub is of the upmost importance."

She glanced around the landing one last time with a frown. Angus crossed his fingers behind his back, hoping Hartley Windspear wasn't about to dive into a detailed definition of the words "safety," "upmost," and "importance." Dougal covered his mouth with his hand, coughing heartily for several seconds, just in case. The projectogram kept his silence, however, and Catcher Sparks finally headed back down the stairs. There was nothing they could do but follow.

"Talk about bad timing," Dougal mumbled as they kept a safe distance.

"I just hope Hartley Windspear doesn't go wandering off while we're gone," Angus said under his breath.

Catcher Sparks led them swiftly across the library and down to the lost property department. She hurried past every closed door until she reached the very end of the gloomy corridor.

"This is the entrance to your emergency shelter," she said, pointing to a heavy-looking trapdoor set into the floor. "You will be completely safe inside it. Nothing will be able to penetrate the rock around you. In the event of another attack on Perilous, you must remain here until somebody comes to fetch you."

The room had already been equipped with food, water,

blankets, candles, and three rolled-up sleeping bags. It had all the coziness of a damp mountain cave, and Angus hoped they'd never have to use it.

For the next half an hour Catcher Sparks forced them to practice opening the trapdoor and diving inside as quickly as possible. As soon as the lightning catcher let them go, they raced back up to their rooms, only to find Germ and their dinner waiting.

"Rogwood brought your food up just after I arrived," Germ said, beaming at them all. "I had to hide in one of the bedrooms until he'd gone."

"Which bedroom?" Indigo asked sharply, glancing over her shoulder. Hartley Windspear was still hiding in her room.

"Calm down, sis, I wouldn't dare enter your private little world without written permission." Germ rolled his eyes at Angus and Dougal.

Angus ate quickly, shoveling several potatoes into his mouth at once as Germ filled them in on all the latest news from the rest of the Exploratorium.

"Everyone's already talking about what happened in the Lightnarium. Gudgeon's interrogating every lightning cub, to find out who ran after the lightning moth. There's also a rumor going around about Dougal's ghost."

Dougal, who had just taken a large gulp of juice, instantly spat it out again, causing the fire to hiss and crackle.

But Angus couldn't help grinning. "This is brilliant. Hey, we could creep down to the lightning cubs' living quarters and give Percival Vellum the fright of his life. Dougal's ghost could make a special appearance in the boys' bathrooms."

"Yeah," Dougal said when he'd finally recovered. "My ghost could warn him not to spend his whole life acting like an incredible idiot."

By the time they'd finished their desserts, Germ was still showing no signs of wanting to leave, and he settled himself in for an evening in front of the fire. Normally, Germ's entertaining company would have been very welcome. But with Hartley Windspear still lurking in Indigo's bedroom with important storm prophet secrets to reveal . . .

"Does anyone fancy a game of Pursuit?" Germ asked as Angus stacked the empty dinner plates on the corner of the table.

"Er, maybe another time," Dougal said, glancing at his watch. "Shouldn't you be writing an essay for Doctor Fleagal on something revolting like swamp water welts?"

"Nope, I've just finished a whole project on the treatment of fog mite bites, which means you get the pleasure of my excellent company for the entire evening." Germ balanced his feet on a footstool, his arms stretched lazily behind his head.

"But what if Catcher Sparks comes back to collect our dinner plates and catches you up here?" Indigo said. "She's already annoyed with us for what happened in the Lightnarium."

Dougal nodded. "Indigo's right. You should probably leave, just in case." He stood up, grabbed Germ's coat, and opened the door into the landing.

"Whoa, I can tell when I'm not wanted," Germ said, still sounding cheerful and not in the least bit hurt. "But if you ever need help scaring the pants off Percival Vellum, I'm always available. See you later."

As soon as the sound of Germ's footsteps had disappeared down the stairs, Indigo yanked her bedroom door open and they hurried inside. There was no sign of Hartley Windspear anywhere.

"Where's he gone now?" Dougal said, kneeling on the floor and checking under Indigo's bed.

"I've got no idea." Angus stared around the room, scowling. "What happens to projectograms when there's no one around to see them, anyway? Do they just disappear?"

"I don't believe this. We were seconds away from hearing one of the biggest secrets in the history of Perilous," Dougal said, miffed.

Angus checked behind the curtains and under the bedcovers, but it was Indigo who finally found the projectogram hiding in her closet. It took fifteen minutes to coax him back into the sitting room.

"Er, right," Angus said after the door was closed behind them. "We're ready to hear all about the last storm prophet secret now."

The projectogram stared at them blinking.

"Try the password again," Indigo suggested.

"Snowdrops."

Hartley Windspear pulled himself up to his full height. "Snowdrops. A password created by Principal Delphinia Dark-Angel to unlock crucial information regarding the last storm prophet secret," the projectogram said. "To be revealed to no one but Angus McFangus, Dougal Dewsnap, and Indigo Midnight."

Dougal groaned. "We're never going to find out anything useful at this rate."

"Shhhh!" Indigo hissed. "Let him speak."

"Before hearing this secret, however, you must each enter into a solemn agreement to tell no one else what I'm about to reveal," the projectogram demanded.

Angus motioned to Dougal and Indigo and led them swiftly into a huddle on the far side of the room, determined not to make this decision alone. "What do you reckon? Should we be making any more promises to Dark-Angel?"

"It's definitely risky." Dougal glanced back over his shoulder at the projectogram. "What if Dark-Angel's using old Hartley Windspear to trick us? She's already tried to have us kidnapped and killed."

"But what if there really is a storm prophet secret?" Indigo said. "What if it could help Angus find his fire dragon, or help us defeat my dear old uncle Scabby?"

Dougal gawped at Indigo, startled. "You hardly ever call him that."

Indigo smiled.

"So, should we agree to keep quiet, or not?" Angus asked.

Indigo nodded. Dougal shrugged and sighed loudly. "What's one more deadly promise when we've already made dozens?"

"Er, yeah, we agree not to tell anyone anything," Angus said as they rejoined the projectogram.

Hartley Windspear took a deep breath, cleared his throat, and arranged his robes so they billowed dramatically in a brisk holographic breeze.

"Many years ago, in the days of the early lightning catchers, when real dragons still roamed freely across the Imbur marshes and nested in the swamps . . ."

"Ha!" Dougal snorted. "Real dragons, my eye. He's making this up just to scare us."

Hartley Windspear continued unabashed. "It was discovered in those ancient times that when a storm prophet died, his or her fire dragon blazed above, visible to all and shedding its scales, which rained down as golden droplets of light. The scales hardened around the prophet's body like a toughened shroud, a spectacular suit of golden armor."

Angus could almost feel the scales falling onto his body as the projectogram spoke.

"In 1777, tiny samples of these golden scales were used in a series of dangerous experiments. These, however, were not the first tests ever performed with the fire dragon scales."

Angus glanced over at Dougal and Indigo as Hartley Windspear paused to scrape his mossy teeth with a blackened fingernail.

"More than thirty years earlier, in 1740, it was discovered that four of the storm prophet shrouds were different from the others: Moray McFangus, Zachary and Zephyrus Bodfish, and Gideon Stumps each had four blue scales hidden deep within his armor."

"Nobody's ever mentioned those before," Angus said, amazed.

"The scales were a magnificent sight to behold; the color of a deep-blue sky, as intricate as a butterfly's wing, and as tough as hardened steel," the projectogram said. "They had no effect on ordinary lightning catchers, but when crushed into a fine powder, mixed with water, and given to the sons and daughters of the original storm prophets, the scales revealed their true power. The storm prophet descendants were not only able to predict when violent weather was about to strike, but they all reported seeing four distinct fire dragons at their moments of darkest need and peril."

Angus stared at the projectogram, shocked. "*F-four* dragons?"

"Each of these creatures resembled the carving on the tomb from which the scales were taken, and the fire dragons of Moray McFangus, Zachary Bodfish, Zephyrus Bodfish, and Gideon Stumps appeared to exist again. The storm prophets were then set against a series of mighty storms and terrible tempests, against lightning so fierce and frightening it turned the hair of all who saw it to the color of pure, spun silver. The skies lit up for a thousand miles in every direction—"

"Oi! Stop making stuff up and get back to the bit about the dragon scales," Dougal said before Hartley Windspear could get completely carried away.

The projectogram adjusted his robes and glared at Dougal before continuing. "All storm prophets successfully used the fire dragons to control the largest and most severe storms that could be flung in their direction. The effects were temporary but extremely powerful while they lasted."

"This is unbelievable!" Dougal said.

"This is how we're going to defeat Dankhart, you mean," Angus said, facing his friends with a rush of excitement. "You said it yourself— What use is one fire dragon against a whole storm? But imagine if I could use four fire dragons. I mean, I'm the only living storm prophet. I'm the only person in the whole of Perilous who can try."

Angus suddenly had a glorious vision of himself and the four powerful fire dragons that he would send swooping and diving about a storm-filled sky. Dozens of admiring lightning catchers and cubs would watch, stunned, as he tore the cloud apart and sent it packing straight back to Castle Dankhart.

"So where are the blue dragon scales now?" he asked eagerly, almost expecting to see them lying on the table among the empty dinner plates.

"Such was the importance of the discovery that all

lightning catchers involved in the experiments were sworn to secrecy," Hartley Windspear said in serious tones. "Only one scale from each of the tombs remained after the experiments were completed. They were placed under the protection of four different guardians. The guardians were never told what they had been asked to protect. They each took a solemn vow of secrecy and were instructed to impress upon their descendants the significance of the scale as a family heirloom, which should be passed from generation to generation."

"Then why doesn't Dark-Angel just get the scales back from these guardians?" Indigo asked.

"As an extra precaution the identities of the four guardians were also protected, written only in a series of complicated puzzles and riddles that were secured inside a box. The box was placed in a secret safe in the principal's office, to be passed down to each new principal in turn. But the names of the guardians were never spoken of again and were slowly forgotten in the peppermint-scented, wispy fogs of time."

"Why doesn't Dark-Angel just open the box and solve the puzzles to find out who the guardians are?" Angus asked.

"Oh!" A sudden look of understanding crossed Dougal's face. "Dark-Angel doesn't know how to solve the puzzles!"

"So, that's why she's sent Hartley Windspear?" Indigo asked.

Angus nodded. "Dark-Angel needs help. She already knows Dougal's brilliant at solving puzzles and stuff. If anyone at Perilous can work out who those four guardians are . . . "

Dougal gulped. "But I've never done anything like this before. I mean, what if I can't solve the puzzles?"

He turned to Hartley Windspear for some answers, but the projectogram had clearly said all he was allowed to on the subject and was now staring out the window, looking bored. Indigo, on the other hand, was pointing nervously at a small box on the mantel above the fireplace, which none of them had noticed before.

"That definitely wasn't here earlier," she said. "Dark-Angel must have left it when she brought Hartley Windspear up to Miss Vulpine's rooms."

"That's not . . . I mean, that can't be *the* box, can it?" Dougal asked. "It looks way too small for puzzles and riddles."

Angus picked it up carefully, his heart suddenly beating fast. The box was made of plain wood and felt extremely light. He opened it slowly, getting ready to run if it contained anything dangerous, vicious, or breathing.

"Oh, it's a beautiful bracelet," Indigo said as Angus placed the box on the table where they could all see it.

Dougal frowned, prodding it with his finger. "Why did Dark-Angel leave that up here?"

But Angus understood in a heartbeat. The bracelet was delicate and clearly very old, with an intricate setting of twisted silver strands. And sitting at the very heart, glinting under the light fissures above, was a tiny blue fire dragon scale.

8
THE STORY OF SCABIOUS

Angus, Dougal, and Indigo stayed up late into the night discussing the shocking revelations that Hartley Windspear had just delivered. A snowstorm raged outside as they shuffled their chairs closer to the fire for warmth. The projectogram hovered behind them, listening to their conversation with a vacant expression.

"So this dragon scale must have been passed down through the Dark-Angel family for centuries," Indigo said, holding the bracelet up to the light and admiring it from all angles.

"Or it could have been passed from principal to principal," Angus said.

"But why is Dark-Angel getting us to find the rest of the dragon scales?" Indigo handed the bracelet over to Dougal, so he could look at it closely for the fourth time.

"Obvious, isn't it?" Dougal said. "We're the only ones she *can* ask. Dark-Angel doesn't know that *we* know she's working for Dankhart, so she thinks she's safe. And she can't exactly ask any of the lightning catchers for help if she's planning to hand the scales straight over to your dear old uncle Scabby. I mean, she's already given him one set of dragon scales."

"So, she's . . . she's just using us?" Indigo said.

"Of course she's using us. She deliberately sent Hartley Windspear up here with an amazing story about secrets and puzzles and four fire dragons, making Angus believe he's the only person in the whole Exploratorium who can save us."

"And then all she has to do is sit back and watch while we zoom around Perilous trying to find the rest of the scales for her," Angus said. "She must have been planning this since she found us in the testing tunnels. I bet that's the real reason she hasn't handed us straight over to your uncle."

Indigo frowned. "But why has she given us her own dragon scale? Why not just get us to find the other three?"

Angus paused. "I didn't think of that."

"Yeah." Dougal's forehead suddenly creased. "That part doesn't make any sense."

They all stared at the scale for several silent moments.

"At least we know one thing for sure: there'll be no more fracture lightning storms in the library until we solve those puzzles," Dougal said. "We'll be safe from Dankhart and Dark-Angel until we've done exactly what she wants."

"Can you imagine how powerful my uncle Scabious would be if he ever got his hands on the blue dragon scales?" Indigo said quietly.

Angus felt violently ill at the thought. "I bet he could restore his own storm prophet powers in a second."

"Perilous wouldn't stand a chance," Indigo said, sounding desperately worried.

"Which is why we can't tell Jeremius or Rogwood about any of this," Angus said, determined. "For a start, they'd never let us search for dragon scales."

Dougal snorted. "They'd have us transported to a cloud-spotting station on Tasmania if they even got wind of it."

"And they've already got loads of problems trying to create a storm to destroy the lightning tower," Indigo added.

"So, we're all agreed." Angus looked pointedly at both his friends. "It's up to us three. We've got to solve the puzzles and find the scales. We'll lead Dark-Angel on a wild-goose chase, do everything we can to help save Perilous, and make sure Dankhart never sets his black diamond eye on those scales."

"Yeah, brilliant," Dougal said, suddenly sounding extremely nervous. "But what happens when Dark-Angel comes up to Miss Vulpine's rooms and asks how we're getting on?"

"Simple. We pretend that the puzzles are too hard to solve," Angus said. "Then when Dankhart's fracture lightning storm comes, I can crush the dragon scales, mix them with water, and see what happens."

"But it's incredibly dangerous. You could be killed," Indigo said.

"If Dankhart sends any more lightning storms over to Perilous, we could *all* be killed." Angus swallowed hard. "Anyway, there might be a bigger problem. It happened yesterday, in the Lightnarium when Dougal was almost struck by lightning." With the excitement of Hartley Windspear's sudden arrival in the sitting room, there had been no time to tell his friends about the continued absence of his own fire dragon. "There was danger all over the place, and I didn't feel anything. It was like my fire dragon didn't even exist anymore."

Dougal and Indigo exchanged surprised glances.

"Maybe you're just a bit rusty," Indigo suggested. "I mean, it's been ages since you've done any lessons."

"Maybe," Angus said, feeling very uncertain.

"And you didn't exactly need to be a storm prophet to tell what was about to happen in that Lightnarium," Dougal added, stirring the fire up with a poker. "Gudgeon had already warned everyone not to do anything stupid. Maybe your fire dragon didn't think any warning was necessary?"

Angus knew they were only trying to help him. But he had an uncomfortable feeling that something far more serious was going on. What if the flames of his fire dragon had been extinguished for good and there was nothing he could do to ignite them again? If that were true, there would be nothing he could do to help his friends, the lightning catchers, or his mum and dad.

When they finally went to bed at 2:45 in the morning, his dreams were instantly filled with yet more terrifying fire dragon battles, each of which ended with his own dragon injured, spiraling out of control, and plummeting toward a violent demise. Each time, he woke with a dreadful start, his sheets sticking to his sweat-soaked limbs, his brain buzzing with fear and panic. It was some time before he finally drifted into a deeper, more peaceful sleep.

The next morning he felt exhausted and anxious. Catcher Sparks arrived shortly after he climbed out of bed, and delivered their breakfast, but not before Hartley Windspear hid himself in the bathroom.

“Dark-Angel must have told him to keep out of sight when we’ve got visitors, so he doesn’t get caught,” Angus said quietly to Dougal.

“It’s a pity he didn’t remember that yesterday when Sparks came up to get us,” Dougal said with a shake of his head. “He almost got himself caught before he could tell us anything useful. We’ll have to keep an eye on him if he’s going to be unreliable.”

Fifteen minutes later Catcher Sparks marched them down to a different section in the lost property department, which looked almost identical to the one they'd already worked in.

"When you're quite ready, McFangus," she said impatiently as Angus tried to stifle a huge yawn and the one that was threatening to follow right behind it.

"Sorry, miss."

"Everything in this room was accidentally left behind by visiting lightning catchers," Catcher Sparks said. She picked up a ticking traveling alarm clock shaped like a fluffy cloud and inspected it with obvious disdain. "Once you have cataloged each item, a list will be circulated around the other Exploratoriums in an attempt to trace their owners."

"That's if there are any Exploratoriums left to circulate it to," Dougal said darkly.

"Don't talk such nonsense, Dewsnap," Catcher Sparks said sternly. "We're doing everything we can to stop Dankhart and his fracture lightning storms."

She left a few minutes later, closing the door behind her.

"How can anybody lose a set of tartan bagpipes?"

Angus held up the strange musical instrument as they started to tackle the mountain of objects. According to the label, it had been in the kitchens when it had been sat on by Catcher Howler.

"Yeah, you'd think any lightning catcher would notice if they'd gone home without their camping stuff," Dougal added, pointing at a heap of cooking pots and tent poles now moldering in the corner.

They worked silently after that, cataloging each item and placing it neatly on the shelves. With thoughts of plummeting fire dragons, dragon scales, and ancient puzzles whizzing around inside his head, Angus found it almost impossible to concentrate on any of the rubber boots, measuring instruments, or automatic, spin-drying umbrellas. And he spent several fruitless minutes trying to catalog a bag of Cradget's magnetic marbles before he realized they belonged to Dougal.

Midway through the morning, Catcher Sparks returned to check on their progress, leaving them with three tall glasses of milk and a stern warning not to sit around, talking.

"I wonder if Dark-Angel's sent the puzzles up to Miss

Vulpine's rooms yet," Angus said as soon as Sparks had gone.

He took the wooden box containing the dragon scale out of his pocket, so they could all have another look at it. Dougal had already removed the scale carefully from its silver setting, in case they needed to crush it and use it in a hurry.

"For goodness' sake, don't lose it in here," Indigo warned. "We'll never find it again."

"Hey, speaking of finding things . . . You'll never guess what I've just read in this old book." Dougal cleared a space on the shelf beside them and showed them the cover of something called *The Complete Lightning Catcher Compendium: A Visitor's Guide to Who's Who and What's What at the Perilous Exploratorium for Violent Weather and Vicious Storms*. "There's some really interesting stuff in here about Adrik Swarfe and what really happened when he left Perilous."

Dougal opened the compendium and flicked to a chapter called "The Swarfe Family."

"What does it say?" Indigo asked.

"A lot of stuff about dangerous experiments with

high-voltage lightning . . . but then it says that Humphrey Dark-Angel somehow discovered that Swarfe was planning to betray the lightning catchers. It sounds like he went down in the testing tunnels to confront Swarfe."

"Humphrey Dark-Angel?" Angus asked, surprised. "But wasn't he Dark-Angel's brother?"

Dougal nodded solemnly.

"So, what happened?" Angus asked.

Dougal turned the book around so Angus and Indigo could see a terrible picture of a heap of fallen rock. "Swarfe deliberately set off an explosion so he could escape without being followed. The testing tunnel collapsed. Humphrey Dark-Angel got caught up in the explosion, and he was buried under the rock."

"Oh, my," Indigo murmured. "So, the lightning catchers just left him in there?"

Dougal nodded. "They held a ceremony several days later and put up a plaque to mark the spot."

"But this just makes the whole thing a hundred times worse," Indigo said, looking upset. "How can Principal Dark-Angel betray the lightning catchers when Swarfe killed her only brother?"

Angus shook his head, more mystified than ever.

At noon a siren suddenly sounded. Catcher Sparks appeared and marched them straight to their emergency weather shelter, where they were forced to eat their lunch and wait for the evacuation drill to end. Their afternoon session in the lost property department dragged by at a snail's pace. Angus accidentally dropped a bag containing hundreds of shiny, green, highly absorbent storm beads—normally used for soaking up large spills and floodles—which they then spent several hours chasing all over the room.

"What are floodles, anyway?" Indigo asked, lying flat on her stomach and stretching her fingers under a shelf where some of the beads had rolled.

"They're like puddles, only much, much bigger," Dougal said. "Watch out!" he warned as Angus put his foot down on a small cluster of beads and skidded crazily across the floor. "These things are lethal when they're dry."

The high point of the day came when Indigo discovered an envelope addressed to Percival Vellum, which had somehow got muddled up with a pile of old weather reports left in the Lightnarium by a visiting lightning catcher.

"What's inside it?" Angus asked, trying to look over Indigo's shoulder.

"But we shouldn't read it. It's addressed to Percival Vellum," Indigo said.

Dougal snatched the envelope out of her hand. "It's also an item of lost property, and Sparks told us to catalog everything." He opened it swiftly before she could stop him. "It looks like a letter from someone called Auntie Mavis. It says, 'To my darling little nephew, Cheeky Peeky Perci.'

"Ha!" Dougal snorted loudly. "She's sent him a family photo, too."

The photo showed Valentine Vellum sitting on a beach somewhere with two thuggish-looking, beefy toddlers. The twins were dressed in matching straw hats and looked like they were about to throw matching tantrums.

"Those two were ugly little squirts even when they were younger," Dougal said, making a face.

Angus grinned. "I'm surprised they didn't break the camera lens with scowls like that."

"I'm definitely taking this upstairs." Dougal stuffed the letter and the photo into his pocket. "You never know when we might need to blackmail those two gargoyles."

As soon as they'd finished their duties for the day, all three of them shot back up to Miss Vulpine's rooms.

It was obvious that nothing had been delivered in their absence except three plates of steaming hot chicken stew and three bowls of apple crumble. Hartley Windspear was sitting in one of the armchairs, staring into the fire. There was no sign of any puzzles.

"I can't just sit here all evening." Angus slumped in the chair next to the projectogram while Dougal placed the photo of the Vellums in full view on the mantel above the fireplace. "I've got to do something useful."

So far, their search for information in the library on fracture lightning and storm prophets had got them nowhere. All they'd found was an ancient chart showing rocket lightning strike patterns and a book called *Historical Hungarian Hailstones*, written by somebody called Murdoch McFangus, who was a distant cousin of Moray.

"I've got to practice my storm prophet skills," Angus said. "It won't be much good if we find the dragon scales and I can't even control my own fire dragon."

Indigo checked the clock on the wall. "Well, we can't do it now. It's dinnertime. The whole Exploratorium will be swarming with lightning catchers. We'll have to wait until everyone's gone to bed."

Therefore, much later that evening, long after darkness had fallen, they crept down the secret tunnel and out into the corridor outside the library.

"Ahhhhh!" Dougal took a deep breath, exhaling slowly. "It definitely smells better out here. The air in that library's starting to get a bit stuffy."

"Yeah, I almost miss the aroma of burned engine oil drifting down from the experimental division," Angus agreed.

They set off slowly, creeping toward the kitchens. It was extremely pleasant to be wandering the familiar corridors and passageways of Perilous again. Angus felt an odd sort of ache inside his chest at the thought of everything they were missing out on, including lessons and mealtimes in the kitchens with Clifford Fugg and Theodore Twill flinging insults and food at each other. Even arguing with the Vellum twins was starting to sound appealing.

They dived straight down the nearest stone tunnel without meeting anyone. There was no sign of Doctor Obsidian or any other lightning catchers as they reached the bottom and the door to the testing tunnels.

Dark-Angel had been as good as her word. The storm prophet room had been neatly arranged for practice sessions, with a box of labeled projectograms and storm globes, racks of wet-weather gear and rubber boots, and even two seats for Dougal and Indigo to sit on as they watched him.

"Wow! I wasn't sure Dark-Angel actually meant it," Angus said, admiring the large array of equipment.

"Yeah, you could train an entire team of storm prophets down here without ever going outside," Dougal said, impressed.

"Um, I suppose we should just get started, then?" Angus said.

He pulled on a large yellow coat and matching boots. Then he flipped through a box of tiny projectograms that came with their own pocket-size viewer, trying to decide which one might shock his fire dragon into appearing at last. Would a torrential Mexican downpour do the trick, perhaps? Or a fognado or a hurricane or a long-lasting lightning storm?

"I'll try this one first," he said, selecting a projectogram that promised a fierce glacial blizzard.

He slotted the plate into the back of the box.

Click!

"Oh no, not again!" He'd been transported straight to the research department with towering shelves and low-hanging sofas surrounding him on all sides. Ancient Catcher Grimble was drooling in an armchair close by, twitching like a rabbit.

"These projectograms must have been mislabeled, too, just like the last lot." Angus ripped the tiny plate out.

"We'll be sharing this tunnel with yodeling yetis any second now," Dougal said, peering anxiously into the darkness.

Angus picked the next projectogram without even bothering to read the label.

Click!

For several seconds he was convinced that nothing had appeared, that the projectogram was faulty. He was just getting ready to declare the whole training session a total disaster when he saw it. Hovering along one side of the tunnel was a large shimmering image. It looked like an old, faded photograph showing two laughing children sitting beside each other on a trunk. Somewhere behind him, he heard Indigo gasp. Angus felt his stomach knot. All three of them had seen the photo before. It showed Indigo's mum, Etheldra, and her brother, Scabious.

"What on earth is that photo doing in the projectogram box?" Dougal asked as he and Indigo left their seats to stand beside Angus.

His question was answered almost instantly. A figure appeared in the tunnel behind them. She was tall and slender, with long brown hair.

"M-mum?" Indigo rushed toward her. But the projectogram walked straight past without acknowledging her daughter and continued into the darkness ahead. Indigo followed without hesitation. Angus and Dougal trailed behind her, only stopping when Indigo's mum walked through a doorway and entered a small room filled with books, where a younger-looking Rogwood was sitting by a fire.

"Thank you for agreeing to talk to me today, Etheldra,"

Rogwood said, smiling kindly at her. "I will just explain for the purposes of this projectogram that we are in the process of gathering and recording as much information about Scabious Dankhart as possible for future generations of lightning catchers. This follows a winter of exceptionally severe black snow blizzards, giant hailstone showers, and rancid rainstorms, which have all come from Castle Dankhart."

"This must have been recorded ages ago," Angus said as Rogwood paused to straighten his beard. "Rogwood's beard's much shorter than it is now." There were also fewer crinkles around his eyes and nowhere near as many rips and tears on his leather jerkin.

"Er, Indigo, are you sure you want to listen to this?" Angus asked awkwardly.

But Indigo nodded and stood her ground.

"Etheldra," Rogwood finally began, "since you grew up at Castle Dankhart and spent much time with your brother, Scabious, I believe you can give us some interesting insights into his early life."

Indigo's mum smiled sadly. She took a deep, steadying breath before talking. "Scabious wasn't interested in the weather as a boy. I believe he hated living at the castle almost as much as I did. Our mother was a great support and made our lives as interesting and fun filled as possible. She tried to keep us separated from the monsoon mongrels, the weather experiments, and from our father. My brother's biggest ambition was to travel the world when he was old enough, to visit the great pyramids at Giza, Niagara Falls, and Stonehenge."

Angus gawped at a startled-looking Dougal. A visit to Stonehenge was also one of Dougal's greatest ambitions.

"But everything changed when our mother and father were tragically killed in a weather accident."

Angus glanced sideways at Indigo, who was soaking up every word her mum said, with a deeply troubled look on her face.

"When our parents died, our uncle, Greville Dankhart, took control of all work at the castle until Scabious was old enough to do it himself. Scabious was frightened," Indigo's mum said, her eyes suddenly filling with tears. "He was barely more than a boy, still grieving for the loss of our mother, and he wanted nothing more than to escape the dreary castle and leave Imbur Island forever.

But our uncle had his own plans. He began to separate Scabious and me at every opportunity. He slowly poisoned my brother's mind with dreadful tales about how the original monsoon mongrels—Nathaniel Fitch, Tobias Twinge, and Nicholas Blacktin—had been banished from Perilous, driven out by their fellow storm prophets. Uncle Greville told Scabious that these brave monsoon mongrels had then been forced to protect themselves against the storm prophets by turning the weather into weapons. I only learned the truth about the first monsoon mongrels when I escaped the castle and came to live in Little Frog's Bottom. I tried to contact Scabious many times, to explain that our uncle was feeding him nothing but dreadful lies. I believe he would have listened to me then, but I learned later that none of my letters ever reached him."

Indigo was now watching her mum with a look of misery.

"Scabious was young, with no one to support him. In time he came to believe everything Uncle Greville told him, including the greatest lie of all: that the lightning catchers had broken into Castle Dankhart and deliberately caused a dreadful explosion in the experimental chambers that killed both our parents. He was told again and again that it was his duty to punish the lightning catchers. Uncle Greville also told my brother that he had descended from those first storm prophets, and fueled his imagination with tales of the great fire dragons that should have been his destiny." Indigo's mum paused, taking a deep breath before she continued. "The longer Scabious spent with our uncle, the more he was convinced by the vicious lies. He will not be happy until Perilous is destroyed, but I fear even that would not satisfy him now."

Rogwood nodded. "People who act from such rage and fury rarely find relief when their plans reach completion."

"I used to believe that the gentle, openhearted brother I once knew was still buried deep inside Scabious," Indigo's mum said sadly. "But as the years passed, I have lost all hope. He has never tried to contact me. I fear what may happen if he ever attempts to convince Geronimo or Indigo—"

The image suddenly faded. Angus turned just in time to see Indigo rip the plate from the back of the box and put both objects into her pocket. She ran to the door and left the testing tunnel without a backward glance, hiding her face.

"Whoa!" Dougal said as soon as she'd closed the door behind her. "At least that finally explains why her dear old uncle Scabby's so twisted. Do you think we should talk to Indigo about it?"

Angus thought for several moments, with Etheldra Midnight's words still ringing in his ears, and then shook his head. When it came to the Dankhart side of Indigo's family, it was better to pretend it didn't exist.

Angus and Dougal waited several minutes, to give Indigo some time to compose herself, and then followed her back up to the library without investigating any more projectograms.

Angus woke early the following morning, even though it was a Saturday, still thinking about the projectogram and the damaging effect it was likely to have on Indigo. He got dressed quietly, so as not to wake Dougal, and yawned his way into the sitting room for an early breakfast. Hartley Windspear was standing by the fireplace.

"Er, morning," Angus said warily, hoping the

projectogram wasn't about to launch into a long-winded explanation of where the word "morning" came from. Hartley Windspear stared back at him but said nothing.

Breakfast had already been laid out on the table with some delicious-smelling muffins. Angus was just reaching out to test if they were still warm when he spotted it: Sitting by the doors that led out to the roof terrace was a wooden chest. Long and narrow, it was covered in elaborate carvings and dust.

Angus raced back into his bedroom, his heart suddenly pounding hard inside his rib cage. Dougal was now leaning against his pillows, rubbing his eyes.

"A wooden chest has turned up. I think Dark-Angel's finally sent the puzzles for us to solve," he said.

"You're kidding!"

Dougal grabbed his glasses and leaped out of bed. He dragged on his bathrobe as he followed Angus back into the sitting room, where they found Indigo, already fully dressed. There were dark circles under her eyes. It was obvious that she'd slept badly after the upsetting incident in the testing tunnel. But she smiled warmly at them now.

"Do you think it's safe to open?" she said, keeping a

wary distance from the mysterious chest. "I mean, there could be anything inside it."

"Yeah," Dougal agreed, tightening the knot on his bathrobe's belt. "We've only got Dark-Angel's word for it that it contains some puzzles. And she's not exactly trustworthy."

Angus grabbed a poker from the fireplace. He approached the wooden chest cautiously and jabbed it hard from every direction possible. Nothing happened. They studied it for several moments more, watching for any troubling signs of oozing. But the chest sat benignly in the sitting room, offering no clues about its contents.

"There's only one way to find out what's inside it," Angus eventually said. "But if this thing starts to rattle, we run and close the door, agreed?"

Indigo nodded. Dougal took a deep breath, knelt down beside the chest, and tried to lift the lid. "It won't budge. It must be locked."

"I can't see a keyhole anywhere," Indigo said.

Dougal sat back on his heels and scratched his head. "Then how are we supposed to get it open?"

"Maybe Dark-Angel's slipped another note or some

instructions under the chest?" Angus picked up one end of it carefully as Indigo lifted the other. Dougal lay flat on his stomach and stuck his head underneath it.

"There's nothing under here except horrible green carpet. It doesn't make any sense," he said, shuffling out of the way as Angus and Indigo placed the wooden box back onto the floor. "Why would Dark-Angel leave us a chest we can't open?"

"Hartley Windspear!" Indigo suddenly said, making Angus and Dougal jump. "He's pointing to another note."

It had been placed against a pot of marmalade that was half hidden by the muffins. Indigo reached over and grabbed the parchment.

"Is there a key inside?" Dougal asked hopefully.

Indigo shook her head and turned the note around so they could both see the single word scribbled across it.

"'Bluebells'?" Angus said, reading it aloud.

Hartley Windspear pulled himself up to his full height. "Bluebells," he repeated in serious tones. "A secret password set by Principal Delphinia Dark-Angel for the revealing of important information only to Angus McFangus, Dougal Dewsnap, and Indigo Midnight."

Angus felt his pulse begin to race. Maybe Dark-Angel was trying to make them feel important on purpose, with passwords and puzzles and projectograms, but he quickly decided he didn't care. Finally, they were doing something to help save Perilous, stop Dankhart, and prove to Jeremius and Rogwood that they could do more than sit safely inside the library like good little lightning cubs.

"Hang on a minute," Angus said, stopping the projectogram before he could really get started. "Let's take Hartley out of here for a bit. I don't fancy spending all day cooped up in this tiny sitting room with the smell of burned carpet. It's far too cold and snowy to sit outside on the terrace, but there must be loads of sections in the library where we can't be seen from the doors, somewhere we can really spread ourselves out."

Dougal raced back into the bedroom to get dressed as Indigo gathered together a good supply of muffins, toast, and crispy bacon and wrapped them in some napkins. A few moments later, Angus and Dougal lifted the chest.

"Whoa!" Dougal staggered under the weight as they carried it toward the stairs. "If I'd known it was this heavy, I would have made you and Indigo carry it!"

Fifteen minutes later they'd settled themselves well away from the main library doors, behind some bulky cabinets containing a collection of rare early lightning catcher journals. The wind howled across the domed glass roof above, scattering a flurry of snow, but the familiar smell of old books felt extremely comforting.

"The identities of the dragon scale guardians were protected by a series of puzzles," Hartley Windspear began after they'd placed the chest on one of the study tables and Indigo had repeated the secret password.

"You've already told us that about a hundred times," Dougal said impatiently, trying to hurry the projectogram along. But Hartley Windspear would not be rushed.

"The original puzzles were created by Constantine Cradget. He—"

"Hang on a minute; this is a Cradget's puzzle?" Dougal interrupted, astonished. "I didn't know they'd been around that long."

"Cradget's has no records of any such puzzles ever being created," Hartley Windspear continued. "But some verbal instructions regarding the opening of the chest have been passed down over the centuries."

"Thank goodness for that." Dougal looked highly relieved. "I thought we might have to attack it with dessert spoons."

"These instructions *must* be followed to the letter," the projectogram warned sternly, wagging a finger at all three of them, "or the contents of the casket may be destroyed and lost forever."

"Uh-oh." Dougal's face suddenly fell. "Is it me or does that sound a lot like a self-destructing puzzle?"

"It could be the first one Cradget ever made," Indigo said, looking amazed.

Dougal's cheeks blanched. They had already encountered several self-destructing puzzles the previous term. They were volatile, unpredictable, and liable to explode with just a few seconds' warning.

"First, to open the chest, you must slip your finger underneath the lip of the lid," Hartley Windspear said, directing his comments at Dougal. "A lever must be pushed to one side until a click is heard."

The projectogram stopped and waited, staring benignly at them.

"What? He's not expecting us to do it now, is he?" Dougal said, startled.

"Er, I think that's exactly what he's expecting," Angus said.

"But I'm not ready. I'm still digesting breakfast."

Hartley Windspear, however, refused to say any more until Dougal agreed to follow his instructions.

Dougal took a deep breath; wiped his greasy, bacony fingers on his napkin; and pushed the chest into the center of the study table to give himself plenty of room to work. He slipped his finger under the lip of the lid and slid it slowly along until—

Click!

"I did it!"

The lid sprang open, and Angus caught a faint whiff of almonds and spiced pear, as if the chest had once been used for storing delicious treats. Inside, it was divided into three equal compartments, each with a domed lid.

"As you can now see, there are three separate puzzles to solve," Hartley Windspear said as they peered inside. "Each will reveal the name of a dragon scale guardian. But the puzzles *must* be solved in sequence, from left to right. If this procedure is carried out incorrectly—"

"Let me guess," Dougal said. "The whole thing self-destructs?"

Hartley Windspear nodded gravely and then continued. "To open the first compartment on the left . . ."

"Hold on, I'm not ready yet," Dougal protested again. But the projectogram plowed on through his instructions regardless.

"Turn the lid through 360 degrees, in a clockwise direction, three times."

"One." Dougal counted as he gripped the lid and twisted it slowly. At first it was reluctant to move. "Two." An odd sound was coming from inside the chest, as if tight knots of string were slowly being severed. "Three."

With a loud pop of stale air, the lid shot upward, spinning wildly.

"Look out!" Angus dived beneath the table, pulling Dougal and Indigo down with him as the lid careered around the shelves. It slashed viciously through a row of books, sending scraps of paper floating to the ground like confetti.

Clang!

The lid collided with the corner of a bulky cabinet,

which sent it spinning in the opposite direction.

Zoom!

It shot across the top of the table, slicing through the remains of their breakfast before finally clattering to the floor, and silence fell in the library once again.

Dougal scrambled out from under the table and rounded on Hartley Windspear. "You could have warned us that was about to happen. That thing nearly killed us!"

"Congratulations." The projectogram scowled. "You have now successfully opened the first compartment."

"Yeah, no thanks to you."

"The rest is up to you. The message from Principal Dark-Angel ends."

Without another word the projectogram turned and drifted away, humming quietly to himself.

"So, what's inside the first compartment?" Angus looked eagerly over Dougal's shoulder as they turned their attention back to the chest.

Dougal carefully scooped out what appeared to be a yellowing paper sphere the size of a baseball.

"It's got words scribbled across the surface." Dougal held it up close to his glasses, inspecting every inch of it.

"What does it say?" Angus asked impatiently.

"It's a bit difficult to read. There are loads of ink blots, and words have been crossed out, as if someone wrote them in a hurry." The paper crackled with age as he turned it. "But I think it says, 'Pick at the clues clasped in your hand.'"

"What does it mean?" asked Indigo.

"Pick at the clues, pick at the clues . . . Just give me a few minutes to think about it, will you?"

Dougal took the paper ball and disappeared around the other side of the tall cabinets, leaving Angus and Indigo to clean up the mess made by the spinning lid. Angus paced restlessly between two study tables. Then he tried to count the number of snowflakes now falling on the glass roof above. He was just considering arranging some of the books on the shelves into size order when Dougal appeared with an excited smile on his face.

"I think I know what I'm supposed to do," he said, placing the paper ball on the table. "I've literally got to *pick* at the clues."

Dougal scratched at a tiny wrinkle of paper with his fingernail and slowly peeled a tissue-thin layer away to reveal another identical layer underneath.

"I don't believe it! This is one of Cradget's famous onion-layer puzzles," he said, sounding awestruck. "These things are legendary. I mean, Cradget's hasn't made any for hundreds of years. I never thought I actually get to solve one."

"An onion-layer puzzle?" Indigo asked.

"Each piece of the puzzle peels off when you solve it, like the layers of an onion," Dougal explained eagerly. "There could be three, four, or even five more layers beneath this one."

"Can't you just forget about the puzzles and peel the paper off until you get to the middle?" Angus asked hopefully.

"No way, this is a Cradget's product, remember? If I do that, the entire puzzle will probably self-destruct. This next clue looks much more difficult than the first one, and there're definitely no wrinkles to pick at this time. It's got a complicated paper knot instead. See?" Dougal showed them the intricate paper tie that had been secured with a baffling number of clever twists, folds, and loops. "It could take me days to figure how I'm supposed to undo it."

"Can we do anything to help?" Angus asked, feeling extremely disappointed. He'd had high hopes that they'd know the name of the first guardian before the morning was over.

But Dougal shook his head. "It's better if you just leave me to it. I'll need plenty of space and some peace and quiet if I'm ever going to crack this."

Angus quickly decided, however, that if Dougal failed to reach the center of the puzzle in a few days' time, he'd take his chances and attack it with a sharp pair of icicle slicers from the Rotundra.

9

SILAS SEVENSTAR

Angus found the next seven days intensely frustrating. Dougal worked hard on solving the first puzzle, but his progress was painfully slow. He sat hunched in the corner of the sitting room, his back turned toward the fire, mumbling to himself about "impossible paper locks" and "sneaky hidden layers" and snapping at anyone who interrupted his thoughts. The chest was now sitting under Dougal's bed, where they'd hidden it after opening the first compartment, to prevent anyone else from spotting it. And Angus could do nothing but wait.

Angus tried to keep himself occupied during the long dark evenings by borrowing several books from the library on great lightning catchers through the ages, but he had so many worrying things to think about now, that the words swam before his eyes. Storm prophet training was proving to be almost impossible, due to lightning catcher activities inside the Exploratorium. After several unsuccessful attempts to sneak down to the testing tunnels, they had finally given up.

Just to add to his concerns, Indigo had been much more subdued than usual since they'd seen the projectogram of her mum. She had taken to sitting in her room for large portions of the evening, listening to the projectogram over and over again, only joining Angus for card games when he asked her directly. He finally tried to broach the tricky subject of her mum's revelations one Sunday afternoon as they sat close to the fire.

"Are you all right?" Angus asked quietly. He checked over his shoulder. Dougal was sitting in the far corner with his head in both hands. "I mean, it must have been really hard hearing your mum talk about your uncle Scabious like that."

Indigo nodded. "My mum just sounded so sad. I mean, imagine if Germ suddenly started doing terrible, awful things with the weather. He'd still be my brother, no matter what."

"Yeah, but Germ would never hurt anybody," Angus said. "Unless it involved lancing snow boot boils or scraping off crumble fungus, of course."

Indigo smiled sadly. "I know Uncle Scabious is a maniac, and he's done some dreadful things that can never be forgiven. But I was just thinking, what if his life had turned out differently? What if his mum hadn't died in an experiment and he'd traveled the world, like he'd always wanted?"

It was a bizarre thought. "There would be no lightning tower, for a start," Angus said. "No fracture lightning storms threatening to destroy every Exploratorium on the planet."

"And instead of being my dear old uncle Scabby, he could have been more like Jeremius or your uncle Max. I wouldn't have to hide the bleckles on my hand, either." Indigo pulled her sleeve up for a change, revealing the five spots in a triangular formation that so cruelly marked her out as a Dankhart. "I just can't help wondering if there's a tiny bit of the old uncle Scabious still hidden deep inside him. I—"

"Can you two shut up? I can't hear myself think!" Dougal barked suddenly from the corner of the room, bringing the troubling conversation to a swift end.

The following day, Rogwood brought their dinner up to Miss Vulpine's rooms, along with news they had all been dreading.

"I'm sorry to tell you that Exploratoriums in New Zealand, the Sahara desert, and Switzerland have been attacked by fracture lightning storms in the same night," he said sadly as they helped themselves to curry and rice.

Angus put down his fork, suddenly losing his appetite. "What happened, sir?"

"The attacks occurred very quickly and with little warning. One of our finest and most experienced lightning catchers, Patricia Seacliffe, who works at the Exploratorium in Wellington, New Zealand, braved the storm just long enough to send a silver lightning moth up into the cloud. When it was struck down, it still had traces of the storm particles stuck to its wings."

Dougal sniffled, clearly remembering Norm's final dramatic moments in the Lightnarium.

"Those particles are being analyzed here at Perilous, as we speak," Rogwood said. "We are hoping they can tell us more about the complicated storm structure, which may in turn help us with our efforts to destroy the lightning tower. Sadly, all three Exploratoriums were burned to the ground during the attacks. I'm afraid there was nothing anyone could do to save them."

Rogwood left them with the latest copy of the *Weathervane*, which contained ten whole pages of deeply upsetting pictures of the stricken Exploratoriums. Angus felt a shiver of anger travel through his body.

"It says here the London office is monitoring the situation closely. All Exploratoriums are on high alert," Indigo said, reading some of the article. "But Trevelyan Tempest says it's almost impossible to predict where the storms will strike next. The attacks are following no particular pattern."

"Of course they're following a pattern," Dougal said. "Dankhart's using all the smaller Exploratoriums for target practice."

"Or there could be another reason, of course," Indigo said, looking thoughtful.

"What do you mean?" Angus asked, tearing his gaze away from the pictures.

"In the bone merchant's, Uncle Scabious made loads of threats about covering half of England in giant snow-storms and stuff?"

Angus frowned. "Yeah, so?"

"So none of these storms have been cataclysmic, have they?" Dougal said, catching on quickly. "What if something's gone wrong with your dear old uncle Scabby's plans? What if the fire dragon scales aren't working properly? Maybe they've been sitting down in the damp crypt for too long, or they've got dragon scale rot or something."

"But he still managed to destroy three Exploratoriums in one night." Angus pointed to the evidence in the magazine. "And the one in the Sahara was much bigger than the other two."

"The Saharan Exploratorium," Hartley Windspear suddenly said. He'd been standing quietly in the corner of the room ever since Rogwood had left. "Built in 1701 and specializing in heat-wave warnings, drought observations, and sun-strength readings, the Exploratorium is home to the famous indoor oasis and training desert and to Hazel Humbert, inventor of the man-made shifting sand dune. It is also the birthplace of Silas Sevenstar, the last of the storm prophets."

Angus stared at the projectogram. "What are you talking about? I've never heard of a storm prophet called Silas Sevenstar."

"Just ignore him," Dougal said. "He's probably got his wires crossed."

"And Rogwood must have mentioned Silas Sevenstar when you were in the Inner Sanctum," Indigo said.

Angus scrunched his eyes up tight and thought hard. "Nope, I definitely would have remembered a name like that."

"Please, Mr. Windspear, can you tell us more about Silas Sevenstar?" Indigo asked very politely.

"Born on the twenty-seventh of July 1699, to the daughter of Jasper Flinch, he was a third-generation storm prophet."

"A *third*-generation storm prophet?" Angus said, surprised. "But Rogwood said there weren't any after the second generation."

"Quiet and scholarly, Silas Sevenstar came to work at Perilous in 1725 and was particularly interested in the perils of frozen undergarments and their effect on body temperature, on which he wrote many important research papers."

Dougal snorted with laughter.

"Silas Sevenstar, however, suffered from ill health."

"Yeah, I'm not surprised if he spent his entire life wearing frozen underpants," Dougal said.

"And it was only at the moment of his early death in 1742, when his fire dragon became momentarily visible to those gathered around him, that his storm prophet abilities were discovered."

"You're kidding." Angus gazed at Hartley Windspear.

"Yeah, I know," Dougal agreed. "Imagine if a huge great fire dragon suddenly appeared out of nowhere and started melting golden scales all over the place."

"According to his final wishes, Sevenstar was buried in an unadorned grave in the Perilous crypt," Hartley Windspear continued.

"I think I've seen it!" Angus said. "It was the only tomb down there that wasn't covered in lightning bolts and fancy decorations. I wonder why Rogwood never mentioned him."

"Maybe he ran off to join the monsoon mongrels," Dougal suggested.

"Then why is he buried in the Perilous crypt?" Indigo said.

"Can you tell us anything else about him?" Angus asked the projectogram hopefully.

But Hartley Windspear folded his arms across his robes. "Further information regarding Silas Sevenstar is password protected."

"Protected?" Angus said puzzled. "By who?"

"Principal Delphinia Dark-Angel."

"Why would Dark-Angel restrict information on one of the storm prophets?" Indigo asked.

Angus frowned. "And who is she protecting it from?"

"You could ask Rogwood about it next time he comes up to our rooms," Indigo suggested.

"Yeah, but then I'd have to tell him who we heard it from." Angus pointed at Hartley Windspear, who wasn't supposed to be in their rooms at all.

"Maybe we can guess Dark-Angel's password, then."

Dougal looked eager to try. "So far she's been using the names of flowers, so let's try . . . 'daffodil'!"

Hartley Windspear scowled at Dougal and said nothing.

"Okay, what about 'hyacinth,' then?" Angus said.

"Or 'lily'?" Indigo added.

The projectogram continued to glare at them and refused to tell them any more about the mysterious storm prophet, no matter how many passwords they tried. He did, however, spout out some boring facts about beeswax, and all three of them hurried to their bedrooms shortly after.

Angus was woken only a few hours later by Dougal, who was shaking him by the shoulders.

"I've done it! I've solved the first puzzle!" he said proudly as Angus sat up and squinted at his friend in the sudden light. Dougal was still fully dressed; he had tired black smudges under his eyes; his hair was sticking up at odd angles, where he'd scratched his head in frustration. But he was now beaming from ear to ear.

"I finally got through all the layers on the puzzle, and the name of the first dragon scale guardian was written at the center. Look!"

Dougal shoved a thin slip of paper under his nose.

Angus stared at it, trying to focus on the words . . . and instantly felt his spirits sink.

"Vesper Vellum? The first guardian is a Vellum?"

"The Vellums are one of the oldest families on the island," Dougal said with a shrug. "Vesper Vellum must have been working here at the time or something."

"So if Vesper Vellum passed the dragon scale down through his family as he promised . . ."

"It probably belongs to Valentine Vellum now," Dougal said, confirming Angus's worst fears. "Vellum's obviously got no idea what it really is, or he probably would have handed it over to Dankhart, or Dark-Angel, ages ago."

Angus stared at the name on the slip of paper, hoping it might miraculously morph into a friendlier one.

"Anyway, we can worry about Vellum later," Dougal said, holding up a second scrap of paper. "We've also got instructions on how to open the second compartment in the chest."

Angus pulled on his bathrobe and slippers, and helped Dougal drag the chest out from under Dougal's bed. They carried it into the sitting room and placed it in the middle of the floor. Then Angus knocked quietly on

Indigo's bedroom door. "She definitely won't want to miss this."

Two minutes later they were all standing in front of the ancient chest once again.

"According to this, to open the second compartment I've got to turn the lid 180 degrees to the left, then 360 degrees to the right," Dougal said, checking the instructions carefully.

"Wait. Don't touch anything yet!" Angus grabbed Dougal's wrist. "The last time we opened one of these compartments we almost got knocked unconscious by a spinning lid."

They snatched up anything they could find—chairs, footstools, and cushions from the armchairs—and piled the items high around the chest, building a makeshift blast barrier. As an extra precaution, Indigo dragged the down comforter from her bed and wrapped it around them in case of flying debris.

"Ready," Angus said after they'd pulled the curtains across all windows.

Dougal concentrated hard as he turned the lid 180 degrees to the left. The movement produced a series of odd clicking sounds, as if something was being tightly wound inside the chest.

Dougal gulped. "I don't want to worry anyone, but this thing feels like it's about to blow."

With shaking fingers he turned the lid to the right.

"Get down!"

Dougal dived behind the blast barrier. Angus pulled the comforter over his head, expecting the worst, but as the seconds slowly began to tick past, he stuck his head out cautiously.

"Isn't the lid supposed to open?"

"Maybe it's stuck," Indigo said.

Dougal reached forward warily and gave the lid a prod. Nothing happened.

"Should I try following the instructions again?" he said, looking doubtful.

Before Dougal could attempt any solution, however, the strange clicking noise inside the chest resumed, suddenly reaching a crescendo.

Bang! Crack! Bang!

The racket was incredible, like an enormous storm vacuum being dropped on top of a thousand dainty teacups. Angus pressed his hands over his ears as sound waves reverberated around the tiny sitting room, causing an ugly picture frame on the wall to crack. Several dinner plates shattered along with what felt like his eardrums. And then a ringing silence fell.

"Typical," Dougal yelled, giving his left ear a good scrabble with his finger. "The one thing we didn't protect ourselves against—sound!"

"Do you think anyone else heard that?" Indigo turned to face the door anxiously.

They waited, expecting to hear thunderous footsteps on the stairs at any minute, but thankfully, no one came.

Dougal approached the chest with caution and peered inside the second compartment. "The lid must have crumbled away to dust," he said, brushing some of the fragments from around the rim. "And the second puzzle's tiny." He reached in and pulled out what looked like a tightly folded cube of ancient paper that was the size of a sugar lump. "There's no writing on this one. I wonder what I'm supposed to do with it."

Angus and Indigo watched as Dougal considered the puzzle from all angles, holding it up to the light, rattling it next to his ear, rolling it between his hands to test the weight. Angus was just about to suggest they leave it until the morning when—

"I think I've got it!" Dougal said, making Angus and Indigo jump. "You've got to unfold it. There's a tiny edge of paper sticking up on one side. I can feel it with my thumb."

They moved the cushions and chairs back to their normal positions to make room as Dougal gently teased the cube apart. He flattened the whole thing out into a surprisingly large sheet of parchment.

"Self-expanding paper," Dougal said. "It was invented eons ago by someone called Boris Bolax. You can crease it up into tiny shapes, and it only expands again when you unfold it and release the pressure."

"But it's just a blank sheet of paper," Angus said, disappointed. "There aren't even any puzzles or clues on it."

"There aren't any instructions, either." Indigo crawled carefully around the outside of the parchment on her hands and knees, studying every inch of it. "What if they've just faded away over time?"

"Shhhh!" Dougal hissed. "Just let me think for a minute."

He sat with his legs crossed, his head in his hands. Angus waited anxiously.

"Oh!" Dougal scrambled onto his feet a moment later and dived across to the table to grab a dinner knife from one of the shattered plates. "There's a seam along one edge of this paper, see." He held it up to the light. Angus wasn't sure he could see anything.

"I think I'm supposed to slit it open like an envelope." He started carefully at one end with the blunt knife, keeping a neat line. "Ha, I was right!" Dougal looked deeply impressed with his own cleverness as the paper finally unfolded into an even larger sheet that covered the entire floor of the sitting room. Tissue thin and yellowing with age, it was littered with strange symbols that Angus didn't recognize. They looked a lot like they belonged on a pyramid in ancient Egypt. There were storm clouds with bizarre curly lightning bolts, triangular hailstones, and loads of interlocking sun symbols with scowling faces.

"I don't believe it! These are really old weather glyphs," Dougal said.

"What are weather glyphs?" Indigo asked.

"They were invented by the very earliest lightning catchers as a sort of secret language, to protect some of their greatest discoveries."

"Why have we never heard of them?" Angus asked.

"Because we've got better ways of protecting our secrets now, so nobody's used them for hundreds of years. I'll have to get a book to help me decipher them, if I can find one, but even then, it won't be easy. Each of the glyphs has a specific meaning, and they were often made up on the spot by the lightning catcher as he or she wrote out the document."

"There must be something on weather glyphs in the library," Indigo said, automatically glancing over her shoulder toward the door.

"But it's two-twenty in the morning." Angus stared at the clock on the wall, which was somehow still working even after it had been struck by shards of shattered mirror.

"So?" Dougal was undeterred. He folded the puzzle carefully to the size of a book and slipped it into his pocket. "I won't be able to sleep now, anyway. Are you two coming with me or not?"

They quickly carried the wooden chest back into the

bedroom and shoved it under Dougal's bed. Then they crept down the stairs and searched through the library—Angus and Indigo still dressed in their pajamas, slippers, and bathrobes—trying to read titles by the light of the moon. Angus took a huge pile of reference books to a cozy table in a sheltered corner, where he could snuggle down into a comfy chair. He flicked through endless chapters, scanning each page for any mention of the weather glyphs. After half an hour of searching, however, the words began to blur before his eyes, swimming in and out of focus as his head drooped and nodded.

"Angus!"

He woke with a loud snort. Indigo was looming over him. Daylight was now flooding through the library windows and the glass roof overhead. He'd been asleep for hours, his head resting snugly in the pages of a book about forecasting symbols.

"What's happening?" he asked, stretching out a crick in his neck.

"Dougal's finally found some books on weather glyphs," she told him excitedly. "They were hidden at the back of the balcony behind a whole stack of ancient books on sea breezes. He's already heading back up to Miss Vulpine's rooms."

Angus followed Indigo in a daze, feeling ravenously hungry and desperately tired. He tripped his way up the secret stairs behind her, looking forward to a hearty breakfast. When they finally reached the sitting room, however, they were met by the bizarre sight of Jeremius having a heated argument with Hartley Windspear.

"I demand to know how you got into this part of the library without permission," Jeremius said.

"That information is password protected," Hartley Windspear said stoutly.

Jeremius shook his head in apparent frustration. "I am a senior lightning catcher at this Exploratorium. I don't need a password. Somebody must have let you out of the Inner Sanctum and in through the locked library doors. You will tell me who that was."

Hartley Windspear kept his silence and glared at Jeremius.

"Er, what's going on?" Angus asked, shielding his eyes from the light that was now streaming in through the open curtains.

Jeremius spun around. "How long has this projectogram been here?"

"A couple of days. He just sort of turned up," Angus lied. If he told Jeremius that the projectogram had been sent by Dark-Angel, who now knew they were alive and who had set them on a dangerous quest to find some blue fire dragon scales that would eventually allow him to control four fire dragons, he had a feeling it wouldn't end well.

"These walking encyclopedias are an absolute menace. He shouldn't have left the Inner Sanctum."

"But he's not causing any trouble," Angus said. Although Hartley Windspear could be intensely irritating at times, they'd all grown used to having him around. He'd also given them some extremely useful information. "You could just leave him here. We don't mind."

"Unfortunately, that's not an option," Jeremius said. "If he tells anyone that he's seen you three hiding up here in the library, it could put you in danger and ruin all our plans. I'll take him back to the Inner Sanctum myself. I just came to tell you three the good news."

Angus glanced at Dougal and Indigo, mystified.

"A fierce snowstorm is about to hit Perilous," Jeremius explained.

"Is it coming from my uncle Scabious?" Indigo asked, horrified, as Dougal raced to the window to search the skies for any looming storm clouds.

"Don't panic, you two. The storm is completely natural."

Indigo let out a long sigh of relief. Dougal lingered by the window for several moments, just to make sure.

"According to the forecasting department, however, the storm may last for a number of days, and the heating system has just developed a major problem, which will also take some time to repair."

"Er, what's so good about that?" Dougal asked, shivering automatically.

"Under the circumstances, Principal Dark-Angel has decided to send everyone home for the week. The rest of the lightning cubs left Perilous first thing this morning."

"So you're letting us out of the library?" Indigo asked hopefully.

"Better than that," Jeremius said with a grin. "It's about time you three had a change of scenery. I'm taking you

to Dougal's house on Feaver Street until the storm blows over."

"Seriously?" Angus felt his spirits soar, only to sink again a moment later. With Mr. Dewsnap and Jeremius watching over them, how would they decipher any weather glyphs or do any kind of storm prophet training?

"We leave in an hour," Jeremius said, checking his weather watch. "Dress warmly. The storm has already taken quite a hold."

10

THE BARD OF IMBUR ISLAND

Angus, Dougal, and Indigo waved good-bye to Hartley Windspear as Jeremius guided him down the stairs.

"How are we going to work on the weather glyphs at Feaver Street?" Angus asked, as soon as the coast was clear.

Dougal shrugged. "Dad will be too busy talking to Jeremius to notice what we're doing all the time. This is going to be brilliant," he added, stuffing socks and sweaters into a bag. "I can't wait to sleep in my own bed."

"We can wander around the house without sneaking about in secret passageways," Indigo said. "We can finally get some fresh air, too."

Perilous already felt deserted by the time they left the library through the main doors. The journey to Feaver Street was short and extremely chilly, with a fierce easterly wind blowing in from the sea. Even with the cold biting at their skin, it felt good to be outside, and Angus admired the spectacular snow drifts and frosted trees all around them as they sat in an open-topped, steam-powered coach.

"Welcome, welcome!" Mr. Dewsnap greeted them when they arrived at Feaver Street feeling cold and ravenously hungry.

Angus felt his spirits lift again. Despite its slightly ramshackle feel, 37 Feaver Street was warm and comfortable and had become one of his favorite places to stay.

"'Tis a pleasure to see you again, young Angus."

"Thanks, Mr. Dewsnap." Angus beamed at Dougal's dad as they shuffled inside. Mr. Dewsnap was dressed in a flamboyant, purple quilted coat. With his jet-black hair, portly frame, and small round glasses, he was almost a mirror image of Dougal.

"And this must be Indigo Midnight," Mr. Dewsnap said, clasping both her hands in his. "I've heard a great deal about you, young lady."

"It's nice to meet you, Mr. Dewsnap." Indigo smiled shyly. "Dougal talks about you all the time."

"Does he indeed?" Mr. Dewsnap chuckled, giving Dougal a tight hug as they passed each other in the hallway. "Did he ever tell you about the time when he was five years old that I caught him stomping about the kitchen in Mrs. Stobbs's shoes?"

"Daaaaad, don't!" Dougal complained, his ears turning pink. "You promised you'd never tell anyone again."

A sumptuous lunch had been laid out on the kitchen table. A fire crackled merrily in the corner of the room. And as soon as all coats, gloves, scarves, and hats had been removed, a marathon eating session began. Angus couldn't help smiling as he helped himself to a plate of roast beef. Mealtimes in Miss Vulpine's sitting room had already become quite monotonous with no other lightning cubs to talk to and very little news coming their way. It was highly enjoyable to hear the sound of other people's laughter and the friendly clink of cutlery. And they soon began to discuss the latest news from Perilous.

"Dankhart's storms are nowhere near as cataclysmic

as we were expecting," Jeremius said after Dougal's dad asked.

"See." Dougal nudged Angus with his elbow. "That's exactly what me and Indigo said."

"Now that he has the fire dragon scales, we should be drowning in calamitous weather, fighting gigantic snowstorms that cover half of England, or lightning storms the size of Imbur Island," Jeremius said. "He could have snuffed out every Exploratorium on the planet by now in the blink of his black diamond eye. Luckily for us, Dankhart seems to be having just as many problems engineering his fracture lightning storms as we are creating our own."

Indigo squirmed in her chair.

"Then how is he still managing to destroy so many Exploratoriums?" Angus asked, shoveling more carrots and potatoes onto his plate.

"Clearly, the storms he has created have been big enough to obliterate some of our smaller outposts. Perilous has a number of protections and defenses that many of our other Exploratoriums simply don't have."

"The atmosphere inside Perilous must be rather

strained, of course," Mr. Dewsnap said, offering Indigo more gravy.

Jeremius nodded. "But that hasn't prevented Clifford Fugg from starting a fire in the research department and almost incinerating the map room."

Dougal dropped his fork on his plate in surprise. "When did that happen?"

"Yeah, and why didn't anybody tell us?" Angus added.

"I'm surprised you couldn't smell it." Jeremius grinned. "The stench lingered in the air for days afterward."

"I hate being shut up inside the library all the time. We're missing everything important." Dougal slumped against the back of his chair.

"Dull though it may be in Miss Vulpine's living quarters, it has so far prevented anyone from discovering you're still alive," Mr. Dewsnap said, peering at them from over the top of his glasses.

Angus quickly shoved another forkful of beef into his mouth and avoided all eye contact with Dougal and Indigo by concentrating hard on the kitchen table. Someone *did* know they were alive . . . Dark-Angel herself. Now that she knew they definitely weren't dead, Dankhart and a whole herd of monsoon mongrels could turn up at any minute in search of Angus's blood.

"What else has been happening inside the Exploratorium?" he asked to fill a slightly guilty-sounding silence.

"I hear on the grapevine that Catcher Trollworthy tripped over the weather cannon on the roof and broke her foot," Mr. Dewsnap said. "And there's also a ghastly rumor going around that Catcher Grimble may have contracted a severe case of crumble fungus from a visiting lightning catcher."

The weather continued to deteriorate as the day wore on, with great storms of snow battering against the kitchen windows, and it got dark outside well before the end of the afternoon. Rogwood appeared just as night was falling, covered from head to toe in snow. And the conversation soon returned to the lightning tower and the progress the lightning catchers were making with their plans to destroy it.

"Things are not going well, I'm afraid," Rogwood said, warming his cold fingers by the roaring fire. "Catcher Sparks and Valentine Vellum are continuing with their storm experiments, but we had an unfortunate explosion in the experimental division about a week ago that has severely damaged our efforts."

"It shook the entire Exploratorium," Jeremius said, sipping a hot cup of tea. "We had to start a rumor about storm vacuums backfiring just to stop anyone asking awkward questions."

He sighed and ran a hand over his tired face. "This is getting us nowhere, Aramanthus. It's been weeks, and all we've managed to create so far are several craters in the Lightnarium."

Rogwood nodded gravely. "I am well aware of that."

"Then we are to pursue my idea of using lightning accelerators?" Jeremius said.

"I believe it is now the only sensible option."

"What are lightning accelerators?" Angus asked.

"It was an idea we were trying out to accelerate the progress of stubborn storms, forcing them to end more quickly," Jeremius said, helping himself to more tea. "But it had the unexpected side effect of making them more violent, so the notion was abandoned some time ago."

"It is perfect, however, for the situation we find ourselves in now," Rogwood explained.

"I don't see how we can possibly hope to destroy the lightning tower when we still have no clear picture of its complete structure," Jeremius said as Rogwood finally moved away from the fire and joined them at the kitchen table.

"But you've already seen it from the weather station," Angus said.

"Yeah." Dougal nodded. "We were so close you could have reached out and grabbed a chunk."

"And there have been lots of pictures of it in the *Weathervane*," Indigo added quietly.

"Unfortunately, what the *Weathervane* doesn't show is that the lightning tower extends down through the roof of the castle and into the guts of the building itself," Jeremius explained. "So far, it's been impossible to gather any accurate information about what's going on below the roofline."

"Which makes it very difficult for us to design something that will destroy the whole structure," Rogwood said. "I fear the time may have come for further exploration."

Jeremius nodded. "I've already put some plans into place. I can reach Castle Dankhart in a matter of hours."

"What? No!" Angus burst out, accidentally knocking over his glass of juice. "It's too dangerous. You'll never get out again!"

"Getting out isn't what concerns me," Jeremius said, clearly trying to make light of it. "If we can't find out more about that lightning tower, we might just as well hand over the keys to Perilous and everything in it. And I know more about the inside of that castle than many of the monsoon mongrels."

"So, you've sneaked into the castle before?" Indigo asked, fishing for details.

Jeremius smiled. "I'm not sure 'sneaked' is the right word, but yes, I've been inside it on more than one occasion. I drew detailed floor plans for *The Dankhart Handbook*. And a couple of years ago now, Dankhart and his monsoon mongrels attempted to release large storms of scarlet sleeping snow across the island, and our efforts to stop them were having very little effect. Somebody had to sabotage Dankhart's plans from inside the castle. I managed to destroy their entire stock of specialized frozen weather crystals before they could use it to create even more storms. It took them years to replace it."

"Is—is that how you got the scar on your chin?" Indigo asked.

"Let's just say destroying lots of weather crystals is not without its dangers." Jeremius brushed the scar automatically with his thumb. "But this time I will only be in the castle for a short time. There are also some very useful tunnels where I can take shelter if things get a bit tricky."

Angus stared at his uncle, horror-struck. Jeremius was trying to ease Angus's concerns with tales of high adventure and lucky escapes. But he'd already lost his mum and dad. What if Dankhart captured Jeremius as well?

"But when are you going?" he asked.

"Soon," Jeremius said, giving nothing away. He refused to be drawn out on the subject any further, and a few moments later Mr. Dewsnap brought out a delicious dessert of hot rhubarb crumble that temporarily ended all conversation.

It was midnight by the time Rogwood finally set off through the storm again, insisting on returning to Perilous to help Catcher Sparks with her latest experiments. Ten minutes later Dougal showed Indigo to a comfortable room that Mrs. Stobbs sometimes stayed in when his dad was away.

"Dad said Mrs. Stobbs was distraught when she heard about the accident at the Canadian Exploratorium," Dougal said as he and Angus left Indigo and carried on up the stairs to the top of the house. "He's told her not to come around for the next few days, because of the storm, so there's no chance of her seeing us by accident." He opened the door to his room, dumped his bags onto his bed, and looked fondly at the walls, which were decorated with pictures of Stonehenge. The room also had a spectacular view across the rooftops of Little Frog's Bottom.

Angus was sleeping in the spare room next door. He pulled on his pajamas, snuggled down under a thick quilt, and listened to the sound of soft snow thudding against his window before falling into a deep sleep.

For the next few days the snowstorm raged outside 37 Feaver Street, but far from spoiling their time away from Perilous, it only made Dougal's house feel even cozier and more welcoming, with roaring fires, soft flickering candles, and endless supplies of hot scones and winter stews.

Dougal spent several hours each day working on the

weather glyphs, which he finally managed to decipher at the end of their fourth day.

"It doesn't make any sense, though." He frowned, showing Angus and Indigo the results of his hard work. Dougal had written what each of the glyphs meant underneath the symbols. A short line at the bottom contained clear instructions on how to open the last compartment in the chest. But the rest of the glyphs . . . Instead of revealing the name of the third dragon scale guardian, they presented the trio with another mystery. Angus read the words out loud, hoping they might make more sense.

"'A rich and riveting tale written by Quintus Quill, the famous Bard of Imbur Island, concerning the adventures of a brave and noble man who trekked through the deep sands of the lost desert and discovered a golden lake of melted sand,'" Angus said. "What's that supposed to mean?"

"Haven't got the foggiest," Dougal said.

"Maybe it's a clue. If we can work out who the brave and noble man was, he might turn out to be the next guardian," Indigo said, trying to sound hopeful.

"Yeah, but how are we supposed to do that?" Angus

studied the strange words again. "I mean, have you ever heard of anyone who discovered a melted lake?"

"Well, whoever it was, their family must have been on the island for hundreds of years, so that rules out Catcher Howler, Miss DeWinkle, and Catcher Mint for a start," Dougal said.

"What about Mrs. Stobbs?" Indigo suggested.

"Yeah, how long has the Stobbs family been on the island?" Angus asked, a small ray of hope flickering in the afternoon gloom.

"Dad says they all lived on the far side of the island, but they've only been here since the 1800s."

Dougal continued to ponder the mystery of the Bard of Imbur Island, but it was impossible to think about it all the time. They split the rest of their days at Feaver Street between playing board games in front of the fire and exploring the attic at the top of the house, which was full of curious objects that Dougal's dad had collected. In the evenings they listened to Mr. Dewsnap's elaborate tales about the time he trekked across Antarctica with a team of dogs in search of mysterious ancient ice rings. Angus wasn't entirely convinced Dougal's dad had ever set foot on the frozen continent, but he enjoyed the thrilling tales as much as he could with the worries and dangers that seemed to be piling up around them.

It was also impossible to stay inside every minute of the day with such tantalizing drifts of fresh, pristine snow collecting on the roof above Feaver Street. And they soon challenged Jeremius and Rogwood to a series of ferocious snowball fights between the chimney pots, pausing only to catch their breath and admire the spectacular views across the rooftops of Little Frog's Bottom.

It was after one particularly brutal battle, where Dougal had been completely flattened by a huge bombardment, that Angus followed Rogwood inside and down the stairs.

"Sir, can I ask you something important?" he began, brushing snow and ice out of his hair as Rogwood stamped his boots in the hallway.

"Fire away, young Angus."

"It's about what happened in the fracture lightning storm and in the Lightnarium, when me, Dougal, and Indigo went for the special lesson with Gudgeon," he said, choosing his words carefully.

"Ah yes, I believe there was an incident with a lightning

moth and a mysterious lightning cub who ran out after it."

"Er, yes, sir," Angus said, not quite meeting the lightning catcher's eye. "But when the lightning struck out, my fire dragon didn't appear, and I haven't seen it for ages."

"Curious." Rogwood considered him carefully. "I have read some documents that talk of Zebedee, one of the Bodfish brothers, experiencing a similar problem. I believe he described the absence of the fire dragon as if it had gone into hibernation."

Angus felt his heart race. "That's exactly what it feels like, sir. But why has it happened to me now?"

"If I remember correctly, when it happened to Zebedee Bodfish, they ran all sorts of tests, but no physical ailment could be found. There was a theory, however, that it might have been caused by a particularly dangerous weather duel during one of the notorious storm prophet battles."

"Storm prophet battles?" Angus said, surprised. Rogwood had only ever mentioned a duel between two young storm prophets before. But "battles" implied something much bigger and fiercer.

Rogwood nodded solemnly. "Soon after Nathaniel Fitch, Tobias Twinge, and Nicholas Blacktin ran off to form the monsoon mongrels, they unleashed a series of deadly storms over Perilous."

Angus thought instantly of the projectogram they'd seen in the testing tunnels, the one with the fire dragons swooping overhead. Had they seen a re-creation of one of the very fights Rogwood was talking about?

"Fearful fire dragon battles raged above the Exploratorium, setting the skies alight with flames to rival those of the Great Fire of London itself. It was during one of these violent encounters that Zebedee Bodfish ran into trouble. As he was still a relatively young storm prophet, his powers weren't fully formed, and the ferocity of the battle pushed him dangerously close to his limits. It was almost as if the power of his fire dragon had been depleted and it needed to rest to regain its strength."

Angus thought quickly back to the last time he'd seen his fire dragon. It had been in the bone merchant's, where he'd sent a dangerous icicle storm chasing after Adrik Swarfe and Victus Bile. Controlling the storm had taken all his strength, and he hadn't felt the presence of his fire dragon since.

"But did the fire dragon return to Bodfish in the end, sir?" Angus asked anxiously.

"It did indeed," Rogwood said with a kindly smile. "And there are no reports that Zebedee ever suffered from the same complaint again."

Angus felt a rush of relief at the news. "How long did it take for him to recover, sir?"

"I believe it was several months before he was able to use his skills again."

Angus did a quick calculation in his head. It had now been almost two months since his own fire dragon had gone into hibernation. But would it appear again before Dankhart tried to destroy Perilous? Would he still be able to use the four blue dragon scales?

"I would be happy to discuss the subject further at another time, Angus," Rogwood said, buttoning up his coat against the raging storm outside. "But I fear I must leave before Feaver Street is snowed in entirely. I will bid you a good day."

All too soon their final evening at Feaver Street arrived.

The snowstorm had finally blown itself out. Angus, Dougal, and Indigo packed their bags, ready to return to Perilous very early the following morning, before the rest of the lightning cubs.

"Did I ever tell you the tale of Deciduous Dewsnap?" Mr. Dewsnap asked, settling down for another evening of storytelling after a delicious last dinner of roasted chicken and parsnips. Jeremius was sitting quietly in the corner of the room by the fire, watching the flames.

Angus grinned across the table at Dougal. Deciduous Dewsnap was one of the most famous members of Dougal's family. Dougal had named his first pet lightning moth, Cid, after his adventurous ancestor.

"A fine and noble lightning catcher, Deciduous was one of the most illustrious Dewsnaps in the history of this island," Mr. Dewsnap said. "As I may have mentioned before, Deciduous and his faithful friend Marmaduke McFangus once joined forces on a hair-raising expedition through the celebrated fog tunnels of Finland."

"Yeah, you might have mentioned it once or twice," Dougal said, rolling his eyes.

"Ah, but did I ever tell you of his famous journey

through the sands of the great lost desert?" Mr. Dewsnap asked. "It was there that he discovered a very curious lake of melted sand, the color of liquid gold. Nothing like it had ever been seen before, or since, for that matter."

Indigo's elbow slipped off the table. Angus swallowed the gulp of hot milk he'd just taken and almost choked. Dougal sat rigid between them both, staring at his dad with owl-like eyes.

"Deciduous paid a famous bard to write a tale celebrating his great achievements, as was the fashion of the time. It was gloriously long, and spectacularly tedious, and took several hours to recite."

"Wh-what was the bard's name, Mr. Dewsnap?" Angus eventually managed to ask.

"I believe it was Quintus Quill, or it could have been Quilltus Quinn."

Angus gawped at Dougal's dad, feeling his heart rate suddenly climb. It could mean only one thing: Deciduous Dewsnap had been the third original dragon scale guardian!

"For goodness' sake, don't make me sit through that dreadful tale again." Jeremius yawned lazily in the corner of the room. "If I had a silver starling for every time I'd been forced to listen to it . . ."

"Er, yeah, Dad, you've told me loads of times before, too," Dougal said, trying to sound convincing. "We definitely don't want to hear it again. Can me, Angus, and Indigo go up to my room instead?"

"Oh, very well." Mr. Dewsnap sighed. "Sadly, you will miss a thrilling tale, and I do tell it extraordinarily well, even if I do say so myself. The McFanguses are mentioned several times, if my memory serves correctly."

Dougal closed the kitchen door as they reached the safety of the hallway outside.

"I don't believe it! The Dewsnaps are dragon scale guardians and I didn't even know it. I thought all we'd ever done was write a few boring history books." Dougal sounded awestruck by the very idea. "There's a portrait of Deciduous in my dad's office. Come on! It might tell us something useful about him."

They hurried inside Mr. Dewsnap's office and closed the door behind them. The room was just as Angus remembered it: large, homey, and overrun with tottering piles of books. Cups of cold tea, shopping lists, and half-eaten sandwiches had been abandoned here and there.

"Dad's got loads of portraits of our ancestors hanging around the walls," Dougal said. "Look for someone with big ears and glasses."

Angus started with the portraits to the left of the door as Indigo turned right. Dougal darted skillfully through the stacks of books to the far wall at the end of the room. It soon became clear, however, that most of Dougal's ancestors had elephant-sized ears and numerous pairs of glasses. Phyllis Dewsnap, a lightning catcher from the early 1900s, wore four pairs around her neck with two more perched on top of her head.

"I think I've found it!" Dougal's voice was muffled by the stacks of books. Angus wove his way between the piles.

Dougal and Indigo were already standing beneath a large portrait on the wall with an ornate frame. The family resemblance was clear. Deciduous Dewsnap had the same round face as Dougal; jet-black hair fell to the collar of his tunic. He was also wearing an impressive blue velvet hat set at a jaunty angle, with a long peacock feather protruding from the side.

"I wonder what he did with the dragon scale," Angus said.

"If he found a way of passing it down to his descendants, then it must belong to your dad now," Indigo said.

"We could just ask him if he's got it," Angus suggested.

"Yeah, but then we'd have to explain how we know about it in the first place," Dougal said. "No, we'll have to sneak into his room tonight before he goes to bed and have a good look around. He'll be up for hours yet, talking to Jeremius, so we should . . . What's wrong with your face?"

Dougal stopped suddenly and frowned at Angus, who had been looking carefully at the portrait.

"It's the peacock feather." Angus pointed with a shaking finger. "Look at the end of it!"

In the gloom of Mr. Dewsnap's office, the single blue fire dragon scale was difficult to spot. It sat almost perfectly camouflaged among the thick brushstrokes and oily layers of ancient paint.

"Angus, you've found it," Indigo said, flabbergasted. Angus grinned.

"We've got to get it down tonight," Dougal said,

determined. "This could be our only chance!"

The painting was set high on the wall. Angus grabbed a chair from behind Mr. Dewsnap's desk and stood on it, but even stretching up on the tips of his toes, he was still several inches short of the lowest edge of the picture frame.

"Here, let me have a go." Dougal grabbed some hefty-looking tomes from the nearest pile and stacked them on the seat of the chair.

The whole tower wobbled precariously as Dougal climbed cautiously to the top of it. Angus held on to Dougal's ankles as he reached up and brushed the scale with his fingertips.

"It's stuck. It's buried under layers of ancient varnish and dust."

"Be careful," Indigo said, watching him anxiously. "Don't break it."

"I *am* being careful." Dougal gave the dragon scale another gentle wiggle. "It just—doesn't—want—to—"

There was a soft click as the office door opened behind them. Angus turned his head sharply, keeping a tight grip on Dougal's ankles. Mrs. Stobbs had entered the room.

She was dressed in a heavy coat, hat, and scarf speckled with snow and had clearly braved the freezing weather outside to collect a knitting pattern or deliver a warming stew to Feaver Street.

The housekeeper stopped dead, frozen like an ice statue in the doorway as she caught sight of Dougal balancing on the chair.

"Oh, great heavens!" She clutched her coat, staring at all three of them with a look of dreadful shock.

Angus and Indigo stared back, speechless with surprise. Dougal, who was concentrating hard on the dragon scale, gave it one final wiggle.

"There, I've got it!" He climbed down off the pile of books and turned around, triumphant, holding the blue scale up to the light like a trophy. "Not bad for someone who's supposed to be dead!"

There was a loud groan and a muffled thump. Mrs. Stobbs had fainted and crumpled to the floor.

11

THE PHOENIX AND THE PHOTOGRAPH

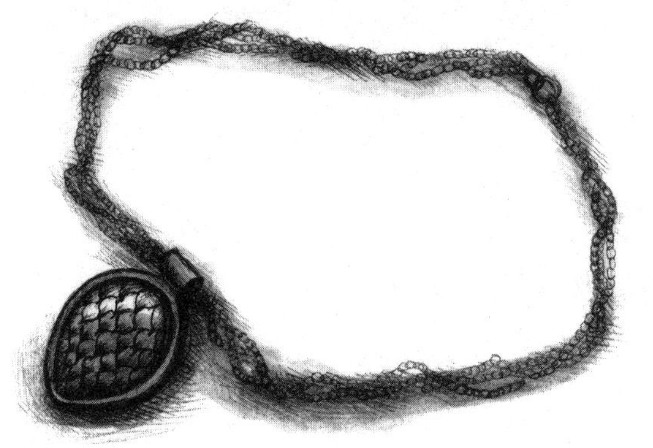

It took quite some time and a great deal of hot tea to revive Mrs. Stobbs. It took even longer for Mr. Dewsnap and Jeremius to tell her the full story of the fake accident at the Canadian Exploratorium and to convince her of the need for absolute secrecy.

"I'm just so pleased you're all safe and sound, my lovelies," Mrs. Stobbs said, still looking thoroughly overwhelmed. "When I read that dreadful report in the *Weathervane* and saw those awful pictures, it was j-just so upsetting." She sniffled, dabbing at her nose with a handkerchief.

Luckily, in the confusion, nobody asked what Angus,

Dougal, and Indigo had been doing in Mr. Dewsnap's office when the housekeeper found them. And it was only after Mr. Dewsnap walked Mrs. Stobbs home again that they finally raced up to Dougal's room to admire the fire dragon scale they'd just found.

"This is brilliant. We've got two scales now and only one clue left to solve." Dougal closed his door and placed the dragon scale on his bed, where they could all see it.

"But we've still got to find the scale that belongs to Valentine Vellum," Indigo said.

"Yeah, and for all we know, he could keep it in a secret compartment knitted inside his socks," Angus pointed out. "We can't just walk up to him and ask him to hand it over. We're definitely going to need a plan."

That night Angus dreamed of the fire dragons once again. A terrible fight raged around him as he desperately tried to wake his own dragon. When it finally appeared, smaller and dimmer than the rest, the other dragons descended upon it, with talons drawn, ripping and tearing, until the wounded creature could take no more. Angus watched in horror as the fire died behind the dragon's eyes and it began to plummet toward the ground, its wings limp and broken, its flames all but extinguished. He braced himself for the moment it would hit the ground, but the impact never came. The dragon transformed gracefully instead into a strange swarm of blue bees. The bees circled overhead and then began to dive at him, trying to sting his arm. A sudden pain stabbed through his veins.

"Ow!" Angus sat bolt upright, wide-awake, breathing hard, as if he'd just run the length of the Lightnarium. The crook of his arm was still throbbing painfully. He rolled up his sleeve to check that no bees had actually flown into his bedroom. But in the early morning gloom it was still too dark to see anything properly. He was just about to swing his legs out of bed and turn on the light when he realized he wasn't alone.

"There now, my lovely, I didn't mean to startle you." Mrs. Stobbs was standing in the corner of the room, clutching a pair of his shoes. "I just came to tell you breakfast is nearly ready, and to take your shoes for a quick polish before you return to Perilous. Heaven knows how you and Dougal manage to get them so dirty," she added, shaking her head.

Angus got dressed as soon as she'd gone, grabbed his

bag, which he'd packed the night before, and dragged it down the stairs to the kitchen. Dougal was sitting by himself at the table.

"Where's everyone else?" Angus asked, helping himself to some buttered toast.

"Indigo's already eaten; she's up in her room finishing her packing. Dad's in his office, and Jeremius left Feaver Street a while ago."

"Why didn't he just wait for the rest of us? We could have gone back together," Angus said, biting into his toast.

"Because I don't think he's gone back to Perilous," Dougal said quietly. "Dad just said your uncle had something *important* to do."

"Oh." Angus understood instantly. Jeremius had left for his dangerous fact-finding mission at Castle Dankhart. Angus placed the rest of his toast on his plate, feeling slightly sick.

Rogwood arrived ten minutes later to escort them back to Perilous. Deep drifts of thick snow had transformed the world outside 37 Feaver Street, covering rooftops, cobbles, and trees with white, wintry hoods.

It was the snowy fields and rooftops that Angus tried

to concentrate on a short time later as the gravity railway took them back up the rock upon which Perilous sat. A blast of sweltering hot air hit them as soon as they entered the building, and it was obvious that the heating had now been fixed. Rogwood took them straight back to the library, where Catcher Sparks was waiting to lock them in again.

"And no slamming doors this time, Dewsnap," she warned. "As far as the rest of the Exploratorium is concerned, this library is still in the grip of a serious fog mite infestation."

For once, Angus was glad that they had the whole library to themselves, and they darted straight up to Miss Vulpine's rooms to retrieve the chest from under Dougal's bed.

"Now that we've got instructions on how to open the third compartment, I can get straight on with solving the last puzzle." Dougal pushed the chest into the middle of the sitting room, where they could all see it. "We've just got to work out how to open it without getting our eardrums blasted or our heads taken off."

Ten minutes later Angus and Indigo had taken cover in the landing behind the half-opened sitting room door.

Dougal—who was now wearing his lightning deflector suit, tinted safety goggles, gloves, weatherproof hat, earmuffs, and snow boots—approached the chest alone.

"According to the instructions, all you've got to do is give the lid five full turns to the right," Angus called out as Dougal knelt down beside the chest.

Dougal took several deep breaths to steady his nerves. Angus crossed his fingers.

The lid turned easily in Dougal's hands, releasing a familiar pop of stale air from the inside at the end of the final turn.

Click!

Dougal gasped and flung himself to the ground with his hands covering his head. Thankfully, there were no explosions or flying lids. But it was obvious that something peculiar was happening inside the chest.

"Why can I smell burning?" Angus asked anxiously.

The answer became obvious two seconds later as smoke began to rise from the third compartment.

"Oh no!" Dougal ripped off his hat and goggles. "I must have done something wrong when I opened it. The last puzzle's about to self-destruct!"

"Quickly, grab it and see what it says," Angus said, hurrying into the room with Indigo right behind him.

Dougal rescued a pyramid-shaped paper puzzle, which was smoldering at the edges. He held it gingerly by one corner as he tried to snuff out the sparks with the cuff of his deflector suit and read the clues at the same time. "It looks like there might be some more weather glyphs, but I haven't seen any of these ones before. I haven't got a clue what they mean. They might as well be written in ancient Egyptian!" He turned the smoking puzzle over in his hands. "The other sides of the pyramid are just the same!"

The edge of the puzzle suddenly began to glow a warning red.

Click!

The puzzle twitched in his hands.

Click! Click! Click!

"It's about to self-destruct!" Indigo grabbed the puzzle and threw it into the cold fireplace.

Bang!

Scorched scraps of ancient paper tumbled through the air around them, burning like fireflies. Angus cowered behind an armchair, listening to the crackle and hiss of the blazing clues, half expecting Catcher Sparks to come storming up the stairs demanding to know why they were trying to destroy the Exploratorium when they'd only just returned.

"I've ruined everything," Dougal wailed as soon as the danger had passed. A thin veil of smoke hung in the air. The floor was now littered with tiny slips of charred paper. Miss Vulpine's curtains, which had already suffered greatly in the fracture lightning storm, had caught the worst of the explosion, and were now even more sooty and singed at the bottoms. "Now, we'll never know who's got the last dragon scale. If Dankhart destroys Perilous, it will be my fault."

"Of course it won't," Indigo said.

"Yeah, maybe we can stick the puzzle back together again." Angus picked up as many burned and blackened fragments of paper as he could find, but they were impossible to read. The clues they contained had been destroyed forever.

"I don't understand it," Dougal said, dropping into one of the armchairs. "I followed the instructions to the letter."

"It wasn't your fault," Angus said. "That old wooden

chest has been sitting in the principal's office for hundreds of years. And it was a Cradget's puzzle, so it was bound to self-destruct at some point."

Angus knelt on the floor to pick up the last of the scraps, but it was hopeless. He sat back on his heels with a heavy sigh, wondering how they were going to defeat Dankhart with just two blue dragon scales. Would Jeremius, Rogwood, and the other lightning catchers manage to create a deadly storm in time? Or had the fate of Perilous just been sealed right in front of them?

"What's that?" Indigo asked suddenly, pointing to a small wooden tile lying at his feet. It was the size of a piece of candy.

Angus picked it up and shrugged. "Maybe Miss Vulpine's been playing board games in here or something."

"But there's another one, and another . . ." The tiles, which were the same color as the carpet, had been difficult to spot at first. "Oh, but they're everywhere!" Indigo said, helping Angus collect them.

Dougal shot to his feet suddenly with a startled look on his face. "Ha! I didn't do it wrong after all. It's a phoenix puzzle," he said, sounding deeply impressed.

"It's a what?" Angus asked.

"A new puzzle rises from the ashes of the old one, like a phoenix from the flames. It's a classic puzzle-maker's trick to make you think you've blown it."

"Yeah, well, it almost worked." Angus smiled at the relief on Dougal's face.

They spent the next fifteen minutes scooping up all the tiles they could find, including several that had shot through the open door, across the landing, and into Indigo's bedroom.

"Lay them all out on the floor," Dougal said, arranging them in neat rows.

There were forty-four in all. Each tile had a tiny piece of an intricate pattern carved upon it.

"What does it mean?" Indigo asked.

"I haven't got the foggiest," Dougal said brightly. "Obviously, all the tiles fit together to somehow reveal a secret word or a picture or a map. But I've never seen a puzzle like this one before."

They continued to find the strange tiles for the next three days inside shoes, behind armchairs, and curtains, until Dougal was certain they'd found them all. He then spent every spare moment hunched over the small wooden squares, shuffling them around in different combinations, mumbling under his breath about "convoluted patterns," and scribbling ideas on a large sheet of paper.

In the meantime the rest of the lightning cubs returned to Perilous. Rogwood paid a rare visit to the library, bringing fresh supplies of peanut butter cookies and the latest copy of the *Weathervane*, which, thankfully, contained no news about Dankhart or any further attacks.

The next morning they also resumed their duties in the lost property department, which gave them plenty of time to discuss the big problem of how they were going to retrieve the second dragon scale from Valentine Vellum.

"We don't even know if he's got it for sure," Angus said as they continued to work their way through the items lost by visiting lightning catchers.

"It could belong to some doddery old uncle who moved to the far side of the island for all we know." Dougal looked up from the phoenix puzzle, which was laid out on a small table in front of him. As Catcher Sparks normally left them alone in the lost property department for several hours at a time, he was using every minute to work on the important tiles.

"There's only one way to find out for sure. We've got to search Vellum's rooms," Indigo said.

"But how are we supposed to get into the lightning catchers' living quarters without getting caught?" Dougal asked, frowning.

"It's not just the living quarters. We'll have to search his office as well," Indigo said.

Angus shook his head. "Winnie Wrascal burned it down at the end of last term and incinerated almost everything. If the dragon scale was in there at the time, it probably didn't survive."

The morning dragged by extremely slowly. Things took a sudden turn for the hazardous when Angus uncovered a box of Christow's mechanical forecasting flies.

"Get these things away from me!" Dougal yelled as the swarm chased him out into the hallway and down the corridor with a very threatening buzz. And he only agreed to return and continue with their work after Indigo had caught the flies in a jar of crystallized honey and sealed the lid.

A far more exciting discovery came late in the afternoon, when Indigo uncovered another glass jar, which contained what looked like the contents of a lint tray.

"I don't believe it! That's storm fluff!" Dougal informed them, placing it on the table and admiring it from every angle.

Angus and Indigo stared at each other, puzzled.

"What's so great about storm fluff?" Indigo asked.

"It's a residue that gets left behind after really big and violent storms. It takes years to build up in any one place, so it's really rare. And it's amazing stuff. It's drawn toward heat, like iron filings to a magnet, which is why it's got to be kept locked inside a jar. Watch this." Dougal demonstrated by swirling his hand across the surface of the glass. The fluff faithfully followed the pattern his fingers were making.

"But why would anyone collect a whole jar of it?" Indigo asked.

"Haven't got the foggiest, but I'm definitely keeping it. You never know when it might come in handy!"

Four days later Catcher Sparks released them from the library and took them to the Octagon for their next special lesson with Gudgeon. She left them with another stern warning.

"This is your last chance," she said as Angus made sure his weatherproof coat was buttoned up tight and his hat was covering his face. "If I hear any reports of reckless or dangerous behavior, you three will remain in Miss Vulpine's rooms until the lightning tower is destroyed. I suggest you follow Gudgeon's safety instructions to the letter, and don't talk to anyone!"

"That's easier said than done with idiots like the Vellums hanging around," Dougal mumbled under his breath as the twins slouched past them, deliberately barging into three third-year girls.

Gudgeon appeared less than a minute after Catcher Sparks left the domed hall, and a deep hush fell. The gruff lightning catcher looked tired and worn. His skin had an unhealthy gray tinge to it, as if sleep had evaded him for several days.

"Last night, the Canadian Exploratorium for Extremely Chilly Weather was attacked by a fracture lightning storm," he announced gravely. "At the same time, Exploratoriums in Dublin and Nova Scotia were also struck. The storms appeared without warning and were more vicious than anything we've seen so far. All three Exploratoriums were completely destroyed."

A frightened buzz broke out all around.

"Oh poor Jeremius!" Indigo whispered, biting her lip. "I wonder if his friends at the Canadian Exploratorium are safe."

Dougal shook his head, looking extremely serious. "All three of those Exploratoriums are much bigger than any of the others Dankhart's attacked so far."

Angus stared at Gudgeon with a terrible sinking sensation in his gut.

"Did all the lightning catchers escape in time, sir?" a tall fifth-year boy asked above the increasing noise.

"It's too soon to say. We've had some messages from survivors, but there are many lightning catchers who are still unaccounted for."

Somebody sobbed at the back of the group.

"It's Prudence Fledwick," Angus heard another lightning cub whisper. "Her mum and dad both work at the Exploratorium in Dublin. She hasn't heard anything from them in weeks."

Angus swallowed hard. He knew exactly what it felt like to lose both parents, to face the devastating prospect that they might never be seen again.

"That's seven Exploratoriums that Dankhart's destroyed now," Nicholas Grubb called loudly, trying to make himself heard. "What are the lightning catchers doing about it, sir?"

"We should destroy the lightning tower before it destroys us!" Felicity Keal, a third year, shouted.

"Sir, or we could mix all the weather samples in the storm archive together, sir, and make a huge superstorm," Nicholas Grubb suggested.

Theodore Twill turned on him with folded arms. "Don't be an idiot, Grubb. Those storm samples would never be strong enough."

Nicholas made a rude gesture in return, and a heated argument quickly broke out.

"Pipe down, you lot!" Gudgeon barked, and an uneasy silence descended once again. "We're doing everything we can, but I'm not about to discuss top-secret plans with a bunch of lightning cubs, so you can stop asking me questions. But it won't be long before Dankhart tries his luck at Perilous again, which is why I'm handing these out." Gudgeon reached into one of the deep pockets in his leather jerkin and pulled out a large handful of small booklets. "Make sure everyone gets a copy, Twill," he said, thrusting them at the lightning cub.

The booklet had a flimsy, hastily cobbled-together feel and smelled of freshly printed ink. There were two simple lines stamped across the plain front cover:

In the event of a catastrophic attack on Perilous, follow emergency evacuation procedures and survival instructions contained inside this booklet.

Angus felt his knees wobble.

"Whatever you do, don't read page six," Dougal hissed.

Angus flicked to the page immediately and then wished he'd taken Dougal's advice. Under the terrible heading "Locating Storm Survivors" was a simple instruction: "Turn the outer dial of your weather watch 180 degrees to activate a location tracker. It will automatically respond to any other weather watches in the vicinity."

"Let's hope we never have to use it," Dougal said, staring

at his own weather watch, as if it had been deliberately hiding secrets from him.

Angus turned to Indigo, to see if she had discovered the same instructions, and froze. Percival Vellum was now standing much closer to them. He was hovering on the far side of a small group of fourth years, staring at them with a deep frown. Angus ducked swiftly behind Clifford Fugg and his tall friends, dragging Dougal and Indigo with him.

"Vellum's looking at us!" he whispered.

"You don't think he's recognized us, do you?" Indigo said quietly.

Angus peered carefully around the side of Clifford Fugg. Percival was now talking into Pixie's ear and pointing in their direction.

"Don't!" Dougal pulled him back out of sight. "If Vellum recognizes us and starts blabbing to everyone else . . ."

"It'll ruin everything," Indigo said. "We'll never be able to find the last dragon scales."

Before they could discuss the matter any further, however, Gudgeon was speaking again.

"Right, you lot, settle down. Since our last training

session in the Lightnarium was interrupted by several unfortunate incidents . . ."

Dougal sank inside his hat and stared down at his feet.

"We'll be going in again today for another look at fracture lightning, so pay close attention!" Gudgeon opened the door to the Lightnarium and disappeared into the dark stone passageway behind it.

"Wait!" Dougal grabbed Angus by the sleeve before he could join the long trail of lightning cubs that followed. "We can't risk it. I don't like the way Vellum's looking at us. We should skip the lesson and go straight back to the library before he can do something brainless."

They waited until the last cub had disappeared through the doorway and then closed it carefully and hurried back to the library.

"We could always threaten those two with the photo we found in the lost property department if they start causing trouble," Dougal said as soon as they reached Miss Vulpine's rooms. He grabbed the picture from the mantel over the fire for another look. "There's no way Cheeky Peeky Perci wants this doing the rounds in the lightning cubs' living quarters. Can you imagine what Fugg, Twill, and Grubb would do if they ever got their hands on it!"

Despite the grim news Gudgeon had just delivered, Angus couldn't help smiling.

"What should we do now?" he said as Indigo took off her coat and hat, flung them on a chair, and took the photo from Dougal for another look. "It'll take Sparks hours to realize we haven't been in the Lightnarium with everyone else."

"I could spend more time on the phoenix puzzle, I suppose," Dougal said. "You and Indigo could go and hunt around the library again for stuff about fracture lightning. We haven't looked through everything yet."

Angus nodded. All searches so far had proved fruitless and incredibly frustrating, but he couldn't just give up.

"Are you coming?" he asked Indigo as he headed for the door.

But Indigo stood motionless, still staring at the picture in her hands.

"I think I've found something. It's Valentine Vellum," she said, pointing to the photo. A small colorful pendant on a chain was just visible over the top of Vellum's shirt. "He's wearing a blue fire dragon scale around his neck."

12

INTO THE DRAGON'S LAIR

The news that Valentine Vellum wore his dragon scale on a chain around his neck kept them up well into the early hours of the morning.

"We could ambush him in the kitchens," Dougal said, raking the fire to liven it up a bit.

"But somebody else might see us," Indigo said.

"Okay, then, how about making Percival do it? We could threaten him with that photo."

But Angus shook his head. "We'd have to tell him we're still alive first."

"So, what are we going to do?" Dougal asked, yawning heartily. "I mean, that photo was taken at least ten years ago. We don't even know if Vellum still wears that pendant."

Angus thought hard, staring into the fire, trying to imagine all possibilities. Somehow, they had to get close enough to Valentine Vellum to see what he was wearing around his neck, and they had to do it without getting caught. He could think of only one extremely risky way.

"We'll have to break into his bedroom while he's asleep," he finally said.

"What?" Dougal yelled, almost falling out of his chair. "Have you completely lost your marbles? I'd rather poke a fog yeti with a pitchfork."

"We can also look for anything that proves he's helping Dark-Angel and Dankhart while we're at it," Angus said. "There must be something in his rooms—a letter or a note or directions to a secret meeting place under Castle Dankhart. I mean, what if Vellum's even causing problems in the Lightnarium on purpose?"

"You think he's deliberately sabotaging the lightning catchers' efforts to make their own giant storm?" Indigo asked.

Angus shrugged. "It could explain why they're having so much trouble."

"It's never going to work." Dougal shook his head vigorously. "If Vellum catches us, he'll take us straight to the Lightnarium and have us vaporized. I bet he's been dying to do it for ages. Anyway, Vellum's room is bound to be locked, and we've got no idea how to get a key."

Two days later, a series of highly distressing pictures of the destroyed Exploratoriums in Canada, Dublin, and Nova Scotia appeared in the *Weathervane*, which Germ delivered to Miss Vulpine's rooms.

"Perilous has been put on high alert, of course," Germ said. "Dark-Angel's got extra lightning catchers on the roof, searching the skies day and night for any signs of rogue storms. They're working around the clock in the forecasting department. Some lightning catchers have turned up from the Icelandic Exploratorium that was attacked a few weeks ago."

"Are they all right? Have they told everyone what happened?" Angus asked, desperate for more details.

"Dark-Angel's keeping them well away from the kitchens, so no one can ask questions," Germ said. "But some of them have been coming up to the sanatorium for treatment, and I may have accidentally overheard them talking to Doctor Fleagal when I was listening— Oops, I mean, sweeping directly outside his office."

"And?" Angus asked impatiently.

"And it's worse than the *Weathervane*'s letting on." Germ sounded extremely serious for once. "The Icelandic Exploratorium was attacked by monsoon mongrels from the inside. They forced their way in when the storm broke and stole loads of equipment, secret designs for new weather machines, and tons of other stuff like storm globes. From what I could hear, the same thing happened in Canada and Nova Scotia."

"So, basically Dankhart's helping himself to anything that can make him even more powerful before he destroys what's left of each Exploratorium?" Angus said.

"I bet that's exactly what he's planning to do at Perilous," Dougal added.

Indigo shivered violently.

"Listen, Germ, you don't know how we can sneak into Vellum's private rooms in the lightning catcher's living quarters, do you?" Angus asked, starting to feel desperate.

"We need to, um, find something really important."

Germ nodded, as if asking how to break into Vellum's rooms was just as normal as asking what the kitchens had prepared for dinner that night. "Vellum's private rooms are right at the end of the corridor, through the last door on the left. But I wouldn't go in there unless you've got a strong stomach," he warned. "The whole room reeks of old socks. That's probably why he keeps the door locked at all times, to stop the stink from escaping back into the Exploratorium."

"How do you know what it smells like?" Indigo asked.

"Doctor Fleagal's always sending me down to the living quarters with tonics and constipation cures," Germ explained with a shrug. "I've been to Vellum's room loads of times before with some powder for stench foot."

Angus grinned at Dougal, his spirits momentarily lifted by the excellent news that Valentine Vellum had been suffering from extremely smelly feet.

"I don't suppose you know where Vellum keeps his keys, do you?" Angus asked.

"'Fraid not," Germ said. "But I can lend you mine if you want." He took a bunch of keys from his pocket and jangled it in front of them. "Old Fleagal gave me a set ages ago, so I can deliver tonics and stuff when the lightning catchers are busy elsewhere."

He removed one of the keys and chucked it at Angus.

"Wow!" Angus caught the key and stared at it. "Thanks, Germ. We definitely owe you one."

"If you're planning to sneak in and steal his secret grow-your-own-brains kit, I can hold him up in the kitchens by slipping some hiccupping powder into his cocoa," Germ offered enthusiastically.

"Er, thanks," Angus said, severely tempted by the offer. "But I think that might complicate things."

"Suit yourself," Germ said cheerily. "But if you change your mind, I've got loads of other ways to keep him out of your hair. All I need is twenty minute's warning and some vomit buckets from the sanatorium, and I can have Valentine Vellum dripping from head to toe in partially digested carrots. That should give you plenty of time to rummage through his sock drawer."

"Germ's brilliant," Dougal said as Indigo's brother left ten minutes later with a cheery wave. "I wonder if he was serious about the vomit buckets."

After several hours of deep discussion they decided to sneak into Vellum's rooms on Sunday night, the quietest time of the week inside the Exploratorium. In the meantime Dougal continued to work on the last puzzle.

"I've started to piece together some of the tiles," he said during one lunchtime as a rainstorm hammered against the windows outside.

Angus and Indigo peered over Dougal's shoulder. He had only managed to complete a small portion of the puzzle so far, but it appeared to show a lavishly decorated shield. Several creatures with tufted ears stood on either side of it. One had what looked like the very tip of a stripy snout.

"What is it?" Indigo asked.

"I think it might be part of a coat of arms, but I can't tell who it belongs to yet. Everyone on this island seems to have one," he said, pointing to a thick book on the table beside him called *Clever Coats of Arms and Ridiculous Family Mottos.*

To make matters worse, there was still no sign of Angus's storm prophet skills returning. It was also getting increasingly difficult to leave the library via the secret passageway, due to the extra activity in the Exploratorium. And trips down to the testing tunnels were now virtually impossible. In desperation, Dougal and Indigo sneaked several unclaimed storm globes out of the lost property department one afternoon so that Angus could practice his skills out on the roof terrace.

"Somebody left these behind in the experimental division about a hundred years ago," Indigo said, handing over one of the dusty-looking spheres. It was a murky afternoon with dull gray clouds and thick sheets of rain, which were perfect for concealing the presence of another storm from the rest of the Exploratorium.

"Some of the Swarfe weather crystals inside them have dried up a bit. But they might still work," Dougal said, giving one of the globes a hopeful shake.

"Thanks." Angus took the sphere cautiously. The last time Dougal had sneaked a storm globe into the Pigsty to test his skills, they'd narrowly avoided flooding the whole Exploratorium.

"Don't worry," Dougal said, as if reading his thoughts. "I've brought a bag of storm beads as well, just in case anything escapes into the sitting room. These things can soak up a whole lake if they have to."

Angus grinned, hoping they wouldn't be needed. "Ready?" He smashed the first globe, stood back, and prepared to face a fierce tempest. Instead of seeing the familiar wisps of storm rise above their heads, however, a thin trickle of gray dribbled out onto the roof terrace.

"Is it supposed to do that?" Indigo asked, nudging it with the toe of her boot.

The dribble spluttered a few times, as if trying to stir itself into a storm, and then sat in a lifeless puddle.

"Oh no, the weather crystals must have curdled," Dougal said.

The rest of the storm globes were just as disappointing, and it was while they were sweeping up the broken glass all around that an unexpected visitor arrived.

"Make sure you clean up this mess properly, McFangus."

Angus swung around, whacking Dougal on the shins with his broom.

"Ow! Watch it, will you?"

Dark-Angel was standing in the open doorway behind them. Angus had never seen her looking so tired and sallow faced before.

"I was just getting in some extra practice, miss," he said hastily, trying to explain.

"I trust you are also making good use of the testing tunnel and the equipment I have provided for your training?"

"Yeah, I've been down there loads, miss." Angus stared at the principal, hoping his face wasn't about to betray the lies he was telling. "I've seen tons of fire dragons and stuff."

"That is excellent news, McFangus. I am very glad to hear it. I believe we may need your skills to help save Perilous from a terrible fate."

"Er," Angus said, not sure what else to say.

"I discovered yesterday evening that Hartley Windspear has been taken back to the Inner Sanctum," Dark-Angel said. "The projectogram informed me that Jeremius discovered him here in Miss Vulpine's rooms. But I am making arrangements for him to return in the next few days, so that he may continue to assist you with your puzzle solving. I hope you are making good progress?" She turned and glanced around the sitting room behind her, searching for the ancient wooden chest.

Angus gulped. Luckily, the chest was hidden in his and

Dougal's bedroom, where Dark-Angel couldn't see that they had opened all three compartments inside it.

"Well, Dewsnap?" the principal asked impatiently. "Have you solved any of the puzzles yet?"

Dougal concentrated hard on his feet. "The puzzles are really difficult, miss. I—I've never seen anything like them before. It's taking loads of time to figure out how to unlock the first one."

"The *first* puzzle?" Dark-Angel sounded surprised. "But I do not recall you having this much difficulty with the Tri-Hard competition last term. Cradget's informed me that you won third prize. Are you now telling me that the puzzles are beyond your abilities?"

"No, miss!" Dougal said, sounding panicked. "I—I just need a bit more time. If I get it wrong, the whole lot will self-destruct, and then no one will ever find out who the dragon scale guardians are."

"I am well aware of the perils," Dark-Angel snapped. "But we do not have much time if the blue scales are to be of any use against Dankhart and his monsoon mongrels."

She shook her head and walked farther out onto the roof

terrace to look at the view beyond, shattered glass crunching under her feet.

"Very well, Dewsnap, you may have more time, but if you fail to make any progress soon, I shall be forced to take matters into my own hands. I will remove the puzzles and find someone who can solve them. Do I make myself clear?"

"Yes, miss," Dougal said.

"Do not let me down, Dewsnap." She fixed him with a hard stare. "I'm relying on you."

Sunday night finally came. At 2:15 a.m., Angus, Indigo, and Dougal sneaked out of the library and through the deserted corridors of Perilous until they reached the entrance to the lightning catchers' living quarters. All was quiet as they tiptoed along the curved hallway, passing leafy green plants in decorative pots, thick rugs, glowing light fissures, and large impressive paintings of previous lightning catchers hanging along the walls.

"How come we haven't got any of this stuff in the lightning cubs' living quarters?" Dougal said quietly as they crept past a door marked Amelia Sparks.

Loud snoring sounds were coming from Catcher

Grimble's room. A light shone out from under Gudgeon's door. Angus hovered outside it for a second, tempted to knock softly and tell Gudgeon exactly what was happening. Indigo, however, pulled him gently onward.

"We've got to find that dragon scale," she whispered. "We might not get another chance."

Valentine Vellum's room was clearly marked at the end of the corridor, just as Germ had described. Angus rummaged in his pocket for the key and took a deep breath.

"Remember, if Vellum's awake or he catches us red-handed, we make a run for it, straight back to the library. He'll have a hard time proving he's seen us if the rest of Perilous still thinks we're dead."

Dougal nodded, looking petrified. Angus turned the key inside the lock as quietly as he could.

It felt like walking into a sleeping dragon's lair. Inside, Vellum's room was surprisingly warm and cozy, with none of the fetid smells that Germ had warned of. Two armchairs had been placed on either side of a large fireplace, where glowing embers still burned, giving them just enough light to see by. There was a writing desk and various bookshelves scattered around the room. Luckily, the inner door to Vellum's bedroom was shut.

"Spread out and get searching," Angus whispered, heading for a tall cabinet next to a bookcase. "There's a good chance Vellum doesn't wear that pendant all the time, and he might have left it in here somewhere."

He checked nervously over his shoulder every few seconds, each time expecting to see a furious Valentine Vellum striding toward them. The cabinet he'd chosen to search was full of old-looking teacups with chips and cracks. Each had a lid, and Angus suddenly realized that Vellum had the largest collection of storms in teacups that he'd ever seen. One of the cups had a whirlwind painted on the side. Another was called Misty Maelstrom, according to the label, and promised "a genuine fognado of milk and sugar inside your morning cup of tea." He moved away from the cabinet, careful not to bump it. The last thing they needed was to set off a whirling weather spiral.

"Have you found anything yet?" he whispered, joining Indigo, who was looking through Vellum's writing desk.

"There's nothing in here but letters from other lightning

experts and some half-finished crossword puzzles. I can't find anything that mentions my uncle Scabious, either, or anything to link Vellum to Castle Dankhart and the monsoon mongrels."

Dougal's careful rummage through a cupboard also proved fruitless. They quickly searched the rest of the room, even checking down the sides of the armchairs, but the pendant was nowhere to be found.

"We've got no choice. We'll have to search Vellum's bedroom," Angus said, feeling his insides lurch.

He grasped the door handle and took a deep breath. "Ready?"

Dougal's face blanched. Indigo nodded, looking determined. Angus opened the door as slowly as he could to avoid any creaking hinges. Moonlight flooded in through a gap in the curtains, throwing a silvery gleam over wardrobes, chests of drawers, bedcovers, and the sleeping figure of Valentine Vellum. The lightning catcher was breathing deeply, undisturbed by their presence, for now.

Indigo crept silently across the room to a large wardrobe; the door had been left ajar. Dougal stood frozen with fear, too afraid to move. Angus looked through Vellum's clothes that had been flung carelessly across a chair, being extra careful not to drop anything that could clatter across the floor. There was nothing in the pockets of his pants but pencils, scraps of paper, and safety goggles. There was no sign of his leather jerkin.

Vellum snorted and turned over suddenly, his forehead creased, his breathing now faster and shallower. Angus swallowed hard. They had to search him quickly.

He tiptoed across the floor, holding his breath, flanked on his left by Indigo. Dougal was now bringing up the rear, several cautious paces behind them. Close up, Vellum was even hairier and more gorillalike than Angus had imagined. His breath smelled spicy, as if he'd eaten a curry for dinner. Angus reached out slowly and peeled the bedcovers back just far enough to see a hint of blue pajamas and the lightning catcher's neck. But there was no sign of the dragon scale pendant.

"Ow!"

The silence was suddenly shattered. Dougal was clutching his foot, hopping about the floor. While creeping closer, he'd accidentally stubbed his toe on the bed, jolting the frame. Angus felt his heart beat painfully hard inside his chest. Vellum's eyelids flickered and opened.

"Mc-McFangus? Midnight? Dewsnap?" Vellum squinted at each of them in turn, half asleep.

"I'm still dead, sir," Angus said quickly, in what he hoped were ghostly sounding tones. "Me, Dougal, and Indigo have come back to haunt everyone at Perilous, and tonight, it's your turn, sir."

But Vellum was already propping himself up on his elbows. "I'm not an imbecile, McFangus. And ghosts don't stub their toes." He made a sudden lunge at Angus, who ducked swiftly out of reach. "Get back here! You've gone too far this time!"

"Run for it!" Angus said as Vellum clambered out of bed.

"When I've finished with you three, you'll wish you *had* perished in the glacier caves!"

They were back through the sitting room in seconds, racing out into the hallway before Vellum could raise the alarm. Angus could hear him stumbling out through the door behind them, barefoot and still befuddled.

At the exact same moment a dreadful sound began to

wail along the corridor. Light fissures flicked on inside the rooms they were hurtling past. For one confused second Angus thought that Vellum had set off some kind of intruder alert. But the truth was even more hair-raising.

"I don't believe it! It's an evacuation drill," Dougal said above the racket. "Why are they doing one in the middle of the night? Talk about a bad time to go dragon scale hunting!"

Doors slammed open behind them. In a matter of moments they would be surrounded by a dozen senior lightning catchers.

Crash!

Spectacular lightning flashed outside a window. It fractured as it struck the walls, sending dozens more bolts in every direction.

"This isn't an evacuation drill," Angus said. Perilous shook around them as a deep roll of thunder vibrated through the night air. "Perilous is under attack!"

They raced away from the living quarters and down several flights of stairs. Lightning catchers and cubs began to appear from all directions, colliding with one another in the chaos.

"Quickly! All lightning cubs to their emergency weather

shelters!" Catcher Sparks hurried past in her nightdress and slippers. "Croxley! Stop those first years; they're heading the wrong way!"

"Should we follow Croxley down to the shelter?" Dougal said as yet another lightning strike rocked the Exploratorium.

"We can't," Angus said. "If anyone does a head count, they'll realize straightaway they've got three extra lightning cubs."

"Then we've got to get down to the shelter in the lost property department!" Indigo was already pushing her way through the confusion. Angus tried to follow, accidentally tripping over somebody's foot in his haste.

"Ooof!"

He fell headlong, crashing straight into something solid.

"M-Munchfungus?" Percival Vellum was staring down at him with a look of shocked recognition as the siren continued to wail. "I knew it! I knew there was something funny going on."

"You three have been coming to Gudgeon's lessons!" Pixie added, pinching Angus on the arm to test that he was really there.

"Keep your voices down, you idiots! It's supposed to be a secret," Dougal hissed.

Percival glared at them. "Why should I care about your stupid secrets, Dewsnap? Why are you pretending to be dead?"

"It's too complicated for your pea-size brain to understand, Vellum," Angus said.

"Just get out of the way!" Indigo added.

Angus, Dougal, and Indigo tried to push past the twins, but Pixie and Percival both refused to budge, forming a brainless wall of muscle across the narrow corridor.

Crash!

Another long streak of lightning hit the wall outside. Percival whimpered, flinching away from it.

"Look, we can't just stand here arguing. That storm's about to burst through one of those windows," Angus said.

Percival trembled from head to toe. "I-I'm not letting you and your friends win this time, Munchfungus. I'm taking you straight to my dad! Just because you're a storm prophet—"

Crash! Crash! Crash!

Fracture lightning finally forced its way through the window closest to them, sending dozens of fizzles and flickers skipping in different directions. Screams of panic broke out all around.

"Arghh!" Percival cowered away from Angus, his face contorted, his arms braced in front of him like two crossed swords. "You're making that lightning strike on purpose, Munchfungus, I know you are, you and that stupid electrified lizard of yours!"

He stared wildly around, as if expecting to catch a glimpse of the enormous fiery creature. The idea came to Angus with another blinding flash from above.

"Y-yeah, that's right, it was me," he said, trying to sound convincing. "I made that lightning strike close to you, but it won't miss next time."

He raised his hands above his head, as if getting ready to control the weather like a magician about to perform a spectacular trick.

"You wouldn't! You can't!" Pixie said in a wild panic.

"If you or Pixie tell anyone that we're still alive, I can send another storm chasing after you in a second. I'll sneak into the lightning cubs' living quarters in the middle of the night, and no one will ever know it was me. So, keep your big mouths shut!"

"Okay, okay." Percival's eyes were wide with dread. "We won't tell anyone, we promise. Just tell your fire dragon to leave me and Pixie alone!"

He scrambled to his feet, grabbed his sister by the arm, and hurried away from them.

"That was the best moment *ever*." A fleeting look of pure joy crossed Dougal's face.

Angus, however, was glad neither of the twins had called his bluff. Even with the fracture lightning striking out all around them, he'd felt nothing stir inside his chest, no hint that his fire dragon had returned from its long hibernation.

"Come on, we've got to get down to the evacuation shelter!"

Walls, pillars, and windows were illuminated by every strike of the lightning that now surrounded Perilous on all sides. They hurtled down more flights of stairs and along several dark corridors, pushing past lightning cubs and catchers as they ran back toward the library.

When they finally reached the entrance to the secret

passageway, however, Angus felt the hairs rise on the back of his neck in warning.

"Wait, something's wrong." He ran along the corridor until he reached the main library doors, which had been flung open wide. The lock was broken and lying in pieces on the floor.

"Percival Vellum!" Dougal said, sounding annoyed. "I bet the ugly little squirt went running straight to his dad as soon as we were gone and told him everything."

"Valentine Vellum must have worked out we've been hiding in the library," Indigo said quietly.

They walked cautiously through the doorway. Inside, it was obvious that all was not well. A howling wind was whistling around the shelves, tossing books through the air like autumn leaves. Rain was falling in the reference section. A gaping hole in the glass roof above showed exactly where a bolt of lightning had smashed through, allowing the storm to enter. But the storm wasn't the only thing that had forced its way into the library, Angus realized with a sinking feeling in his stomach. A trail of wet footprints led up the stairs toward the balcony, where a lone figure stood.

The man had short brown hair and a face like a ferret. Angus recognized him instantly. It was Victus Bile, one of Dankhart's chief monsoon mongrels. It was the first time they'd seen him since he'd chased them through the labyrinth of animal skulls and jars of powdered bone in Crevice and Sons.

"What's he doing here?" Indigo whispered as Angus pulled them both swiftly down a narrow aisle full of bulky weather encyclopedias.

"Dark-Angel must have told your dear old uncle Scabby that we're still alive," Dougal hissed. "I bet she finally got fed up waiting for us to solve the puzzles and find her the dragon scales."

"And now Victus Bile's looking for us?" Indigo said.

"Well, he's not searching for a book on weather fore-casting snails, is he? What do we do now?"

"Oh!" Indigo said, suddenly turning pale. "What if he's come for the blue dragon scales as well? What if Dark-Angel didn't believe us, what if she guessed that we've already found one?"

The scales were sitting in a chest of drawers beside Dougal's bed, vulnerable and easy to find. Angus peered through a gap in the shelves and watched as the monsoon mongrel made his way across the balcony. "We've got to get those scales. If Victus Bile takes them back to Dankhart . . ."

They sneaked along behind the shelves, edging their way toward the stairs and the secret door that led back up to Miss Vulpine's rooms.

Crash!

Dougal flinched at the deafening sound of rolling thunder. Angus glanced up at the roof as yet more lightning flashed overhead. But when he finally dropped his gaze . . . Angus froze, blood thickening in his veins. Victus Bile was now blocking the aisle in front of them.

"Run!" Indigo yelled in a panic.

For the second time that night they fled, running helter-skelter across the library. Angus crashed into a study table and knocked it flying. Indigo sprinted past him, but Dougal had somehow backed himself into a corner while Victus Bile advanced upon him.

"Hey! I'm over here, you big hairy mongrel!" Angus yelled. He grabbed a book off the nearest shelf and hurled it. Victus Bile changed course swiftly and rushed after Angus instead.

Dougal took his chance, darting toward the door that led down to the lost property department. Angus ran blindly, desperately looking for an escape route, but he was now heading straight for the far wall of the library. He slid to a halt on the polished floors and stared wildly around.

"It's a dead end," Indigo said, appearing from the aisle beside him. "I've already looked. There's nowhere left to run!"

Angus clutched Indigo by the arm and tried to double back, but hands reached out and grabbed his sweater.

"You're coming with me, boy! There'll be no escaping this time."

"Geroff me!"

He tugged himself free, staggered sideways, and hit the edge of a tottering bookcase.

Creak!

A heavy pile of books smashed to the floor and knocked him flying, and Angus remembered nothing more.

13
THE GUARDIAN IN THE GALLERY

". . . The lightning catchers didn't see the storm coming until it was too late."

"Our plans are advancing well. Soon, there will be no more lightning catchers to stand in our way."

The words drifted slowly across the air, making Angus's head throb with pain. His mouth felt as dry as a desert, and for some reason his eyebrows were aching. He opened his eyes just wide enough to see that it was now daylight. He was lying on the floor of a room he didn't recognize. The air around him was cool and musty, with a hint of sulfur and the lingering smell of recent explosions.

"You have done well, Victus," the first voice said. "It fits in perfectly with our plans to have Angus and Indigo here at this time."

Angus swiveled his head to the left as slowly as he could. Adrik Swarfe and Victus Bile were standing close by with their backs toward him. The truth hit him with another throb of pain. He was no longer at Perilous. He'd been brought to Castle Dankhart.

"Scabious will be delighted by the news." Swarfe was speaking again. "He has always been keen to explore the McFangus boy's storm prophet potential, and now, at last, his chance has come."

Angus could vividly recall the last time Dankhart had been keen to test his skills. He and Indigo had only been saved by the appearance of an extremely well-timed icicle storm, and his fire dragon. He could feel nothing inside his chest now, however, except his own irregular breathing. He moved his head a fraction of an inch in the opposite direction. Indigo was staring back at him from just a few feet away. She was clearly listening to the same conversation with a look of silent terror on her pale face.

"Dankhart won't get much out of these two unless we revive them with a strong effervescence tonic," Victus

Bile said. He turned and approached Angus and nudged him roughly in the ribs with the toe of his boot. Angus forced himself not to wince, his eyes firmly shut once again. "They've been unconscious since we left Perilous."

"My dear Victus, we will force them through our cloud washing chambers if that is what it takes to bring them back to their senses. Come." Swarfe headed toward the door. "We must inform Scabious that he has some unexpected visitors."

The two men left the room, closing the door behind them with a heavy clunk. Angus waited for several moments, just to make certain they'd really gone.

"Are you all right?" he asked, crawling across the floor as Indigo sat up slowly, rubbing the back of her head.

"I th-think so. I don't remember anything after Victus Bile chased us across the library. Where's Dougal?"

Angus shook his head, trying to recall exactly what had happened. "I saw him heading toward the cupboard that leads down to the lost property department. I bet Victus Bile didn't even see him. He's still safe at Perilous. And we've got to get out of this room before Swarfe comes back with your dear old uncle Scabby."

He scrambled to his feet and was hit by an instant wave of dizziness. He stumbled over to the only window in the room and peered through the grimy glass. It was a very, very long way down; there were no ledges to crawl out onto, no balconies from which they could signal for help—just a deathly drop down a tall tooth of rock that ended in a moat full of crocodiles.

"We'll have to find another way," he said, staring hopelessly around the room instead.

"But even if we do escape, how are we going to get back to Perilous?" Indigo brushed the dust from the floor off her clothes. "It's on the other side of the mountains."

Angus felt his spirits nose-dive. Indigo was right. Even if they did find a way out of the castle, they would be facing a long, treacherous trek with no food, water, or warm clothing. With nothing but their weather watches to guide them, they'd be lucky if they made it half a mile through the winter storms that were still raging through the mountains.

"Well, we can't just sit here and wait for Dankhart and Swarfe to lock us up," he said, determined. "Dougal must have raised the alarm by now. He'll have told Rogwood or

Catcher Sparks. With any luck there'll be a rescue party waiting for us, if we can just get out of this castle," he added, hoping he was right.

"Castle Dankhart," a familiar voice said quietly from the farthest corner of the room. "Belonging to the Dankhart family, the castle is a private dwelling of great importance, with the largest collection of wild crocodiles on the entire island."

Angus spun around on his heels so fast, it made his eyeballs ache. His heart leaped into his mouth at the startling sight of Hartley Windspear, who was lurking in the shadows, his robes billowing gently.

"I don't believe it! What's he doing here?" Angus said, wondering if his eyes were playing tricks on him.

Indigo shook her head, dumbfounded. "The monsoon mongrels must have kidnapped him as well. I wonder what they want him for."

"I don't know, but we can't leave him here. He knows all sorts of important Perilous secrets."

Angus darted over to the door and rattled the handle forcefully, dislodging several puffs of dust, which floated through the air like drifts of gray snow. He kicked the door for good measure. It sprang open suddenly, creaking on its rusty hinges.

Indigo gasped. "Swarfe thinks we're still unconscious, so he didn't even bother locking it."

They slipped into the corridor outside, with Hartley Windspear following close behind. The castle was eerily quiet. For the first few minutes they crept along corridors without catching a glimpse of anyone. There were none of the comforting touches that made Perilous feel like home—no blazing open fires, no colorful posters warning of the dangers of chilblains, or coat hooks groaning under the weight of knitted hats and scarves. The thick walls felt more like a prison than protection against the weather outside. Light fissures ran through bare stone, broken only by an occasional window.

Indigo looked straight ahead, refusing to even glance at their unfriendly surroundings. Angus, however, soaked up every tiny detail. It was the first time he'd been inside the same building as his parents in over a year. His heart began to thump erratically. He'd spent hours imagining what it felt like just to stand within the castle's imposing walls. He'd spent even longer poring over detailed floor plans in *The Dankhart Handbook*, and now that he was actually creeping around inside it . . . Angus shivered, trying to shake off the deeply unsettling sensation that the castle was watching *them*.

Angus stopped abruptly as the corridor opened out into a much larger hallway with doors and stairs leading off in different directions, none of which were marked “Exit.”

“Which way now?” he said, considering their options. There was a grand door made of gleaming, engraved copper, behind which anything could be lurking, including Dankhart’s bedroom or a dining hall where hundreds of monsoon mongrels were eating breakfast.

“Over there.” Indigo pointed to a narrow gap in the wall, where a set of dingy-looking stairs headed down. “Maybe they lead to the lower levels of the castle.”

They tiptoed quietly across the hall, feeling horribly exposed and vulnerable. If any of the doors opened now, they’d be caught without any hope of escape. The steps led to a long gallery with a set of double doors at the far end. Light flooded in through tall mullioned windows set deep into one wall. On the other side of the gallery, huge, ancient-looking tapestries showed monstrous storms and great fire dragon battles where the monsoon mongrels stood victorious, where Perilous lay in ruins, and the storm prophets knelt, vanquished, their heads bowed with shame, their hands tied. Grand portraits of the Dankhart family glared down at them as they hurried toward the end of the gallery, as if they could somehow sense the presence of intruders. Even the ceiling was decorated with elaborate coats of arms showing crossed swords, ancient-looking hailstone helmets, squirrels with tufted ears, and—

Angus stopped abruptly and stared at the impressive shield directly above his head, which was embellished not only with tufted squirrels but with stripy-snouted badgers.

"That coat of arms . . . It's exactly like the one Dougal's been trying to put together in Miss Vulpine's sitting room. Look!" He turned to see if Indigo had spotted the same thing, only to find Hartley Windspear gliding beside him instead. Indigo had stopped thirty feet behind them and was now staring at one of the wooden panels in the wall.

"What's wrong?" Angus asked, hurrying back to join her.

Indigo pointed to some rough notches in the wood. It was

obviously a height chart, marked out in feet and inches. Just two names had been carved at the top: Scabious and Etheldra.

"Me and Germ have got one just like it at home," Indigo said with a sad shake of her head. "I can't believe my mum ever lived in this castle with my uncle Scabious. I mean, this is where she grew up."

Angus was suddenly extremely glad that he'd spent most of his life so far at the Windmill in Budleigh Otterstone. Even with the constant danger from tiny mechanical squids and rampaging blizzard catchers, it still had a far friendlier, homey feel than Castle Dankhart.

"Listen, Indigo, I'm really sorry about your mum, but we've got to get out of this place before somebody finds us. And there's something I've got to show you first." He dragged her back along the gallery and pointed to the coat of arms.

Indigo took a sharp intake of breath. Angus felt his head begin to throb once again as he read the family name draped in painted ribbons across the shield; it was Swarfe.

"Swarfe is the fourth dragon scale guardian?"

"The Swarfes came to the island with Starling and

Perilous," Indigo said, thinking it through quickly. "They've always been really well respected."

"Yeah, right up until Adrik Swarfe ran off to join your uncle Scabious."

"But this is terrible news!" Indigo looked stricken. "It means the last dragon scale is here, somewhere inside this huge horrible castle! How are we ever going to find one tiny dragon scale? We haven't even found any emergency exits or escape routes yet."

"Emergency escape route from Castle Dankhart," Hartley Windspear said quietly from behind them. "To be used as a last resort only, or when being chased by an abominable snowstorm."

Angus stared at the projectogram, astounded.

"You—you know how to get out of here?" Indigo asked.

Hartley Windspear nodded solemnly.

"Then why didn't you say so sooner!" Angus said, exasperated. "We could have been charging around this castle for days like a pair of headless chickens before we found a way out by ourselves."

"*Headless Chicken*," Hartley Windspear said. "The title of a famous modern painting by the renowned Imbur

Island artist, Delia Chook, which is currently hanging in an art gallery at—"

"There's no time for that now," Angus cut the projectogram short. "Just tell us how to get out of this castle."

"Hmmph." Hartley Windspear folded his arms across his chest, looking highly offended.

"Look, I'm sorry." Angus took a deep breath, trying hard to keep his voice calm and steady. "But this is really important."

"Oh please, Mr. Windspear, can't you help us just this once?" Indigo added in an extremely polite voice.

The projectogram stared down his nose at them both, hesitating. "Turn left at the end of the gallery," he finally said, "and head down a set of gloomy-looking stairs that lead toward the castle dungeons and a network of secret passageways underneath."

"The d-dungeons?" Angus said.

"Where Angus's mum and dad are being held?" Indigo added.

Hartley Windspear said nothing. But Angus was suddenly buzzing with the brilliant possibility of a heroic rescue. Up until that moment he hadn't even dared to hope. But if they could somehow free his mum and dad and take them back to Perilous, it would be a glorious, wonderful triumph.

"Listen, Indigo, we've got to make a new plan," he said, hoping Indigo had already come to the same dangerous conclusion. "We can't leave this castle without searching for that fourth dragon scale. We'll never get another chance. I mean, we can't exactly pop back anytime we feel like it and ask Swarfe if we can rummage through his personal belongings."

Indigo nodded, looking determined. "But where do we start? We haven't even got a map of the castle."

"Yeah, but we've got the next best thing." Angus pointed to Hartley Windspear, who had drifted over to one of the tapestries and was gently billowing beside it. "He obviously knows loads of stuff about this place, plus *The Dankhart Handbook* says most of the monsoon mongrels sleep in a turret on the north side of the castle. So, if we can just get old Windspear to tell us where the turret is . . ."

"He could guide us straight down to the dungeons afterward so we can rescue your mum and dad," Indigo added.

"But how are we going to get them out?"

"We'll need a key, or we'll have to find a way to trick the guards outside. It won't be easy," Angus said, feeling like he'd just made the understatement of the century. "But we have to try."

He jumped suddenly at the noise of a door banging somewhere in the distance.

"Come on, we've got to find that scale, rescue my parents, and get out of this stinking castle!"

After questioning Hartley Windspear for several minutes, however, it was obvious that the projectogram had no idea where the north turret was.

"We'll just have to find our own way," Indigo said as they finally left the gallery. "Can you remember anything else from the handbook?"

Angus closed his eyes, trying to picture the floor plans. But it had been months since he'd last studied them, and his memory had become distinctly fuzzy on the subject. "I think we need to head down. There's a central hallway, somewhere on the lower floors, with stairs leading up to all the turrets." They sneaked carefully along dreary corridors of cold stone, flinching at the slightest howl of wind outside the windows or the distant thump of unknown weather machines. The castle was vast. The labyrinth of closed doors and dark corridors was also far more confusing than the handbook had led Angus to believe, and he soon lost all sense of direction. The only thing he could tell for sure was that every set of stairs was leading them down deeper and deeper into the castle. The hot, choking smell of weather experiments began to drift through the air toward them, and Angus was sure they were now getting dangerously close to the heart of Dankhart's weather-making madness, the experimental chambers. There was no sign of any central hallway or turrets.

"This is getting us nowhere," he whispered a few minutes later, after they were forced to hide in a tiny room full of large mops and brooms as a group of monsoon mongrels hurried past. It was the first time they'd seen any of the Dankhart's weather engineers close up. They looked extremely thuggish and frightening.

"Why don't we follow those monsoon mongrels?" Indigo said quietly as three particularly bushy specimens with straggly beards and unkempt eyebrows went scurrying past. "I mean, they must go back to their rooms to change their socks or wash their feet sometimes. They could lead us straight to Swarfe's private chambers."

They followed the group at a distance, hiding in deep shadows and ducking into doorways. Their plans changed swiftly, however, when the monsoon mongrels suddenly altered course and began to stride toward Angus and Indigo instead.

"In here!" Angus dragged Indigo through a plain wooden door on their right before they were spotted. He stumbled to a halt.

They'd walked straight into pitch-black darkness. It took several seconds for his eyes to adjust.

"Whoa!"

They were standing in a gigantic domed cavern. A vast swath of magnificent stars twinkled way above their heads. Angus stared at his weather watch. The face was glowing a soft luminous green, showing him the names of the stars and the positions they occupied in the sky. The big twinkly one directly overhead was called the pole star. Uncle Max had pointed it out at the Windmill, when they'd sat outside on the balcony stargazing. Angus gulped. The Windmill seemed like a very, very long way away now.

"What is this place?" he asked, watching as two comets shot suddenly across the darkness, leaving a trail of silvery dust.

"The dark chamber was devised by Adrik Swarfe," Hartley Windspear said in a spooky whisper, "and is used for nighttime navigation training."

It sounded exactly like the sort of chamber that might exist at Perilous. Angus could easily imagine standing somewhere identical with Gudgeon while he gave them special lessons on how to navigate their way across Alaska in an emergency. The comparison made him feel very uneasy.

They hurried away from the door before any monsoon mongrels came bursting through it. The cavern was cold, damp, and eerie. They stopped frequently to listen for the sound of heavy footsteps. When they finally reached the far side, Hartley Windspear came to a halt in front of a door that had been padlocked from the inside.

"Brilliant. What do we do now?" Angus tugged angrily on the lock, but it held fast.

There was nothing else for it, so they turned around and retraced their steps across the cavern, hoping that the monsoon mongrels had now moved away from the door they'd first come through. It was a long, nervous, bad-tempered journey. Angus tripped over several large rocks, bruising his knees badly. And he was just wondering if they might be going around in circles when a strange bloodred moon began to appear on the horizon.

"Wh-why is the moon all red?" Indigo asked nervously.

"The appearance of a blood moon is caused by a particular scattering of light waves in the earth's atmosphere," Hartley Windspear informed them, "and often occurs when the moon is low in the sky or when there are particles in the air from volcanic eruptions or forest fires. But it is used by the monsoon mongrels to investigate the legends of blood-sucking weather vampires."

"You're kidding," Angus said, almost smirking in the gloom. "I mean, weather vampires are just a stupid legend."

Grrrrrr!

Blood surged through his jugular as a spine-chilling snarl echoed around the cavern.

"Let's get out of here!" He broke into a sprint, trying to stay several desperate steps ahead of the sound of snapping teeth that followed them all the way back to the first door.

Bang!

Angus slammed the door behind them and stood panting in the empty corridor, desperately trying to catch his breath.

"This castle is a death trap!"

Indigo nodded, breathing heavily. "What now?"

"We've got to keep looking," Angus said, determined not to give up yet.

They set off again, investigating every set of stairs that might lead up to the turrets. But after they'd been forced to avoid monsoon mongrels by diving into three storage cupboards, one bathroom, and a room filled with what looked like yeti toenail clippings, Angus was finally forced to admit defeat. Without the help of Hartley Windspear or the maps in *The Dankhart Handbook*, their search for the scale was hopeless.

"There must be something else we can try," Indigo said as they stopped in the same corridor they'd already run down twice before. "We could follow some more monsoon mongrels." Angus sat on the floor with his head resting against the cool stone behind him, trying to get his thoughts clear.

"The castle's too big. We've got no idea where we are."

"But we've got to stop my uncle." Indigo's face was desperate. "We need that blue dragon scale!"

"I know! But if we keep on looking, we're going to get caught and then we'll spend the rest of our lives locked up in your uncle Scabby's dungeons. Then we'll never be able to rescue my parents, or save Perilous, or ever see Dougal again!"

Indigo bit her bottom lip, suddenly looking forlorn.

"Listen, I'm sorry," Angus said, taking a deep calming breath. "But we've already been chased by some weather vampires. What if it's something worse next time?"

Indigo hesitated, clearly thinking of the dangers, before she finally nodded. A few minutes later they set off in search of the dungeons.

They crept warily past study rooms, store cupboards, chart rooms, and the entrance to a badly neglected library, the sight of which would have made Miss Vulpine's blood boil. Piles of mildewed books had been trampled, torn, and left to rot.

Finally, they reached some slippery, dark steps that Hartley Windspear claimed led down to the dungeons. Angus stared expectantly into the gloom around each spiral, wondering if his mum and dad could hear the sound of his footsteps approaching, if they could somehow tell they belonged to friendly feet.

"I think we're getting close to the bottom," he said quietly as a faint light began to flicker in the dimness below.

He slowed down to a cautious creep, but before he could catch a glimpse of any dungeons, or their inhabitants . . .

". . . want my niece and the boy caught before they can find their way out of this castle."

Angus froze midstride. He recognized Dankhart's voice instantly. It sounded cold, hard, and extremely angry. Indigo's uncle was standing just feet away from them around the final bend in the stairs. Angus could see his shadow moving on the curve of the wall, pointing and gesturing angrily at another figure. He gulped silently. It was clear that their escape had been discovered.

"Have some patience, Scabious. They will be found." Swarfe was speaking now. "Sooner or later they will grow hungry or tired, and that is when they will be forced to come out of hiding. There is no escape from the castle."

"Nevertheless, I want it searched from top to bottom, and make sure it is done properly," Dankhart said. "These *children* have already outsmarted you once today, Adrik. See that it does not happen again."

Swarfe's voice hardened. "As you wish, Scabious. But we have already stationed extra guards outside the McFanguses's dungeon. If the boy is foolish enough to come searching for his parents, he'll get a nasty surprise."

Dankhart grunted. "We cannot risk our plans being disrupted by the presence of two meddlesome children. The final storm will be ready to send over to Perilous in precisely fourteen days' time—or so you claim. It must be finished before the lightning catchers make any progress with their efforts to destroy the lightning tower."

"I do not think we need to concern ourselves with the lightning catchers' efforts," Swarfe said with an unmistakable sneer in his voice. "Their experiments are going very badly indeed. They do not have the power to destroy a storm bucket, never mind a powerful and mighty tower."

Angus swallowed hard. There was only one way that Dankhart and Swarfe could know anything about the lightning catchers' plans: Dark-Angel had told them everything.

"That is still no cause for complacency." There was a diamond-hard edge to Dankhart's voice. "If you had done a better job of combining the lightning storm particles and the dragon scales, Perilous would have been finished long ago."

"The process is far more complicated than we were led to believe," Swarfe said. His shadow moved restlessly on the curve of the wall, dangerously close to where Angus, Indigo, and Hartley Windspear stood listening. "I have been telling you for months now that we need extra information about the original experiments in 1777. I believe we are missing some of the crucial details, and until we discover what they are, we might just as well combine lightning storm particles with bread crumbs for all the good it will do."

"But Victus has now found what you were looking for?"

"On my instruction he kidnapped a particular holographic projectogram who has more knowledge of the 1777 experiments than almost anyone else."

Angus stared over his shoulder at Indigo. It was obvious now why Victus Bile had kidnapped Hartley Windspear. It also explained why they'd found a monsoon mongrel lurking in the library. Dark-Angel had told him where to search. Victus Bile hadn't been looking for the blue fire dragon scales, after all.

"I assume you have already begun to question this projectogram?" Dankhart asked.

There was a brief awkward pause. "Unfortunately, the projectogram was placed in the same room as your niece and the McFangus boy."

"So you've foolishly allowed him to escape?" Dankhart said, furious. "Organize a search party, and this time, Adrik, make sure there are no mistakes."

The shadows began to move toward the stairs. Angus turned silently, pushing Indigo and Hartley Windspear back up the steps ahead of him in a panic. His heart was pounding so loudly, he was convinced the sound of it would echo off the walls and give their presence away.

They tripped and stumbled, retracing their steps. Angus could feel his lungs about to rupture, the muscles in his legs burning with the effort of their silent escape.

But their luck had run out at last. When they finally reached the top of the stairs, they were met by the terrifying sight of a monsoon mongrel. Tall and hairy, with a straggly beard covering his chin, he was barring their only escape route.

14
THE STORM NURSERIES

"Angus?" The monsoon mongrel looked almost as surprised to see them as they were shocked to see him. "Thank goodness I've found you! I've been looking for you and Indigo everywhere."

"Stay away from us!" Angus shoved hard and tried to push past him. Any second now Swarfe and Dankhart would appear behind them, and their chances of ever escaping again would be less than zero.

The man lunged forward and grabbed Angus by the arm.

"Let me go!"

"Shhhh!" the monsoon mongrel warned. "Keep your

voice down. It's me, Angus. It's Jeremius. Look at me!"

Angus stopped struggling for a fraction of a second and stared at the face that was now inches from his. The man's eyes were an unusual shade of gray. His ears were small and bear-shaped. There was a very familiar scar across his chin, almost hidden by the straggly beard. The monsoon mongrel winked at Angus.

"Jeremius?" Angus felt his knees turn to rubbery relief. He'd never been so pleased to see anyone in his entire life. He hugged his uncle tightly.

Without another word, Jeremius hurried them away from the stairs and took a sharp left turn down the nearest bare-stone corridor, one with no windows or doors. A few seconds later they heard Swarfe and Dankhart emerge from the dungeons, their voices quickly fading into the distance as they walked in the opposite direction.

"I can't believe you're disguised as a monsoon mongrel." Indigo was still wide-eyed with surprise.

Angus stared at his uncle. "But how did you . . . I mean, what did you . . . ?"

"There'll be plenty of time for explanations later," Jeremius said, checking over his shoulder. "But first, we've got to get you out of this castle, and it isn't going to be easy."

Angus looked sideways at Indigo. Their chances of escaping had suddenly increased by a thousandfold. Jeremius knew his way around the castle, how to get across the mountains without freezing to death, how to contact Perilous and ask for urgent help. But Angus wasn't ready to leave Castle Dankhart yet.

"Hartley Windspear was leading us down to the dungeons so we could rescue my mum and dad," he explained, nodding toward the projectogram who was now drifting about behind Jeremius with a vacant expression on his face. "That's what we were doing when we almost ran into Swarfe and Indigo's uncle. We've got to get them out!"

"We could steal a key, or create a diversion, or set off the fire alarms," Indigo suggested.

But Jeremius was already shaking his head. "I'm sorry, but any kind of rescue mission is out of the question. It's far too risky."

"But . . . you can't be serious?" Angus stared at his uncle in disbelief. He'd expected Jeremius to come up with an even riskier plan, something impossible sounding and utterly brilliant.

"We can't just leave them behind, Mr. McFangus," Indigo pleaded, looking just as flabbergasted. "And Hartley Windspear knows an escape route in the tunnels underneath the dungeons."

Jeremius smiled sadly at them both. "The tunnels under the dungeons will be flooded with monsoon mongrels long before we can get anywhere near an escape route, and we cannot outfox them all. I know it sounds harsh, Angus, but you must believe that your parents know how to look after themselves."

Angus felt his hopes plummet. "I need to go and assess the situation in the rest of the castle," Jeremius said, moving the conversation on before they could argue any further. "But you can't wait for me here. You could be discovered at any minute." He checked up and down the corridor, frowning, and then hurried them all the way to the far end and stopped beside a hatch in the wall.

"Behind this there's a chute that will take you safely to the lowest levels of the castle. Slide yourselves down carefully and wait for me at the bottom. Nobody will be expecting to see you there. *Don't* go wandering off. I will come and find you. And no looking for trouble, understand?" Jeremius hurried away from them and melted into the shadows without a backward glance.

Angus opened the hatch cautiously. Behind it was a long stone chute disappearing into darkness.

"I wonder what's at the bottom," Indigo said, peering inside. Her voice bounced off the walls and traveled down into the unknown.

"I'll go first." Angus sat on the edge and swung his legs over, trying to force all thoughts of his parents to the back of his mind. "Don't follow me for a couple of seconds, okay? That way if I land on a pile of monsoon mongrels, I might be able to give you some warning."

He took a shallow breath, closed his eyes, and shoved off before Indigo could stop him. The chute was well worn and slippery and had so many twists and turns, Angus was convinced he was about to land in the crocodile-filled moat. He bumped and banged his way down, bruising elbows and knees. When he finally shot out the other end, like a cork being popped from a bottle, he fell onto a heap of crumpled blankets and pillowcases.

Jeremius had sent them straight into a large laundry room.

Indigo appeared a few seconds later and landed nimbly on her feet. Hartley Windspear was close behind. The laundry room was extremely stuffy, with a whole bank of whirring washing machines and tumble dryers set against one wall. It smelled greasy and oily, with just the faintest hint of soap. It was obvious, however, that they would not be able to wait for Jeremius among the washing baskets and piles of laundry, for sitting on a chair in the corner, clutching a tub of stubborn storm-stain remover, was a sleeping monsoon mongrel. Angus and Indigo ducked swiftly behind a towering stack of folded sheets that had been left on a small table.

"What do we do now?" Angus whispered as the sounds of snoring drifted across the room. "If that monsoon mongrel wakes up, he'll find us in about two seconds."

Indigo led the way as they crawled out from behind the sheets, across the floor, and out through the open door, with Hartley Windspear bringing up the rear. The sound of voices drifted along the dark stone tunnel outside.

"This way!" Indigo whispered. And all three of them

hurried away from the voices in the opposite direction. "I just hope Jeremius can find us again."

The stone tunnel sloped downward at a steep angle. Two minutes later it came to an abrupt dead end with just one wooden door set deep into the wall.

"Well, we can't go back the way we've just come," Indigo said, listening to the voices, which were now following them down the corridor, drawing closer by the second.

Angus took a deep breath, grabbed the door handle, and pulled it open slowly. They inched their way inside, getting ready to run at the first sign of danger. The tunnel behind the door was very long and dark, with a high ceiling that disappeared into black shadows above. It was also completely deserted. Protruding from the walls on either side was a number of large clear glass domes.

Angus and Indigo peered warily through the first dome . . . and Angus felt his head whirl. Inside was a churning mass of violent-looking weather—cloud, rain, lightning bolts, and winds—as if several storms had been flung into a tumble dryer and set on fast spin. The noise was incredible; a cacophony of what sounded like deep booming drums and screaming ghouls. Angus could feel the force of it rumbling through the floor beneath his feet. The view through the next dome was even more frightening. Lightning fizzed and arced across the surface of the glass like a giant electrified spider. Thick black clouds collided and roiled inside, fighting for space.

"I think we might be in the storm nurseries," Angus said. Hartley Windspear nodded. They had come to the very heart of Dankhart's vile weather-making activities, where the storm that could one day destroy Perilous was being created.

Puddles of water and shattered glass littered the tunnel floor. It seemed not all the domes were storm-tight. Even more worryingly, several domes had deep cracks running across the surface and looked ready to shatter at any second.

"We've got to get out of here," he said, moving quickly down the corridor, which was so long he couldn't even see the end of it.

But before they'd taken another ten paces—

"It's the McFangus boy!" a voice suddenly shouted.

Five of the largest, most unintelligent-looking monsoon mongrels they'd seen so far had burst through the door behind them and were now charging down the tunnel like a herd of wooly mammoths.

"He's with Dankhart's niece. Get them!"

Indigo broke into a sprint, leaping over a large glass-filled puddle, where a storm dome had shattered. Angus followed close behind, checking over his shoulder every few seconds.

"They're gaining on us!" he yelled, feeling his chest tighten.

"But there's a door up ahead, look!"

Angus could just see a glimmer of soft light through an open door in the distant gloom. It was their only possible chance of escape. But the monsoon mongrels were stronger and faster. They'd never make it to the end of the tunnel without being caught.

He jumped over the next puddle, crunching through shards of broken glass. The dome to his left had a number of deep cracks running across the surface.

"Oh!" He skidded to an abrupt halt. "Take off your shoe!" He was already trying to yank his own shoe off his foot without untying the laces.

"What are you doing?" Indigo stopped a few paces ahead, breathing heavily.

"We've got to shatter one of these domes," Angus explained quickly. "If we can fill this tunnel with a storm, we might be able to slow those monsoon mongrels down."

He pulled his arm back, took careful aim, and hit the dome along a crack with the heel of his shoe.

Creak!

Several new splinters formed as the storm inside the dome raged and pushed against the glass, as if it could sense that freedom was just moments away.

Indigo joined in hitting the dome with all the force she could muster. Again and again they struck the glass, desperately trying to liberate the angry storm.

"Stop those two before they flood the tunnel!" One of the monsoon mongrels, the head of the herd, was almost upon them.

Crack!

"I think it's working," Angus yelled.

Crack!

He grabbed Indigo and pulled her clear of the dome as tiny splinters spread across the entire surface with a frosted, snowflake pattern.

Smash!

A furious storm punched through the glass and spilled out into the tunnel, stopping the monsoon mongrels in their tracks. Cloud, rain, wind, and lightning formed a dangerous wall of howling weather between them. Hartley Windspear was instantly blown headlong like a tumbling leaf on the wind. Indigo managed to stand her ground, but Angus was knocked off his feet. Hailstones battered at the skin on his hands and face. Long tendrils of black cloud reached out, tugging at his clothes, threatening to drag him into the depths of the vicious storm and swallow him whole.

"We've got to get out of here!" Indigo hauled him onto his feet, pulling him away from the weather with some difficulty. They turned and ran without looking back as the angry shouts and yells of the monsoon mongrels faded behind them. They raced through the doorway at the end of the tunnel and into a rough stone hall, where Hartley Windspear had been blown.

"Thanks!" Angus said, still trying to catch his breath. "That storm . . . would have shredded me to pieces."

Indigo was already staring around the hallway, searching for a place to hide. Closed doors surrounded them on all sides; the only one that was open led to another long corridor beyond.

"I've got an idea!" Indigo led the way through the open door, making sure they both left a good trail of wet footprints behind them. They returned to the hallway a few moments later in their socks, shoes clutched in hand. "If we can just make those monsoon mongrels think we've run farther into the castle . . ." she said, testing the handle on the plain-looking door closest to them. "It's open!" They shot inside. Hartley Windspear drifted in behind. Thankfully, the room was quiet and empty. Angus closed the door and pressed his ear to the wood. Only seconds later the sound of heavy footsteps thundered into the hallway outside.

"Some of the monsoon mongrels must have forced their way through the escaped storm," he whispered. "I think they're talking about our wet footprints . . . They're running after us through the other doorway. Indigo, you're brilliant! It worked!"

Indigo sank to the floor with relief. Angus slumped against the door and tried to fill his lungs with air again. It felt like they'd been running on empty for hours.

"What are we going to do?" Indigo asked as soon as she could speak again. "How will Jeremius know where to find us now?"

"If he follows the gang of angry monsoon mongrels, it might give him a clue," Angus said, managing a weak smile.

There was nothing they could do but wait it out and hope Jeremius managed to locate them before anyone else did.

"Where are we, anyway?" Angus stared around the room properly for the first time.

It was the most comfortable room they'd seen in the castle so far, richly decorated with patterned rugs, soft light fissures, and red velvet curtains. A large wooden desk sat in the center, and tapestries of swirling snowstorms and illuminated lightning strikes were draped around the walls.

"Maybe we could look for a detailed map of the castle," Indigo suggested. "In case we need to find our own way out after all."

It was better than listening for the sound of footsteps outside the door. Angus trod wearily across the room. He began to look at the papers scattered across the imposing desk while Indigo rummaged through the books on a shelf.

There were several detailed weather reports marked "Urgent," a folder containing some complicated drawings, and a stack of letters, written on thick ivory stationery. An impressive coat of arms, showing a squirrel and a badger, had been printed at the top of each page.

He grabbed the paper and held the page up to the light, his fingers shaking. "I've found it again, that coat of arms, the one that belongs to the Swarfe family!"

Indigo stumbled across the room and tugged the stationery out of his hand. "This must be Swarfe's office. I mean, it makes perfect sense. It's right next to the storm nurseries."

The presence of Dankhart's chief monsoon mongrel was suddenly everywhere they looked. A framed photo showing Swarfe standing next to Dankhart in a great hall sat on the chest of drawers. A row of dusty books on a shelf each claimed to tell the Swarfe family history.

In their desperate struggle to free his parents and flee the castle, Angus had given up all hope of ever locating the tiny blue dragon scale. But now, by sheer good fortune, they had stumbled into one of the few rooms in the entire castle where it might be found. The very thought of it sent a ripple of excitement through the air.

"I'll finish looking through Swarfe's desk. You see if there's anything behind those tapestries," Angus said, his heart suddenly beating with the rhythm of a ticking clock.

Indigo darted over to the closest wall hanging and ripped it aside to search for hidden compartments.

Angus rifled speedily through the desk drawers. Everything was neat and orderly, and there were no bracelets or pendants. There were no portraits of great ancestors, either, he realized, staring around the room for the next place to search. But somehow he sensed that the dragon scale was close. He could almost feel its presence, as if he could reach out and simply touch it with his fingertips.

A closed door sat at the far end of the room. He raced over, yanked it open, and flicked on a light fissure. Inside was a deep closet filled with old robes and lightning deflectors. Boots were lined up along the floor. Angus forced his way deeper in. He found nothing in the corner except a pile of ancient newspapers and a stray sock.

He pushed an old coat out of his face, disappointed. He was just about to abandon the closet when he saw it in the deepest shadows. A tiny lightning bolt had been carved into a wooden panel, so small he wasn't even sure he'd seen it at first. He traced the shape with his fingers. It was exactly like the lightning bolt outside the library, the one that led to a hidden passageway. He took a deep breath and pushed it.

Click.

A small panel in the wall slid sideways. Behind it was a hole just big enough for a fully grown monsoon mongrel to wriggle through.

"Indigo! I've found something!" he called, his voice muffled by the heavy coats hanging around him. He hesitated for a second . . . and then crawled inside.

A small light fissure flicked on automatically above his head. No bigger than the closet that concealed it, the hole was filled with glass jars containing muddy liquids and swirling green gases. There were scrolls sealed with red wax and ancient-looking ribbons, large glittering jewels set in heavy gold, and impressive stacks of gleaming coins. Angus swallowed hard. He'd found Swarfe's secret treasure trove!

He scrambled farther inside, looking for anything that resembled a tiny blue dragon scale. He picked his way carefully past the ominous-looking jars and almost kicked over a large leather pouch containing a strange-smelling yellow powder.

At the very back of the hole was a collection of small enameled trinket boxes. Angus grabbed the nearest box and opened it. It was empty. He tried the biggest one next. There was nothing inside except little balls of dust. He snapped it shut, frustrated. The next box had been lavishly decorated with delicate blue butterflies. Angus felt his heart somersault inside his chest. The wing of the largest butterfly contained a tiny blue dragon scale.

Bang!

Angus froze at the sudden noise. It had come from somewhere inside the office. He slipped the trinket box into his pocket, scrambled out through the hole, and fought his way back through the closet, tripping over several pairs of tall boots. When he stumbled into Swarfe's office once again, Indigo was standing with her back pressed against a tapestry, looking petrified. A monsoon mongrel had entered the room. The man frowned at them from behind a curtain of bristly whiskers.

"I thought I told you two to wait for me in the laundry room." The bristly face broke out into a wide smile.

"Jeremius!" For the second time that day Angus felt immensely glad to see his uncle. "We couldn't wait for you; someone was asleep on a chair."

"And then some different monsoon mongrels chased us through the storm nurseries," Indigo explained.

Jeremius frowned. "But the storm nurseries are incredibly dangerous. You could have been killed."

"Yeah, we discovered that the hard way," Angus said. "How did you find us again?"

"I tried to think of the most dangerous places you could choose to hide, and Swarfe's office was at the top of the list," Jeremius teased. "Plus, Adrik never lets anyone enter his office, and I knew he was in the upper reaches of the castle, so when I saw shadows moving about under the door, I guessed it had to be you two."

"What happened to all the other monsoon mongrels who were chasing after us?" Indigo asked, glancing nervously at the open door.

"I sent them on a wild-goose chase, told them I'd seen

you running toward the kitchens. It was one of my more brilliant moments, even if I do say so myself. But there's no time to gloat now. All the normal escape routes are being heavily guarded. But there is another way."

They left Swarfe's office, checking that the coast was clear in both directions, and headed up a very long flight of narrow stairs that seemed to go on forever. Angus looked back over his shoulder every few seconds, half expecting to see Dankhart racing after them with his black diamond eye gleaming.

Finally, they burst through a door at the top that reminded him of the trapdoor leading on to the roof at Perilous.

"Whoa!" Angus shielded his eyes from the sudden brightness of the outside world. They were standing on the roof of Castle Dankhart. It was surrounded by tall snowcapped mountains and had none of the storm jars, weather cannons, or experimental equipment that normally littered the roof at Perilous. Instead, pushing up through the floor at their feet like a gigantic tree was the mighty lightning tower.

The tower was staggeringly large and powerful. With a man-made metal peak, it soared straight up into the sky above. Wild weather swirled around the top in a vicious vortex, but Angus could feel nothing but a breeze pulling at his clothes and ruffling his hair. Hartley Windspear floated easily beside him, with a blank expression. The whole structure felt alive somehow. With each strike of lightning and every howl of wind, it shuddered, fizzed, and hummed. Angus stood transfixed. The tower was more magnificent and terrifying than anything he'd ever seen.

"Follow me!" Jeremius tugged urgently on his sleeve, yelling above the deafening roar of the vortex.

But somewhere in the distance there was another noise. It was so faint at first, Angus wasn't even sure it was real. And yet there was something strangely familiar about it. . . . He swung around and searched the stormy skies. A cloud was moving low across the mountains. Gray and puffy, it looked odd against the swirling vortex above. It was heading directly for the lightning tower now, with the unmistakable thrum of powerful engines.

"The weather station's coming to rescue us?" Angus yelled.

"I sent out an urgent distress signal as soon as I heard

you and Indigo had been kidnapped." Jeremius grinned. "It's time to go home."

Angus stared at his uncle, speechless. Indigo grabbed Angus by his arm and squeezed it tightly until he'd lost all feeling, but he didn't care. They were going back to Perilous.

"We'll need to get up as high as we can so the weather station can lower the basket down to us. It's not safe to wait around on the roof." Jeremius led the way. They ducked under the nearest metal strut and headed for the steps that went straight up through the heart of the skeletal structure. Inside, the weather felt strangely calm. Angus stared at the kaleidoscope of clashing storms way above their heads. It was a long way up, but he could now see straight through the eye of the vortex, the only calm spot at the very center of the swirling weather that surrounded the top of the tower. He checked his pocket, making doubly sure the trinket box was still sitting safely inside it.

Five, ten, twenty flights of stairs disappeared beneath them as they began to race toward the top, with Hartley Windspear bringing up the rear, pretending to puff and pant. The weather station was finally in position. It hovered dangerously close to the vortex, just visible through the metal struts as they wound their way upward. A wicker basket was already being lowered through the storms and along the outside of the tower. On and on they climbed, the tower now narrowing around them as they reached the upper flights of stairs.

Angus glanced over the side of the rail to see how far they'd come and almost lost his balance. The roof below them was now flooded with monsoon mongrels.

He yelled at Jeremius and pointed to Swarfe and Victus Bile, who were already hurtling up the steps behind them.

"Keep going!" Jeremius shouted. The noise of the vortex was steadily rising the closer they climbed to it. "I'll try to keep them busy until you and Indigo are safely inside the landing basket."

Angus raced past Jeremius and up a final flight of stairs to a narrow platform. He reached out, grabbing one of the ropes that dangled from the bottom of the basket. He and Indigo pulled and guided the wicker through the metal struts and onto the platform at their feet, where it landed safely.

"Get in!" Angus shouted.

Indigo grasped the ropes and hauled herself inside. Hartley Windspear drifted in and stood beside her, billowing. Angus followed, feeling the basket already itching to take off.

"No! We're not going anywhere without Jeremius!" he shouted.

But the landing basket had other ideas. It lurched beneath them, lifted free off the platform, and squeezed through a gap in the metal struts.

"Jeremius, hurry up!" he shouted into the howling wind.

But there was nothing he could do to stop the basket now. Angus watched over the side as Swarfe and Victus Bile ran up the last few flights of stairs with a long trail of monsoon mongrels just seconds behind them. Jeremius grinned at Angus. He pulled a large bag from his coat and tipped the contents onto the stairs beneath him. Hundreds of shiny green storm beads, just like the ones they picked up in the lost property department, began to bounce and cascade down the stairs.

Swarfe tripped and skidded, crashing into Victus Bile, who fell, bottom-first, into the oncoming monsoon mongrels, causing an instant pileup.

Jeremius clambered up the last few stairs, ran across the platform, and heaved himself onto one of the metal struts, balancing dangerously close to the edge of the tower and the sheer drop below.

"He's going to jump!" Indigo shouted, clutching her face in horror. "He's never going to make it! We've already drifted too far away from the tower!"

But Jeremius was undeterred. With one last glance over his shoulder he launched himself into the air, making a wild grab for the straps that were trailing beneath the basket.

"No!" Angus yelled.

He raced to the edge of the basket and searched desperately underneath, hoping to see his uncle dangling there. But the basket had suddenly entered the storm vortex. Thick, dark clouds, driving rain, and lethal lightning descended upon them in a frenzied whirl of wild weather, and it was impossible to see anything. The basket lurched at terrifying angles, threatening to tip them out.

Angus ducked beneath the rim, clinging to the woven ribs around him as they creaked and groaned in protest. They sailed past the top of the lightning tower, still buffeted from side to side by howling winds and vicious storms. He closed his eyes and hoped with every fiber of his being that Jeremius was still clinging on to the ropes underneath them.

15

RETURN TO THE PIGSTY

Clunk!

The loading doors closed beneath them. They were inside the weather station at last. Angus scrambled out of the basket and lay panting on the floor. He felt his head spin as the weather station took a sharp turn and pulled speedily away from the lightning tower.

"Is everyone all right?" Jeremius asked. His anxious face suddenly loomed over Angus, blocking out the light.

Angus felt the knots in his stomach unclench a little at the sight of his uncle, safe and sound. He clambered on to his knees and stood up, his legs almost too unsteady to support his weight. Indigo was pale and shaken, a large puddle of rainwater forming around her feet, but she'd made it through the weather vortex unharmed. Jeremius, on the other hand, looked like he'd been dragged through a hurricane backward. His clothes were ripped and torn, the skin on his hands raw from his desperate struggle to cling to the straps beneath the basket.

"I thought you were going to fall," Angus said when he could finally speak again. "And when we went through the storm vortex . . ."

"I'll admit it wasn't the ideal way to leave a castle." Jeremius smiled wearily, wringing water out of his whiskers. "But it wasn't nearly as dangerous as the time I had to escape from an angry polar bear across some icebergs. We were just lucky the weather station arrived when it did."

"For that, we must all thank young Dougal Dewsnap." Rogwood suddenly appeared in the doorway, looking extremely worried. "He raised the alarm immediately after Angus and Indigo had been kidnapped. An hour later we received an urgent distress signal from Jeremius, and the weather station was the only way to reach you before something calamitous happened."

"And we are extremely pleased to see you, old friend," Jeremius said, clasping Rogwood by the shoulder. "If the weather station hadn't been in place, ready to rescue all three of us, we never would have seen the light of day again."

"I hate to correct you, Jeremius, but there appear to be four of you." Rogwood nodded at Hartley Windspear, who was bent over, doubled, with his hands on his knees, pretending to catch his breath.

"Swarfe had him kidnapped," Angus explained. "We overheard Dankhart and Swarfe talking about it in the dungeons."

Indigo nodded. "Hartley Windspear knows everything about the original dragon scale experiments from 1777."

"And Swarfe's having big problems. He hasn't worked out how to combine the fire dragon scales that Dark-Angel stole with the lightning storm particles," Angus said.

Jeremius frowned at both of them. "But surely Delphinia must have told them everything about those experiments by now."

"Although, if she hasn't, it would explain why the lightning storms haven't been as fierce as we were expecting and why Dankhart hasn't covered half of England in giant blizzards," Rogwood said with a thoughtful expression. "Either way it is extremely fortunate that Hartley Windspear has now been rescued. But it might be wise to conceal him in a different part of the Inner Sanctum for a while, so he cannot reveal anything important to Delphinia."

The projectogram blinked at them benignly.

"There's something else, too." Angus tried to remember every detail of the conversation they'd overheard. "Dankhart and Swarfe have already set a date for the final attack on Perilous. It's going to happen in fourteen days' time."

"And those were Dankhart's exact words?" Rogwood asked. "You're absolutely certain of the date?"

Indigo nodded. "Positive. They had no idea we were listening."

"But this could be precisely what we need to finally give us an edge," Jeremius said, his tired face suddenly animated. "I've been trying to find out the details of their plans for days now, without any success. Dankhart and Swarfe make a point of only ever discussing such important matters in private; none of the other monsoon mongrels have got a clue what's going on until the last minute. Now that we know the date has been set, it means we can strike first."

"But Dankhart knows your plans, too," Angus said. "He knows you're having problems with making storms in the Lightnarium. Swarfe says you couldn't destroy a storm bucket."

"Dark-Angel's been telling him everything," Indigo added.

Rogwood gave them both a small mysterious smile. "This is all extremely useful information. There is no need, however, for you to worry about our plans."

"But what if your storm isn't strong enough?" Angus said. Thanks to Jeremius, they had somehow escaped Castle Dankhart without serious injury, but they were still in terrible danger. "What if I can help? I could use my fire dragon."

"No!" Jeremius took several steps toward him, suddenly looking far more like a terrifying monsoon mongrel than his uncle. "There is no question of you ever facing this storm with your fire dragon. *If* the fracture lightning storm comes, you, Dougal, and Indigo will be safely inside the emergency shelters with the rest of the lightning cubs, and you will stay there until this is over. Swear to me that you won't do anything foolish."

"But what if I can steer the storm?" Angus said, the promise of the third blue dragon scale suddenly weighing heavily in his pocket, and he felt for the trinket box with his fingers.

"Your only job is to keep safe and out of harm's way. You must give me your word, Angus, or I will have no choice but to send you back to the Windmill at Budleigh Otterstone on the first available ferry."

"Okay, okay, I promise," Angus said, shocked by how grave and serious Jeremius suddenly sounded.

"You and Indigo have already done more than enough," Rogwood said kindly. "Rescuing Hartley Windspear and delivering vital information about Dankhart's plans will give us a huge advantage."

Jeremius took a deep breath. "And I could never face your parents again if I allowed you or your friends to do battle with any storm. You must understand it's far too dangerous for any lightning cubs, even those with unusual skills, to take part in this."

Angus frowned at his uncle, wondering if Jeremius also had doubts about his storm prophet talents. Did he think that Angus wasn't really up to the task? That a big battle might finish him off completely? And worse still, what if Jeremius was right? There was still no sign that his fire dragon might come out of its long hibernation. And if the final battle was now only fourteen days away . . .

A moment later Rogwood took them to the upper decks, where mugs of steaming hot chocolate and some warm blankets were waiting for them. It was only when Jeremius had changed into his own clothes again that Rogwood pressed him for more details of his fact-finding mission at Castle Dankhart.

"I managed to steal a full copy of the lightning tower plans," Jeremius said, handing a thick pile of papers and drawings to Rogwood. "The new design has been rushed. I've only had a quick glance at it, but there appear to be some serious flaws that can be exploited. The tower is unstable for a start. It stands far too tall for its foundations."

Rogwood nodded and flicked through the drawings with

interest. "You have done well, old friend. Your career as a monsoon mongrel has proved most useful."

"It's not the first time I've used this disguise," Jeremius explained, turning to Angus and Indigo as he tugged the last of the false hair off his chin. "You might be interested to hear that the other monsoon mongrels know me as Victor Rail."

Rogwood chuckled behind his beard. "Well, if the name fits."

Jeremius grinned. "I thought it had a certain ring to it."

"I don't understand," Angus said. "What's so funny about being called Victor Rail?"

"'Rail' is 'liar' spelled backward," Jeremius said. "It appears nobody at Castle Dankhart was aware of that fact until now."

"But you've only been gone for two weeks. How could you get any of the monsoon mongrels to trust you so soon?" Indigo asked.

"Some time ago now, I turned up at the castle, claiming to be a weather expert from Canada who was interested in joining the monsoon mongrels. It wasn't easy to convince them at first. Swarfe definitely had his suspicions.

But over the years they've come to trust me."

"Years?" Angus said, amazed. "You've been pretending to be a monsoon mongrel for years?"

"I have my own room in their living quarters and a workstation in the experimental chambers. I was even forced to save several monsoon mongrels from a freak explosion caused by some unstable storm particles once, or risk giving myself away. I received high praise from Dankhart himself for my efforts."

Angus stared at his uncle, aghast. "But why didn't you tell me sooner?"

"I wouldn't be much of a secret agent if I went around telling my nephew about my exploits. But I think it's safe to say my cover has been blown. I've just been seen by Swarfe, Victus Bile, and practically every other monsoon mongrel at the castle, helping you and Indigo escape in the weather station. I won't be going back again. There's no reason not to tell you everything now. I'm sorry, Angus," he added. "I couldn't free your mum and dad. I managed to sneak down to the dungeons on several occasions and fill them in on everything that's been happening at Perilous. They wanted me to tell you that they're both very proud of you," he said, squeezing Angus tightly by the shoulder.

Angus nodded and then studied his own knees intently for several moments. He'd been so close to seeing his mum and dad, to telling them his own tales of adventure. When would he get that close to them again?

The journey back was short and uneventful, and Angus was extremely pleased when the friendly lights of Perilous came into view up ahead. He stared out the window as the weather station drifted over the roof. It was now well stocked with buckets of sand, for putting out sudden lightning fires. There were also several portable weather eye machines that could extend all the way up to storm level. Five more cloud-busting rocket launchers had been maneuvered into position since the last time they'd landed on the roof. They cast long shadows over the growing collection of steel storm nets sitting behind them.

As soon as the weather station had docked, a familiar figure came hurrying onboard to greet them.

"You might have told me you three hadn't been crushed to death at the Canadian Exploratorium," Gudgeon said in a gruff voice, hands on his hips. "I've been going to Little Frog's Bottom almost every weekend to visit your parents, telling them stories about what you did at Perilous."

His weary face was a comical mix of relief, anger, and confusion. He pulled Angus and Indigo into a bone-crushing hug. Angus couldn't help smiling. Gudgeon's leather jerkin had a comforting, familiar smell of rust and engine oil about it.

"Nothing's ever simple with you three." The lightning catcher released them with a shake of his bald head. "I should have known there was something peculiar going on. Rogwood says you've been coming to my lessons all along and Dewsnap's the lightning cub who almost got himself killed in the Lightnarium."

"Er, yeah, sorry about that," Angus said, grinning sheepishly. "We wanted to tell you we were there, but Jeremius made us promise not to."

"Ha!" Jeremius snorted. "So, this is all my fault now?"

"You've managed to put Valentine Vellum in a foul mood, anyway," Gudgeon said, looking immensely pleased about it. "He's demanding to know what you three were doing in his bedroom in the middle of the night. There's no need to look so worried." He chuckled. "Dewsnap's already explained everything."

"He—he has?" Angus glanced nervously at Indigo.

"He said you needed to let off some steam after being cooped up in that library for weeks, so you were planning to set off a can of Cradget's hiccupping powder to give Vellum a fright."

"Hiccupping powder?" asked Jeremius, raising his eyebrows at Angus.

"Um, yeah, well, it seemed like a good idea at the time," Angus said, trying to sound suitably ashamed.

"Vellum brings it all on himself if you ask me, going around with that sour face of his, looking like he's got a bad case of belching blisters," Gudgeon said. "I've been tempted to shove him into the storm hollow with the deadly seven once or twice myself."

Angus grinned at Indigo.

"But I'd stay out of his way for a week or two if I were you," Gudgeon warned. "He's still got steam coming out of his ears."

It was great to finally have a proper conversation with Gudgeon. Angus had missed the sound of the lightning catcher's voice immensely. He and Indigo spent the next ten minutes filling him in on all the details of their adventures as they made their way out of the weather station, through the trapdoor in the roof, and down the stairs.

"There's no point sending you or Miss Midnight back to the library, now that Dankhart is fully aware of your miraculous return to the land of the living," Rogwood said as they finally reached the Octagon. Gudgeon said a cheerful good-bye and returned to the roof for the latest weather report, promising to see them again in the morning. "Dougal also made quite a racket when you and Indigo were kidnapped. I should imagine half the Exploratorium heard him. You might just as well return to your own rooms in the lightning cubs' living quarters, where I'm sure you'll be much more comfortable."

"Seriously?" Angus said, cheered by the news that he would no longer have to stare at the dreary brown wallpaper in Miss Vulpine's rooms.

"I'm afraid I'll have to take you to see Principal Dark-Angel first." Jeremius looked less than thrilled. "We've been hiding you right under her nose. She won't be pleased. I'll have to try to explain."

"Perhaps under the circumstances it might be best not to mention anything you heard at Castle Dankhart about dragon scales," Rogwood said, straightening his beard.

Jeremius nodded. "Or Hartley Windspear."

"Or the fact that we now know when Dankhart's planning to attack Perilous."

"In fact, it's probably best if you let me and Rogwood do most of the talking," Jeremius said.

Hartley Windspear waved good-bye to them sadly as Rogwood guided him over to the Inner Sanctum to hide him away from Dark-Angel. When they walked into the principal's office ten minutes later, her usually pale face was almost pink with apparent fury.

"I demand an explanation!" She marched angrily over to Jeremius. "Not only have you violated a position of great trust, but you have put three lightning cubs in grave danger. Had they been with the rest of the second years when the storm struck Perilous, they would have been safe in the emergency shelter!"

The shouting seemed to go on for hours. Rogwood joined them a few minutes later, and it took him quite some time to convince Dark-Angel not to banish Jeremius to a tiny Exploratorium in Fort William or remove his lightning strikes and bar him from ever being a lightning catcher again. Angus felt the angry words wash over him as they stood before Dark-Angel's desk, his body tired, his brain befuddled from lack of food and a hasty, fear-filled climb up an enormous lightning tower.

"I am extremely pleased to see that you, Dewsnap, and Midnight are not dead after all," Dark-Angel said after the shouting finally came to a halt. There was a sudden theatrical shake in her voice as she spoke.

"Um, thanks very much, miss," Angus said uncomfortably, feeling all eyes in the room swivel in his direction.

"Since you have no injuries to report, I will spare you and Miss Midnight a trip up to the sanatorium tonight, but you must report to Doctor Fleagal first thing tomorrow morning and allow him to check you over thoroughly for any signs of delayed shock. I believe a hot meal and an early bedtime are in order. You may go."

Angus and Indigo left her office without a backward glance. Dougal ran to meet them as they approached the stairs that led down to the lightning cubs' living quarters a few minutes later.

"I thought I'd never see you two again!" His face was creased with worry, his glasses smeared with smudged, sweaty fingerprints. "I couldn't believe it when Victus Bile just turned up in the library."

"Yeah, Rogwood said you were shouting your head off after me and Indigo got kidnapped," Angus said, feeling tremendously pleased to see his friend again.

"It was really scary." Dougal gulped. "When I went back into the library it was all eerie and deserted, and I knew he'd taken you. Where have you been for the last hour, anyway? Clifford Fugg said the weather station arrived back at Perilous ages ago. And there're all sorts of rumors flying around about you and Indigo fighting off an army of fog phantoms to escape from Castle Dankhart."

"Er, there definitely weren't any phantoms." Angus grinned.

"But Jeremius did take us straight up the lightning tower to the weather station, and that's how we got away," Indigo explained.

"Jeremius?" Dougal said in total disbelief.

"Yeah," Angus said. "We've just found out he's a monsoon mongrel in his spare time."

"We've got loads of other things to tell you," Indigo said. "We know when Dankhart's planning to—"

But Dougal held up his hand to halt Indigo before she could really get started. "Listen, we can't talk about this now. Rogwood's already had our stuff collected from the library and taken down to our rooms, and everyone's waiting to welcome you back."

"What about the dragon scales?" Indigo asked, looking concerned. "Are they safe?"

"I ran straight up to Miss Vulpine's rooms as soon as I knew you two had been rescued," Dougal said, patting his pocket. "First thing tomorrow morning, I'm finding something like a nice grubby floorboard to hide them under."

It was like walking straight into a solid wall of noise. Angus and Indigo were surrounded by an excited gaggle of cheering lightning cubs as soon as they reached the bottom of the stairs.

"Oh, it's so good to have you back!" Violet Quinn gushed. "We've really missed you!" And she gave all three of them a tight squeeze. Georgina Fox stood beside them, choking back tears. Jonathon Hake and Nigel Ridgely slapped Angus hard on the back.

"We knew something wasn't right," Jonathon said.

"Yeah," Nigel agreed, nodding. "One of the older cubs wanted to take over your room, and Catcher Sparks wouldn't let anyone touch it."

"At first we thought she was just being sentimental."

"Until we remembered she hasn't got a soppy bone in her body," Nigel said.

Angus laughed along with everyone else. He'd missed his fellow second years more than he'd realized. Thankfully, most of them seemed to accept the fact that they weren't dead after all with cheerful curiosity.

"All right, Angus?" Nicholas Grubb pushed through the crowd and gripped his hand tightly. "I told Rogwood there was something fishy going on. I knew you weren't going to the Canadian Exploratorium over Christmas, but everyone kept telling me I'd got it all wrong."

"That's because you're always wrong about everything, Grubb," Theodore Twill said, making several younger lightning cubs snigger.

"Shut up, Twill. At least my socks don't give off noxious gases," Nicholas said cheerfully. "Everyone except Twill's invited back to my room for a welcome home party!"

He steered Angus, Indigo, and Dougal down the curved hallway. "Come on," he said, smiling. "Everyone wants to know if Dankhart takes his black diamond eye out at night and soaks it in a glass of water."

The celebrations went on for hours. Angus ate as many potato chips and cookies as he could get his hands on and thoroughly enjoyed playing a mad game of human dominoes, which involved lots of falling about on the floor. The only lightning cubs who didn't look pleased to see them were the Vellum twins, who kept a sulky distance from everyone, muttering to each other in a corner.

"This is brilliant! I can't believe Vellum's keeping his big mouth shut for once," Dougal yelled over the noise of a rowdy screaming competition that some of the older lightning cubs had organized. "He must be really scared you're going to set a storm on him. It must be killing him," he added, waving at the twins, who scowled back angrily.

Halfway through the evening, Angus was forced to give a speech about not being dead, at which everyone cheered, despite the fact that he could think of nothing interesting to say on the subject.

"But why was Rogwood hiding you in the library in the first place?" Edmund Croxley asked when Angus had finished.

"It was because of his mum and dad," Indigo explained quickly, her face turning red with embarrassment as everyone turned to look at her. "They've been working on a top secret assignment in Nova Scotia for ages now, and Dankhart wanted to know all about it."

"Yeah, Dankhart thought it would help with his lightning storms and stuff," Dougal said, trying to make Indigo's story sound even more believable. "And Rogwood thought Dankhart thought Angus would know all the details."

The party became even more boisterous when Germ appeared after a long day in the sanatorium. He found some records by the popular Imbur band, the Typhoon Trappers, and started a sudden craze of hazardous dancing. It was well after midnight when Catcher Mint finally sent everyone to bed, banning all lightning moth races and ghost-story telling.

Angus returned wearily to his room and closed the door for a welcome moment of solitude. He was pleased to see that the Vellums hadn't sneaked in during his long absence and stolen anything, not even the book his uncle Max had given him about Imbur Island facts and frippery. In fact, everything was exactly the way he'd left it months before, from the mud-caked shoes he'd abandoned on the floor to the empty candy wrappers strewn across the bedside table.

"Oi! Are you coming into the Pigsty or what?" Dougal poked his head into Angus's room a moment later from the entrance that was concealed behind a moth-eaten wall hanging of a violent typhoon.

Angus grinned and followed Dougal. Indigo was already busy trying to light the fire with some kindling.

"Ah! That's more like it." Dougal sank happily into his favorite armchair. "It's great to be back in the Pigsty. I definitely won't miss old Vulpine's dodgy taste in wallpaper. So, tell me everything that happened at Castle Dankhart," he said.

Angus and Indigo described every detail of their nail-biting adventure, including the moment that Jeremius had found them hurrying out of the dungeons.

Dougal let out a low whistle. "I mean, we knew he was doing dangerous stuff but actually living at Castle

Dankhart? And at least we know when Dankhart's planning to attack Perilous now."

When Indigo told him about their dash through the storm nurseries and their discovery of the Swarfe family coat of arms, however, Dougal was devastated.

"But that's the worst news possible! We'll never get our hands on all four dragon scales now."

"Er, yeah, we will," Angus said. And he drew the trinket box carefully out of his pocket, setting it down on a small table in front of them.

"Whoa!" Dougal jumped out of his chair as if he'd just been attacked by a swarm of book fleas.

"You found the third dragon scale?" Indigo said, aghast. "Why didn't you tell me?"

"I couldn't. Jeremius came bursting through the door and we had to leave."

Dougal picked up the box, shaking his head in wonder. "So, actually, we should be really glad that the monsoon mongrels kidnapped you."

"Yeah, I'm thinking of sending them a thank-you note," Angus said, smiling.

"It also means we've only got one scale left to find,"

Indigo said, easing off her shoes and warming her toes over the fire. "I just wish it didn't belong to Valentine Vellum."

"He wasn't exactly thrilled when he found us snooping about his room in the middle of the night," Angus said.

Dougal grinned. "It was almost worth it just to see the look on his face. Dark-Angel tried to convince him it was nothing more than a stupid prank. He wanted us to spend the next month scraping storm salts off the walls in the Lightnarium as a punishment, but Dark-Angel told him we'd been through enough already."

"At least he doesn't know why we broke into his room, so he's probably not expecting us to do it again," Angus said, thinking it through.

"A-again?" Dougal glanced from Angus to Indigo with a look of panic on his face. "But why would we go anywhere near Vellum's rooms again?"

"Because we've still got to find the last dragon scale," Indigo said.

Angus nodded, feeling a sudden pang of guilt at deliberately breaking the promise they'd made to Jeremius only hours ago. But seeing the dreadful storm nurseries and the power of the lightning tower at Castle Dankhart had only made him more determined to help save Perilous. Taking shelter when the storm finally hit the Exploratorium just wasn't an option.

"We'd better find that scale soon, too," he said. "We've only got fourteen days."

"It's thirteen days now," Indigo said, glancing at her weather watch. "It's already past midnight."

Dougal turned paler than a spooky fog and had to sit with his head between his knees for several minutes before he stopped feeling sick.

16
THE LAST DRAGON SCALE

The next morning, the skies overhead darkened to a deep black, several vicious storms broke out, and a nervous atmosphere fell over the entire Exploratorium. All celebrations came to an abrupt halt. Everywhere they went, lightning cubs and catchers could be seen nervously peering out of windows, watching the skies.

The library was declared free from fog mites and opened once again. Miss Vulpine, however, was far from happy about the state of her rooms, and she stormed into the kitchens to complain about it the morning after Angus and Indigo returned from Castle Dankhart.

"Scorch marks all over the carpet, holes burned

through the walls, and as for the roof terrace . . ."

"That wasn't our fault, miss," Angus said quickly. "It got struck in a lightning storm."

"But that does not explain how my curtains ended up five inches shorter than they used to be."

"I don't know what she's complaining about," Dougal mumbled quietly as she stomped out of the kitchens again, frightening several first years who clearly had overdue library books. "I thought those scorch marks livened the place up a bit."

Things improved slightly, later that afternoon, when Mrs. Stobbs appeared in the lightning cubs' living quarters with a special batch of homemade peach and honey muffins.

"It's a welcome-back-to-Perilous gift for you and your friends, my lovely," she said, presenting Dougal with a large basket. The delicious smell of melted honey was mouthwatering. "And if you ever need any extra socks or gloves to help keep this dreadful weather out, I'll have my knitting needles ready in a jiffy."

Later that evening, Dougal put the dragon scales in a tin box, which he then hid on a ledge inside the chimney in the Pigsty. "Nobody's ever going to look for them up there," he said, brushing soot off his hands.

The atmosphere inside the Exploratorium went from bad to worse two days later when alarming pictures of the lightning tower appeared in the latest copy of the *Weathervane.* Even more storm clouds had gathered above it in a swirling mass, almost completely obscuring the castle beneath.

"It didn't look that bad when we saw it," Angus said as he, Indigo, and Dougal studied the pictures in the kitchens.

"Uncle Scabious must be collecting some extra weather and sending it straight down to the storm nurseries," Indigo said with a look of deep unhappiness.

She had barely mentioned their ordeal since returning to Perilous. Angus had been plagued by a series of very real dreams that had once again been filled with the fury of the storm prophet duels. Each time, his fire dragon had fallen from the skies, broken and battered.

Later that day a series of powerful explosions, which appeared to come from the Lightnarium, rocked the whole of Perilous.

"Things aren't going well with the lightning accelerators, and time is running out fast," Jeremius told them the next evening when they spotted him in the kitchens having a late dinner. "We've got ten days left." Angus felt his stomach clench at the looming deadline. "Unfortunately, Valentine Vellum is still having all kinds of problems with the storms breaking apart before the lightning accelerators can do their work."

Angus shot an anxious glance at Dougal and Indigo, deciding that the time had finally come to air their doubts about the lightning catcher. "Um, we've been wondering for ages now if Valentine Vellum . . ."

Jeremius shook his head. "I know what you're going to say. You wouldn't be the first at this Exploratorium to raise questions about Valentine's loyalty. But I think I can assure you that Valentine is the least likely person in the whole of Perilous to betray us to Dankhart or to sabotage our experiments."

"But how can you be so sure?" Angus asked, confused.

"When Adrik Swarfe fled from Perilous, he was very keen for Catcher Vellum to go with him. Swarfe and Vellum were great friends. They had always shared similar ideas on the use of lightning and were both keen to locate the lightning vaults. But when Swarfe eventually made his move, Valentine flatly refused to go with him."

"But why?" Dougal asked.

"Valentine Vellum is a lazy, selfish creature of habit who enjoys the comforts of his existence as a lightning catcher. I believe he did not find the thought of life at Castle Dankhart particularly attractive. He and Swarfe quarreled furiously, and in the end Adrik left alone. So, it is very much in Valentine's interests to do everything he can to help us defeat the threat from Castle Dankhart. He would be in for a rough time of it should Dankhart ever take control of Perilous."

Angus stared at his uncle, feeling shell-shocked.

"I can understand your doubts about Valentine," Jeremius said, smiling. "It would seem, however, that he is nothing but a bully who likes to pretend he's more important than he actually is."

"But Pixie and Percival Vellum are always bragging about how close their dad is to Dark-Angel, that their dad knows loads of important stuff," Angus said, still not a hundred percent convinced.

Jeremius nodded. "I won't deny that Valentine has a certain . . . influence over Dark-Angel, which none of us have ever quite got to the bottom of, particularly since Delphinia appears to loathe Valentine just as much as the rest of us."

"Then it could still have something to do with my uncle Scabious," Indigo said, her face contorted as she said his name.

"It is possible, but I'd be more likely to believe another explanation."

In the days that followed, all first-year lightning cubs were hastily sent home following a sudden outbreak of pustular mold. Large portions of the experimental division, research department, and forecasting department were sectioned off and wrapped in a protective coat of plastic. Notices appeared in the kitchens announcing that all lightning cubs would be evacuated in the next few days.

"I wonder if there really has been an outbreak of mold," Dougal said as they sat in the Pigsty one evening. The wind was howling and wailing outside.

"I reckon Rogwood and Catcher Sparks have made the

whole thing up. They must be trying to evacuate the Exploratorium before Dankhart's deadline," Angus said.

"They could have come up with something less revolting, though." Dougal checked his hands quickly for signs of pustules. "Just thinking about it is making me itch."

Angus stared into the fire with a familiar feeling of panic rising inside his chest. They had eight days, or possibly even less now that the lightning cubs were being evacuated, to find the last dragon scale, to get ready for the final attack on Perilous, to shock his fire dragon out of hibernation. They'd discussed the serious problem of how to find the last elusive dragon scale over and over since their return to Perilous, and they were still no closer to an answer.

"We already know the dragon scale isn't in Vellum's private rooms," he said, bringing the subject up for the hundredth time. "He's not wearing it around his neck, either."

"It's unlikely to be in the Lightnarium." Indigo repeated what had already been said time and time again.

"Yeah." Dougal shivered. "Who'd be mad enough to keep anything in there?"

"So, unless he's got it at his home in Little Frog's Bottom, it's got to be in his office," Angus said, coming to the same conclusion they'd reached the last dozen times they'd talked through all the possibilities.

"But we still don't know where his office is," Indigo pointed out. "And we can't ask Jeremius, Rogwood, or Gudgeon without giving ourselves away."

Dougal sighed. "This is getting us nowhere."

"But there must be a way," Angus said, kneading his temples with his knuckles.

Dougal stared into space, apparently thinking hard for several moments. "Oh! I have got one idea, but you're not going to like it."

"Go on," Angus said, eager to hear any suggestion, no matter how dangerous or ridiculous.

"Vellum's desperate to use us as lightning bait, agreed?" Dougal said. "And out of the three of us, he definitely hates Angus the most."

Angus nodded. "He'd stick me at the top of the lightning tower if he got half a chance."

"Then why not ask Germ where his office is and go there to apologize for breaking into his rooms? Tell him all the rumors are true, that we really were going to set off a can of hiccupping powder in there and that the whole thing was *your* idea," Dougal said, "and then grovel at his stinking feet."

Indigo frowned. "How's that going to help us?"

"It helps because if Angus gets Vellum frothing at the mouth with anger, he might just march Angus out of his office and straight up to Dark-Angel's."

"Er," Angus said, wondering if Dougal was suddenly feeling the strain of the last few months and was starting to lose his marbles. "I still don't see how that helps."

"Isn't it obvious?" Dougal asked, smiling. "If Vellum drags you out of his office, it means me and Indigo can sneak in and search every nook and cranny for his dragon scale pendant! I mean, Dark-Angel won't actually expel you or anything, not until we've found all her dragon scales, anyway, and even then, she's more likely to hand us over to Indigo's dear old uncle Scabby, so what have we got to lose?"

Angus glanced at Indigo. There was no guarantee that the plan would actually work, and despite what Dougal said, there was plenty of opportunity for all *three* of them to end up in front of Dark-Angel, threatened with expulsion. Expulsion, however, was the least of their worries.

Indigo bit her lip, looking extremely troubled, but as none of them had any better ideas, they had no choice but to trust the hare-brained scheme would work, and they spent the next hour discussing their plans in detail.

Luckily, since Perilous was mere days away from being obliterated, there was no time to sit around feeling anxious about the plot. The following evening, after a very nervous dinner, they made their way slowly to Vellum's office, using detailed directions given to them by Germ.

Vellum's office was on the far side of the kitchens, where the smell of dinner still lingered in the air. They passed several locked doors, one marked "Lightning Fissures Control Room," another which contained something called lightning coils, according to the sign on the door.

"Ready?" Angus asked, feeling completely unprepared as they stopped outside the lightning catcher's office.

"No! Wait!" Dougal pulled a glass jar from his pocket. It was the one containing storm fluff that he'd taken from the lost property department.

Angus frowned. "What did you bring that for?"

"In case we need to make a quick getaway," Dougal said, checking the seal and stuffing it back into his pocket.

Indigo took a deep breath and knocked quietly on the door before any of them could change their minds. Then she and Dougal slipped into an empty office close by, keeping out of sight.

"Yes, what is it?" an irritated voice said.

Vellum shot to his feet as Angus shuffled awkwardly into his office. Angus took a quick glance around the room. The walls still had a slightly charcoaled look about them after the fire that Winnie Wrascal had caused. The rest of the office was extremely ordinary with shelves, filing cabinets, and box files arranged around the edges of the room. Angus could see nothing that resembled a blue fire dragon scale.

"What do you want, McFangus?" Vellum asked, scowling at him.

"Sir, I've come to, um . . ."

"Spit it out, boy. I haven't got all day."

"It's about the night we broke into your bedroom, sir," Angus suddenly blurted out.

There was a long, tense silence. Vellum marched out from behind his desk and glared down at him.

"So, you've come to confess everything," he said with a snarl.

"Yes, sir," Angus said, being careful not to look Vellum in the eye. "I'm sorry, sir. It was only supposed to be a stupid prank."

"How touching, an apology. But I'm afraid I don't buy it, McFangus. You've never bothered taking responsibility for your actions before now."

"Er . . ." Angus said, suddenly sensing that their plan might already be in trouble.

"Unless you have anything more interesting to say, you will leave my office immediately. I am extremely busy with important lightning catcher business. I haven't got time for any more of your juvenile jokes."

"But, sir, d-don't you want to punish me?" Angus asked, desperate for something to say. "I mean, it was all my idea."

"Your idea?" Vellum turned on him suddenly, his eyes narrowing. "If I thought I could get away with it, I would march you straight into the Lightnarium and let a stormful of fracture lightning use you as target practice, McFangus. Nothing would give me greater pleasure."

Angus took a step backward, deciding it might have been a mistake to invite Vellum to punish him.

"I should have insisted that Dark-Angel expel you last year when you were caught roaming around the lightning vaults." Vellum's left eye was suddenly twitching. "But you were mumbling ridiculous stories about fire dragons, and everyone believed you."

Ridiculous stories? Angus felt himself bristle. But he couldn't lose his temper now. It would ruin the whole plan.

"You are a typical McFangus, boy. You have a very high opinion of yourself, which nobody else shares."

Angus clenched his fists.

"Your whole family suffers from the same delusion, and that's what landed your parents in their cozy little dungeon. You're nothing but trouble."

"That's a lie!" Angus shouted out the words before he could stop himself. "My mum and dad ended up in a dungeon because they were trying to save Perilous, to stop

Dankhart from stealing a map of the lightning vaults for your best pal Swarfe."

Vellum's face was now as black as a thundercloud. "What did you say to me?"

"Everyone knows you were big friends with Adrik Swarfe before he ran off to Castle Dankhart."

"And what is that supposed to signify?" Vellum's voice was rising dangerously. "Out with it, boy, or are you too afraid to say what you truly mean?"

"It means everyone wishes that you'd left with Swarfe. You don't belong at Perilous. So why don't you do everyone a favor and join the monsoon mongrels. Or wouldn't they have you, *sir*?"

As soon as he'd said the words, he knew he'd gone too far. Vellum was advancing upon him, fury etched into every crease of his scowling face. He grabbed Angus roughly by his collar, yanked the door open, and dragged him outside.

"Nobody speaks to me that way in my own office, boy!" Vellum yelled, spittle flying from the corners of his mouth. "You're coming with me!"

Angus glanced with some difficulty over his shoulder.

Dougal and Indigo were already sneaking into Vellum's office. They were both watching him with extremely anxious expressions.

Vellum marched him swiftly down the corridor and straight past the kitchens without pausing for breath.

"Er, isn't Principal Dark-Angel's office back the other way, sir?" Angus said as Vellum hauled him toward the stairs that led up to the Octagon.

"I have no intention of taking you up to the principal's office, McFangus," Vellum said, increasing his pace so Angus was forced to break into a jog just to keep up. "I am taking you for a private session in the Lightnarium instead."

Angus swallowed hard. Dougal's plan had worked *too* well. Vellum had completely lost his head. The lightning catcher's hold tightened on his collar.

"You are a willful and ignorant lightning cub, McFangus, with very little potential; a storm prophet with no skills other than to fool those around you into thinking you are something special. It is time to prove once and for all that you are not."

They had already reached the top of the stairs. The

Lightnarium was just steps away. Angus tried to tug himself free, but the lightning catcher had him in an iron grip. He stared around the Octagon, desperately searching for help. For once, the domed hall was completely deserted. There was no one to reason with the enraged lightning catcher, no one to suggest a less lethal form of punishment.

Suddenly, a siren began to wail, shattering the quiet around them. Vellum flinched at the noise, his grip loosening slightly. Doors banged open. Catcher Sparks and her team began to emerge from the experimental division. Angus had never been so pleased to see the lightning catcher.

"Get down to the evacuation shelter now, McFangus," Vellum said loudly, finally releasing him. "But make no mistake, we will finish this later."

Angus turned and fled without looking back.

He hurtled down toward the kitchens, where lightning cubs, confused and anxious, were running in all directions, shouting and pointing at the darkening sky just visible through the windows.

"Oh, thank goodness you're okay!" Indigo was pushing

her way through a group of hysterical third years with Dougal trailing close behind.

"We thought Vellum was going to kill you," Dougal said with a shudder. "You should have seen the look of loathing on his face when he dragged you out of his office."

"Did you find the dragon scale?" Angus asked, deciding now was not the moment to reveal where Vellum had been planning to take him.

"We searched everywhere," Indigo said. "But there's nothing in his office except safety manuals and reports."

"And some old coats and stinking boots stuffed inside a cupboard."

"We were just looking through his filing cabinets when the siren went off," Indigo explained.

Dougal covered his ears with his hands. "Why does a stupid siren start wailing every time we search one of Vellum's rooms?"

"Maybe it's just another practice drill," Angus said hopefully. But the noise continued, louder and more urgent as the seconds ticked past.

Large groups of lightning catchers were pushing their way past the kitchens now, shouting and looking extremely serious. “Over there!” Angus yelled as Jeremius, Rogwood, and Gudgeon charged through the crowd, creating a ripple of bodies as they went. “Jeremius!” He waved frantically until his uncle pushed through the tide to reach them. “What’s going on?”

“Another big lightning storm is approaching Perilous.”

“But Dankhart must have changed his plans,” Dougal said. “I mean, he’s seven days early.”

“Which means we’ve got to get up to the roof, board the weather station, and fly over to that lightning tower without delay.” Jeremius glanced over his shoulder at Rogwood and Gudgeon, who were waiting impatiently. “Get yourselves down to the emergency shelter and stay there until it’s safe to come out again.”

He turned and ran, dodging between Catcher Greasley and Catcher Howler, who were dragging extra storm nets along the floor behind them.

“But it’s too late.” Angus watched his uncle go with a sinking feeling. “The storm’s already heading toward Perilous.”

“Destroying the lightning tower won’t make any difference now,” Indigo said.

Dougal swallowed hard. "And it won't stop your dear old uncle Scabby from burning Perilous to the ground, either, just like all those other Exploratoriums."

"We've got to go back to Vellum's office and find that scale," Angus said above the noise. "It's the only way to stop Dankhart. It's now or never!"

They ran, pushed, and shoved against the surge of fleeing lightning cubs and then darted back to Vellum's office, closing the door behind them.

"We haven't got much time. Search everything again!" Angus said.

He ripped the drawers out of Vellum's desk and turned them upside down, scattering the contents far and wide. Dougal swept armfuls of books off their shelves and onto the floor, where he and Indigo scoured the pages for secret treasure compartments or hidden keys.

"Oh!" Indigo gasped a moment later when the siren stopped abruptly.

Dougal gulped. "What now?"

They stood motionless, listening to the unnatural silence, their ears still ringing with the siren's last wail.

"I can hear the storm," Indigo said as thunder rumbled in the distance.

The walls of Vellum's office trembled in a very disconcerting fashion, as if several earthquakes had occurred right beneath the very rock upon which Perilous sat. The floor seemed to buckle and shake beneath them until the last of the thunder had faded.

"It's no use. The dragon scale isn't here," Dougal said. His glasses had been knocked askew in the mad search, his face and hands smeared with long streaks of dust. "We've got to get down to the emergency shelter before the storm breaks."

Angus stared hopelessly at the disheveled room. They'd utterly failed in their quest. Perilous would be destroyed.

"McFangus!"

Angus spun round on his heels. Vellum was standing in the doorway. His face was a vision of pure rage. "Explain why you and your friends are ransacking my office!"

"Sir, you've got a blue fire dragon scale, and we need it now," he said, throwing caution to the wind. There was no time to make up any kind of story. "It comes from the body of a storm prophet, and we think it's here, in your office."

"That's what we were looking for when you found us in your bedroom," Indigo added swiftly.

"What is this gibberish?" Vellum sneered. "Perilous is under attack and you are still trying to fool me with preposterous stories. I will take great pleasure in dealing with your outrageous behavior later, but right now, you must get out of my office and down to your emergency weather shelter."

"It's been passed down through your family for centuries," Angus continued, standing his ground, "to keep it safe from Dankhart and the monsoon mongrels. It can help give me extra storm prophet powers. It's the only thing that can stop Dankhart."

Vellum's face darkened. "If you think I'm doing anything to help you, McFangus, after the insults that have been hurled at me inside my own office . . ."

A sudden crash of fracture lightning illuminated Vellum's angry face. A deep roll of thunder shook the walls of his office. It sounded like the Lightnarium had been cracked open right outside his door.

"Please, sir, there isn't much time," Angus begged. "You've got to give us the dragon scale!"

"I haven't the faintest idea what you're talking about, McFangus. You will leave my office immediately, or I will remove you myself."

"Wait!" Dougal scrambled across the messy pile of books that he'd created. "I can prove that we're telling you the truth, sir." He took a photo out of his pocket and shoved it under the lightning catcher's nose. "You're wearing the dragon scale in this picture. It's around your neck on a chain. Look!"

Vellum snatched the photo out of Dougal's hands and stared at it for several seconds without moving, but a dramatic change came over his face. His eyes widened, his thuggish brow line traveling upward in surprise. His free hand dipped briefly into one of the pockets in his leather jerkin, checking its contents, and Angus understood. The dragon scale pendant was sitting in Vellum's pocket.

"Where did you get this photograph?" the lightning catcher demanded angrily.

"We found it in the lost property department," Dougal explained hastily.

"Please, sir!" Indigo said. "We're not trying to trick you. We know you care about Perilous. We know you've been working with lightning accelerators and storms in the Lightnarium. You want to stop Dankhart just as much as we do."

Vellum stared at Indigo as another crash of lightning illuminated his entire office. There was an agonizing pause. Then Vellum thrust the photo into his leather jerkin and turned his back on them all.

"Get out of my office and don't ever come back!"

Angus felt his last hopes evaporate. The dragon scale was just inches away, but there was nothing more they could do, nothing more they could say to persuade Vellum of the truth. Would three dragon scales be enough to halt the storm? Would three fire dragons come to his aid instead of four? He was already heading swiftly for the door when it happened. Dougal plucked a glass jar from his pocket. He shook the contents vigorously and removed the lid.

"Hey, sir!" he yelled.

Vellum turned on his heel and—

Pooof!

A fuzz of storm fluff descended instantly on the lightning catcher, drawn toward the heat of his body, covering him from head to toe in a soft downy coat. It was an astonishing sight, as if Vellum had grown a long beard and aged a hundred years in a matter of seconds. For a moment time stood still, then . . .

"D-Dewsnap!" Vellum spluttered, spitting fluff out of his mouth. "You've gone too far this time!"

Angus's hand was in Vellum's pocket before the lightning catcher could scoop the storm fluff out of his eyes. His fingers closed around the dragon scale pendant . . . and he tugged it free.

"Run!"

They raced out of Vellum's office as quickly as their legs would carry them.

"Dougal! That was genius!" Angus said, letting out a sudden whoop of victory as they ran.

Dougal flushed crimson. "Well, somebody had to do something. Vellum's an even bigger jerk than we thought. Why didn't he just give us the dragon scale?"

Angus felt his pulse begin to race. Now, finally, they had a chance to fight the storm before it destroyed the

Exploratorium and everything around them. There was another flash of lightning.

"Come on," he said, breaking into a sprint. "We've got to get the other scales."

It was a desperate dash down to the lightning cubs' living quarters. Signs of a hasty evacuation met them at every turn. Dougal burst into his room and darted straight toward the Pigsty to retrieve the rest of the dragon scales from the tin box that he'd hidden up the chimney. They hurtled back up the stairs two minutes later, only to find a familiar figure waiting for them at the top.

"Oh thank heavens, I've found you at last, my lovelies!" Mrs. Stobbs said, sounding close to tears. She gasped at another flash of lightning.

"Mrs. Stobbs?" Dougal said. "What are you doing here?"

"Everyone is looking for you. Catcher Grimble is refusing to seal up the emergency weather shelter without you. Follow me quickly, before the whole Exploratorium falls around our ears."

"What do we do now?" Angus whispered. Mrs. Stobbs was hurrying them toward the entrance hall. "We've got to get up to the roof. We can't do anything to stop the storm from down here."

The stairs that led up to the Octagon came into view. There was no time to come up with a plan. As they passed a broom closet on their right, Angus yanked the door open and bundled the housekeeper inside before she could protest.

"I'm really sorry, Mrs. Stobbs!" he yelled, slamming the door shut. "We'll explain everything later!"

"I'm never going to hear the last of it when Dad finds out we've stuffed her into a cupboard!" Dougal groaned.

They ran before the housekeeper could emerge and headed through the door that led to the staircase up to the roof, again taking two steps at a time. Angus reached the trapdoor first. He pushed his way through and straight into the most alarming scene he'd ever witnessed.

17

STORM JARS AND ROCKET LAUNCHERS

The storm cloud was gigantic. It filled the starless skies in every direction, stretching from one side of the island to the other and to the dark horizon beyond. Booming rumbles of thunder shook the roof beneath their feet. Fracture lightning flitted through every part of the swirling mass, but none struck out at the Exploratorium. Angus swallowed hard. He could instantly feel the prickle of electricity in the air. A gusty wind snatched at his hair and clothes. It was as if the whole storm was waiting for the perfect moment to launch a frenzied attack.

Lightning catchers darted urgently from one storm vacuum to the next, checking suction pipes, adjusting nozzles. They fastened down the lightning shelters, which looked far too flimsy to withstand the colossal storm. Angus, Dougal, and Indigo quickly took cover behind a large pile of steel storm nets before they were seen.

"This is *really, really* bad." Dougal looked petrified. "There's no way a hundred fire dragons could defeat that!"

"But I've got to do something!" Angus tried to shout above the wind that caught each of his words and whisked them away on a swirling coil of angry air.

"Angus is right," Indigo yelled, holding on to her hair as it whipped around her face. "We've got to crush the scales and mix them with some water."

"Water!" Dougal slapped his forehead with the palm of his hand. "I totally forgot. We've got nothing to mix the dragon scales with."

"But there must be something up here we can use," Indigo said, looking desperately from one dry-weather machine to the next.

The cloud above looked as if it held a whole ocean full of water, but none of it had fallen yet. The roof was as dry as a dinosaur bone.

"Over there!" Indigo pointed suddenly to a sad collection

of moldy-looking storm jars that had been heaped together and abandoned on the far side of the roof. From a distance it was impossible to see what, if anything, they contained.

Angus squinted at the jars, wondering if it wouldn't be quicker and easier just to make a mad dash back through the trapdoor and down to the kitchens for a jug of water. He glanced over his shoulder. The whole trapdoor area was now swarming with lightning catchers. They'd have to take their chances with the storm jars.

"We've got to get a closer look at those jars," he said, hoping they contained something more than dust.

They kept to the deepest, darkest shadows, creeping quietly behind Catchers Howler, Winnie Wrascal, and Catcher Greasley, who were each manning one of the storm vacuums. Angus almost collided with Catcher Mint, who came hurtling out of nowhere carrying a trumpet-shaped storm snare. Dougal accidentally tripped over some emergency fire buckets filled with sand, which the wind instantly caught and sent spiraling up into the sky above.

"What's *she* doing up here?" Indigo said into Angus's

ear as Dark-Angel appeared a moment later, striding across the roof with a great air of urgency.

"Why hasn't she gone skipping off to join your dear old uncle Scabby?" Dougal sounded shocked. "I mean, if Perilous is about to be destroyed . . . Isn't that what she wanted?"

"Hold those suction pipes steady!" Dark-Angel bellowed as she finally joined the group of lightning catchers.

"It's no use!" Winnie Wrascal shouted above the roar of the wind. "The storm's too big, and the vacuums aren't strong enough."

"Then we must try the cloud-busting rocket launchers," Dark-Angel commanded. "Aim for the center of the storm, where it will have the greatest effect."

There was a sudden outbreak of activity around the massive machines as Angus, Dougal, and Indigo crept slowly past them in the deep shadows behind. Up close, the steaming rocket launchers were an impressive sight, with giant harpoons attached to the fronts.

"Three, two, one, firing!" Dark-Angel shouted.

Rocket after rocket shot straight up from the roof like a volley of enormous fireworks, with fiery comet tails.

Angus pressed his hands over his ears as he, Dougal, and Indigo clambered through an old pile of ropes.

Boom! Boom! Boom!

Each rocket exploded deep inside the storm cloud. The blast was so loud and sonorous, it shook the ribs inside Angus's chest. The gigantic cloud was momentarily lit up from within.

"I don't believe it. It didn't make any difference," Dougal said, pointing. "The storm cloud looks just the same."

"Send another barrage up!" Dark-Angel ordered. "We may have weakened the structure of the cloud. Now is the time to strike again!"

After four more attacks, however, it was obvious that the cloud-busting rocket launchers had failed to disperse the storm. If anything, the cloud seemed even more violent and threatening than before. And if the storm jars contained nothing but dust . . .

The jars, when they finally reached them, sat in the shelter of a giant rusting funnel. More than half contained nothing but a fine coating of silt and dirt. Several others had been smashed by large hailstones or clumsy feet.

"There!" Dougal raced over to a single tiny jar that

contained a small cupful of water. He lifted the lid and sniffed warily at the clear liquid inside. "It's definitely rainwater," he said. "As long as it didn't fall from a poisonous storm cloud or a shower of rancid rain, it should be safe enough to drink. Now, all we've got to do is figure out how to crush the dragon scales. It isn't going to be easy. They're as tough as armor."

Angus stared at Dougal and Indigo in horror. In their desperate quest to find the small blue scales, they'd never actually considered how they were going to mash them into a fine powder.

"We could stomp on them!" Indigo shouted over the whooshing sound of yet more rockets being launched into the storm.

But Dougal shook his head. "It's way too risky. What if half the scales stick to the bottom of our shoes or they accidentally get mixed in with some stray storm particles?"

Angus searched around his feet, looking for something strong enough to crush the scales. "The storm jars! We could use one like a giant rolling pin."

"It might just work," Dougal said, suddenly looking more hopeful. He grabbed a clean handkerchief from his pocket, laid it neatly on the roof, and placed the scales carefully on top.

Angus tipped the heaviest-looking jar he could find onto its side and rolled it across the scales, pressing down hard until they each began to snap, break, and splinter.

Crunch! Crunch! Crunch!

"You two had better stand back," Dougal warned as he scooped the crushed scale dust into the center of the handkerchief before a sudden gust of howling wind could scatter it across the roof. "Who knows what's going to happen when I mix this stuff with the rainwater. I mean, if these scales really do contain the essence of four fire dragons, there could be spontaneous flames or deadly sparks or some serious frothing."

Dougal took a deep breath, tipped the dust into the tiny storm jar, replaced the lid, and gave it a hearty shake. He then set the jar down carefully on the roof and scrambled behind the large rusting funnel where Indigo and Angus had already taken shelter. The rainwater instantly began to fizz and bubble. The jar shook violently as foam filled every inch of the glass container. There was a blinding flash of tiny sparks.

Snap! Snap, snap, snap!

And then all activity inside the jar ceased. The only sound that remained was the distant voice of Dark-Angel yelling orders at Winnie Wrascal.

"Is—is it over yet?" Dougal asked, peeping out from behind the funnel, his face illuminated by yet another flash of lightning.

Angus approached the glass jar cautiously. It now contained a strange oily-looking liquid the color of topaz.

"Do you think it's ready to drink?" he asked.

"I haven't got the foggiest," Dougal said, sounding worried. "Just don't shake the storm jar up. It might set the whole thing off again."

Angus nodded. This was it. The moment he'd feared since he'd first learned that the blue dragon scales existed. If his own fire dragon awoke, if he could control the other four fiery creatures, then maybe he could help save Perilous. But what if his talents had deserted him for good?

His throat suddenly felt thick and tight, as if his swallowing muscles could already sense the importance of the oily drink he was about to take. He wiped his clammy hands on his pants, but before he could reach out and grasp the neck of the storm jar . . .

"McFangus! Dewsnap! Midnight!" Catcher Sparks was sprinting across the roof toward them, her long leather jerkin flapping in the howling wind. "What in the name of Perilous are you doing on the roof? You should have been down in the emergency weather shelter with the rest of the lightning cubs half an hour ago. Explain yourselves!" she demanded, almost incandescent with anger. "If I had a silver starling for every time I'd found you three lurking in dangerous places, I could have bought Castle Dankhart by now, had it taken apart stone by stone, and saved us all a great deal of bother."

"I, um," Angus said. Before he could think of anything more intelligent to say, her eyes fell on the storm jar.

"And what, might I ask, is this?" She snatched it up from the roof and gave the contents a shake.

"It's nothing, miss, it's just some fruit juice from the kitchens," Indigo said hurriedly before the lightning catcher could stir up the contents again or, worse still, open the jar and take a swig for herself.

Catcher Sparks raised a single eyebrow at her. "Fruit

juice does not have bits of grit floating around in it, Midnight. If I find that you, McFangus, and Dewsnap have stolen a dangerous vial of experimental storm solution from my department, there will be serious trouble."

Crash! Crash! Crash!

Fifty bolts of lightning suddenly struck out from the cloud. The storm was finally hitting back. Tired of being pummeled with rockets and harpoons, it was now attacking the roof with long lashes of terrible lightning, which fractured on impact and danced in every direction. Storm vacuums burst instantly into flames and melted into twisted piles of metal where they stood.

"You three are coming with me!" Catcher Sparks yelled, herding them hastily past the mangled machines.

Angus ducked instinctively as yet more lightning flashed around them.

Crash! Crash! Crash!

Flames began to leap and spread across the roof. And other parts of Perilous had also been hit. Angus could feel the explosions as they shook the Exploratorium; the whole rock was being pounded by a relentless battering ram of raging weather.

"We've lost all contact with the forecasting department!" Catcher Greasley shouted at a large group of senior lightning catchers as they hurried past. "The Rotundra's on fire. There are reports of fracture lightning entering every part of the building."

"We must deploy the storm nets," Catcher Howler said, choosing twenty lightning catchers to help him in the task. "We might be able to pull the cloud apart and damage its internal structure. Nobody is to leave this roof until an evacuation order is given!"

"The rest of you follow me!" Catcher Greasley charged in the opposite direction, heading for the weather machine with ladders and grappling hooks.

In the distance they could see Dark-Angel organizing another volley of rockets from the cloud-busting machines. Angus stumbled sideways as Winnie Wrascal pushed past them, helping an injured Catcher Mint. Moments later they were standing beside the trapdoor that led back down into the Exploratorium.

"For once in your lives you will do exactly as I say!" Catcher Sparks shouted above the chaos. "You will go straight down to the emergency weather shelter and stay there with the rest of the lightning cubs."

"But, miss—"

"No arguments, McFangus! Take this storm jar with you and give it to Catcher Grimble when you reach the shelter. I will be having words with you later about where it came from and what you were planning to do with it. That's if there is a later."

She thrust the storm jar at Dougal, forced them down through the opening and onto the stairs beneath, and slammed the door shut before they could protest.

The sound of the storm diminished instantly.

"What now?" Dougal clutched the jar tightly to his chest, in case anyone tried to snatch it.

They dived out of the way as a crowd of lightning catchers sprinted up the stairs behind them from the direction of the Octagon. They were heading straight for the roof.

"McFangus!" Miss DeWinkle said. "Take your friends and get down to the emergency weather shelter immediately."

"We can't give up now," Angus said, dismissing the idea of the shelter as soon as Miss DeWinkle had disappeared through the doorway. "You saw what was happening up there. The lightning catchers are getting pulverized. And I'm the only person who can stop it!"

Choking black smoke began to drift up the stairs toward them as he said it. From deep within the Exploratorium there were sounds of a fresh explosion and the distant yells of warning. Perilous was beginning to crumble.

"Give me the dragon scale mixture, quickly! I have to—"

Angus stopped suddenly and listened. Something on the roof had changed; something that was causing the hairs on the back of his neck to stand up on end in warning.

"The storm's stopped," Indigo said, her eyes focused sharply on the trapdoor above their heads.

Angus could no longer hear the deep rolls of thunder or the sound of lightning catchers yelling. An eerie silence had fallen.

"Maybe they've pulled the cloud apart with the storm nets," Indigo said, sounding unconvinced.

Dougal frowned. "If they'd just destroyed the storm, they'd be singing and dancing all over the roof."

There was only one way to find out for sure. Angus pushed the trapdoor open slowly, half expecting to see Catcher

Sparks still glaring down at him from above, with nostrils flaring. But the roof was now strangely deserted. There were no lightning catchers manning the rocket launchers or grappling hooks. Dark-Angel had disappeared. The rest of the weather machines lay steaming and abandoned. Some had been destroyed by the lightning or lay toppled over on one side, coughing and spluttering pathetically. The storm still hovered overhead, dark and ominous, but for the time being, at least, it had ceased its attack.

Dougal slipped the tiny storm jar into his pocket for safekeeping as they clambered out onto the roof.

"Where's everyone gone?" Indigo said, looking extremely worried.

Several figures emerged from the shadows as she said it. More were suddenly spilling out from one of the largest tented shelters. Angus swallowed hard. He instantly recognized two of the people now heading toward them. They were Adrik Swarfe and Scabious Dankhart.

18

THE FIRE DRAGON STORM

"Angus, how fortunate to meet you here," Swarfe said, smiling at him. He was dressed in a long coat with his collar turned up against the howling wind, his goatee neatly combed and waxed to a point. Dankhart wore robes of deepest black, to match the dark glittering of his diamond eye. The deep pockmarks and scars on his face were illuminated dreadfully by the flickering lightning above.

A large dirigible weather station hovered close to the edge of the roof. It had clearly brought Dankhart and Swarfe, along with dozens of monsoon mongrels, straight to Perilous.

Angus glared at Dankhart. This had not been part of

the plan. Facing the worst storm ever to attack Perilous was bad enough without having to deal with the very monsoon mongrels who had created it.

"What have you done with the lightning catchers?" Angus asked, facing Swarfe and Dankhart square on, sounding much more fearless than he actually felt. Dougal stood shoulder to shoulder with him. Indigo joined them both in silence, her chin lifted defiantly as she glared at her uncle.

"We have simply confined them to one of their own shelters until we are ready for the storm to finish what it has already started," Swarfe said.

"The end will be quick," Dankhart added. "The lightning will find every stray lightning catcher and strike without mercy."

"But Perilous is only the beginning," Swarfe said, sounding excited. "Once it has been reduced to a pile of rubble, and the last of the lightning catchers have been killed or forced to become monsoon mongrels, we can carry out the next phase of our plans. We will create storms of cataclysmic power and hold the world to ransom. Without the lightning catchers to protect humankind from the worst of the weather, it should be a delightfully enjoyable task. You will witness for yourself the grandness of our ambitions, Angus. We have great plans for *your* future."

Angus swallowed, trying hard not to think of the devastation the catastrophic storms would cause. He had to keep the monsoon mongrels talking for as long as possible, until he could somehow retrieve the storm jar from Dougal's pocket, drink the dragon scale mixture it contained, and let it work its way through his body.

"But if the fracture lightning storm above Perilous is as dangerous as you claim, won't it kill you along with everyone else?" he said, surreptitiously scanning the roof for anything that would help save them. One solitary fire bucket, filled with sand, sat close to his feet. The remnants of several storm vacuum suction pipes lay in smoldering ruins. There was nothing else within reach.

"A clever observation, Angus, but you need not be concerned for our safety." Swarfe sneered at him. "Scabious and I now have the means to control any storm."

"Finally, we have achieved our greatest dream and regained the storm prophet powers that were rightfully ours," Dankhart said.

"And for that we must thank you, Angus."

"M-me?"

"Once we discovered the good news that you were still alive, the possibilities seemed endless. Your blood was the catalyst that was needed to rekindle our own dormant storm prophet strengths. I used it in a special compound of my own invention," Swarfe said.

Angus stared at the monsoon mongrel, confused. "But you haven't taken any of my blood."

"And now that our powers are finally reborn," Swarfe continued, ignoring his words, "they will be made stronger and more invincible still by the blue fire dragon scales."

Angus felt the veins constrict inside his heart. He was no longer the only living storm prophet. Even if his own fire dragon suddenly returned from its long hibernation, he would now be woefully outnumbered. And if Dankhart and Swarfe got their hands on the blue dragon scales, they'd be unstoppable. The power of the first storm prophets would be theirs. Perilous wouldn't stand a chance.

"I d-don't know what you're talking about," he said, trying to sound convincing. Dougal's hand shot automatically to his pocket where the tiny storm jar sat.

"Oh, but I think you do, Angus McFangus. That is why you stole a trinket box from my office when you and Miss Midnight came to Castle Dankhart."

"When you kidnapped us, you mean," Angus said, attempting to shift the conversation away from dragon scales of any color.

"Call it what you want, it does not change the facts." Swarfe was watching him shrewdly. "I heard a whisper, long ago, about the existence of some rare and powerful dragon scales, but I assumed the early lightning catchers had used them up in their foolish experiments. I never dreamed that my own family would be the guardians of such an extraordinary gift." Swarfe was advancing on him now. "The blue fire dragon scales, Angus. We know you've already found them. Where are they?"

Angus stood motionless. He, Dougal, and Indigo hadn't fooled Dark-Angel for a minute. She'd clearly known all along that their hunt had been successful. Had she simply been waiting for the right moment to carry out her final betrayal?

He glanced to the left, trying to catch Indigo's eye. There had to be something they could do. The monsoon mongrels would find the tiny storm jar in Dougal's pocket in a matter of moments.

Boooom!

The deafening sound of an explosion suddenly filled the air. It came from beyond the storm cloud. Every head turned instinctively toward the mountains in the distance, where a plume of smoke was now rising. A deep growling rumble echoed through the air.

"Swarfe!" Dankhart roared. "What is this?"

Angus snatched up the fire bucket close to his feet and flung its contents high into the air. Sand cascaded around them. Picked up by the howling wind it swirled and shifted, covering Dankhart, Swarfe, and the monsoon mongrels.

"Run!" Angus grabbed Dougal, shielding his eyes with his other hand, and darted after Indigo, who was already sprinting across the roof, desperately searching for a place to hide from her uncle. They skidded past a burning rocket launcher, leaped over some discarded fire buckets, and scrambled behind a stack of storm nets before the monsoon mongrels could fight their way through the sudden sandstorm.

"The lightning catchers must have destroyed one of

the vortices above the castle," Indigo said, staring back toward the mountains.

"Vortices don't leave a trail of smoke behind when they get blown to bits!" Dougal pointed out excitedly. "They must be doing some real damage to the lightning tower after all."

Angus watched the burning cloud now forming in the sky, hoping with every molecule in his body that Jeremius, Gudgeon, Rogwood, and the rest of the lightning catchers were still safe, that they'd somehow managed to destroy the tower and rescue his mum and dad. But that still left Dankhart, Swarfe, and the deadly fracture lightning storm to deal with.

"Quickly, give me the dragon scale mixture."

Dougal pulled the tiny storm jar carefully out of his pocket. "Hold your nose and drink it straight down in one go," he advised.

Angus took a deep breath and drank deeply. It tasted like entrails. Thick and sticky, the disgusting concoction coated the inside of his mouth like a mouthwash made from goose fat. Larger bits of crushed scales scratched the sides of his throat as the whole mixture slid slowly down into his stomach. A horrible chalky residue had already collected at the bottom of the storm jar. Angus swirled it around and gulped it down, trying hard not to retch.

"S-so what happens now?" he spluttered, wiping his mouth with the back of his hand.

He stared at his fingers, his feet, his legs, half expecting them to transform at any second into pure flame or to find himself suddenly protected by a golden armor of glimmering dragon scales. His vision was blurred; his stomach felt cold and leaden. But as the seconds continued to tick past . . .

"Nothing's happening."

"It must take a few minutes to work," Indigo said, looking desperately worried.

"We haven't got a few minutes. I—"

Their conversation was halted abruptly by the sound of someone sobbing. A dreadful, pitiful wail echoed around the roof.

"What's your uncle Scabby doing now?" Dougal peered through the holes of the storm nets, attempting to get a clear view of Dankhart and Swarfe. Angus and Indigo looked over his shoulder.

Two monsoon mongrels were dragging a struggling figure out from one of the lightning shelters. Angus recognized her instantly. The monsoon mongrels had somehow found Mrs. Stobbs and forced her up onto the roof. They held her tightly by the arms, making the housekeeper sob with fright.

"Oh no! The monsoon mongrels must have grabbed her after she got out of the broom closet!" Dougal's voice was faint with worry.

"I have no quarrel with the Dewsnap boy's housekeeper," Dankhart said coolly into the night air. He turned slowly on his heels, clearly searching each shadow and wrecked weather machine for any sign of them. "I will release her unharmed, if you and your friends hand over the blue fire dragon scales. If you refuse to cooperate, however, the housekeeper will feel the full fury of the fracture lightning storm."

"You've got no business being inside Perilous, frightening these lightning cubs half to death," Mrs. Stobbs said with a trembling voice.

"Silence!" Dankhart shouted, making the housekeeper sob once again.

"This is all our fault! We've got to help her!" Dougal turned to Angus with a desperate pleading in his eyes. "Can't you do something?"

Angus sank to the ground, took a deep steadying breath, and closed his eyes. He had to act now. The dragon scale mixture had to work. He tried to picture familiar flames and fiery scales swooping through the night air around them. He thought of all the times his fire dragon had ever appeared, and he clutched his chest, willing the fire to burn behind his ribs . . . but nothing came.

"It's no use! The mixture isn't working."

Crash! Crash! Crash!

Lightning struck out suddenly from the storm cloud. It fractured as it hit the roof and danced dangerously between machines.

"Get down!" Indigo grabbed the edge of a storm net and dragged it over their heads.

Whoosh!

Something swooped low overhead. Angus ducked, feeling a scorching trail of heat. He saw the flick of a fiery tail as it disappeared into the storm cloud.

"Fire dragons!" he shouted above a deafening roll of thunder.

"My uncle's trying to flush us out of hiding," Indigo yelled.

Dougal cowered under the steel nets. "That's if he doesn't kill us first!"

Angus watched, horrified, as two powerful creatures with blackened, shimmering scales dipped below the cloud and sped across the roof with fearsome speed. The fire dragons were immense, more frightening and dreadful than anything he'd ever seen in his nightmares. They wove their way expertly through the cloud, whipping up the storm into a frenzy of flashes and sparks. Dankhart and Swarfe had already mastered the dangerous art of controlling the vicious storm. He didn't stand a chance.

Crash!

Lightning struck at the roof again, lashing out at storm vacuums and tented shelters.

Crash!

The storm nets had been hit. Angus shot to his feet and ran blindly, quickly losing sight of Indigo and Dougal in their mad scramble to avoid the fracture lightning.

Monsoon mongrels descended upon him from a dozen different directions.

"Get off me!" He twisted and struggled against the hands now holding him. They dragged him across the roof to where Dankhart and Swarfe stood waiting.

"We have wasted enough time." Dankhart was striding toward him. The fire dragons had disappeared from the sky—for the time being, at least—but the smell of their smoldering heat still lingered in the air like the scent of victory. Dougal and Indigo were being hauled by Victus Bile across the roof. "I am tired of these games, McFangus. You will give us the dragon scales before we destroy Perilous and everyone in it."

"I've already searched these two, Scabious, and found nothing," Victus Bile said.

Angus glanced around in desperation. He needed more time. His insides still felt cold and flameless.

There was a sudden disturbance behind Swarfe and Dankhart. Dark-Angel came stumbling out from the direction of the rocket launchers, where she'd clearly been sheltering from the lightning. She pushed through the circle of monsoon mongrels that now surrounded Angus, Dougal, and Indigo. Her leather jerkin was ripped and torn. There were several deep cuts across one cheek.

Angus felt his last hopes plummet down to his shoes. Dark-Angel had come to join the monsoon mongrels at last. Dankhart welcomed her with open arms.

"Delphinia, you have joined us at a very fortunate moment, for I promise you it will be one of the greatest in the history of Perilous. And we must thank you for your help."

"We already knew she was helping you!" Dougal said suddenly, yanking his arms free from Victus Bile's grasp. "Angus and Indigo saw her handing over dragon scales in the bone merchant's."

A strange smile crossed Dark-Angel's lips, as if she was proud of them somehow.

"I have also brought the special payment we discussed before you kindly agreed to steal the fire dragon scales for us," Dankhart continued.

Two monsoon mongrels brought another figure forward from the shadow of the weather station that still hovered at the edge of the roof. Pale and thin, his ragged clothes hung from his bony frame. But there was no mistaking the resemblance to his sister.

"Humphrey?" Dark-Angel's voice broke. Her face lit up with a brief glimmer of hope. But she did not attempt to reach her brother.

"I will release your brother as soon as you have persuaded Angus and his friends to hand over the blue fire dragon scales that they have been so busy collecting," Dankhart said.

Dark-Angel glanced at Angus, Dougal, and Indigo with a look of great surprise.

"The power of the first dragon scales you gave us proved to be a great exaggeration," Indigo's uncle continued. "They had no effect when added to lightning storm particles."

"There is a simple explanation for that, Scabious," Dark-Angel said, standing tall. "The scales I gave to you did not come from the tomb of Moray McFangus."

A shock wave rippled around the entire roof at her words.

"Did you truly think that I would betray my lightning catcher oaths and the whole of Perilous for the hollow promises that you made? The return of my kidnapped brother for the price of the dragon scales? I could never place Perilous in such a dangerous position. I had no intention of handing you any dragon scales that would help your cause. I took them instead from another storm prophet, Silas Sevenstar."

Angus stared at Dougal and Indigo, suddenly holding his breath. They had heard about the mysterious storm prophet from Hartley Windspear. What was Dark-Angel playing at?

Swarfe scowled. "She is lying, Scabious. I have no knowledge of any such storm prophet."

"That is because he kept his talents a secret, Adrik. His powers were only revealed when he died and his fire dragon appeared. He was buried in an unmarked tomb and forgotten by many. But I discovered that Sevenstar was sick, that he passed his illness on to his dragon. I gave you diseased dragon scales," Dark-Angel said. "They looked identical to the ones found on any other storm prophet, but they would be worthless when added to storm particles. If you do not believe me, you are welcome to check the tomb of Moray McFangus. You will find none of his scales missing."

Dankhart swept forward and struck Dark-Angel hard

with the back of his hand. The force of it knocked her to the ground, where she lay, her face twisted with pain.

Angus started toward her, but Dougal pulled him back. Dark-Angel had been on their side all along. She had tricked Dankhart so thoroughly they had all believed in her guilt.

"You have acted very foolishly, Delphinia," Swarfe said as she struggled to her feet, clutching her jaw.

"On the contrary." Dark-Angel faced him again. "It was worth the risk. I kept my brother safe without helping you in the slightest. But I am curious. You have been extraordinarily well informed of our own experiments in the Lightnarium and of our intentions to destroy the lightning tower. And since I have given you nothing but some worthless dragon scales, you must have received your information from somebody else."

Angus stared around the roof, as if the real traitor might suddenly appear from behind a storm vacuum. It had to be someone who knew exactly what Jeremius and Rogwood had been doing with lightning accelerators and who knew that he, Dougal, and Indigo had discovered blue fire dragon scales.

His eyes shifted past Swarfe and Dankhart to the monsoon mongrels holding Mrs. Stobbs by the arms. The housekeeper's face was still terrified and shocked. Almost as shocked as the moment she had discovered they were still alive at 37 Feaver Street.

Mrs. Stobbs had appeared at the exact moment they'd discovered the dragon scale in Mr. Dewsnap's office. She'd also materialized in his bedroom the morning after, when he'd woken up from a dream about a swarm of bees stinging his arm, a sting that had caused real pain, as if someone had drawn his blood. His blood had since been used to restore the storm prophet powers of Swarfe and Dankhart.

"It was Mrs. Stobbs!" he blurted out, the truth hitting him like a snow bomb bombardment.

"Wh-what are you talking about? Of course it wasn't." Dougal was staring at the housekeeper, stunned. "She's been trying to help us."

"I'd never do anything to harm you or your friends, my lovely," Mrs. Stobbs said, looking appalled by the very suggestion.

"But she's always popping in and out of Dark-Angel's

office. She could easily have heard Jeremius, Rogwood, and Gudgeon talking about experiments in the Lightnarium. She was in my room, too, when we stayed at Feaver Street. She took my blood and gave it to Swarfe and Dankhart."

"Enid, is this true?" Dark-Angel asked, looking almost as surprised as Dougal.

Angus watched the housekeeper's face as her usual caring expression was suddenly replaced by an ugly glare of cold fury. Mrs. Stobbs jerked her arms free of the monsoon mongrels.

"Nobody ever questioned my presence as I was delivering tea and cake. But it was easy to fool the lightning catchers," she said, looking proud. "Easy to help Dankhart gain a position as the librarian, Mr. Knurling, to help Swarfe break into Perilous with the lightning heart, to set off ice diamond storms."

"Y-you set off the ice diamond storms?" Dougal said.

"And when I discovered that you and the McFangus boy were still alive and taking something from the portrait of Deciduous Dewsnap, I reported it straight to Victus."

"You have been an invaluable source of information, dear cousin," said Victus Bile with a sneer.

"Cousin?" Dougal took several steps away from her with a look of deep revulsion.

"It is time to bring this drama to an end," Dankhart said, staring impatiently up at the storm cloud. "We have been delayed long enough by the McFangus boy and his friends. If they will not give us the dragon scales, we will destroy Perilous and take all three of them back to the castle."

Crash! Crash! Crash!

Lightning hit out at the storm nets and rocket launchers, showering every part of the roof with deadly fractures. Monsoon mongrels yelled in fright and scattered far and wide, diving for cover. In the confusion, Dark-Angel grabbed Dougal and Indigo and pulled them urgently away from Swarfe and Dankhart.

"McFangus!" she shouted. "You must come with me, now!"

But Angus was already running in the opposite direction. He skidded to a halt thirty feet away and clambered up onto a storm vacuum that was now lying on its side. He stared up at the sky as two blackened fire dragons suddenly appeared, swooping through the underbelly of the storm.

Dankhart and Swarfe stood beneath the heart of the cloud. They were going to unleash the full power of the tempest and destroy Perilous. He had to fight back with flames.

Bang! Bang! Bang! Bang!

A firestorm burst through a wall in his chest as four magnificent dragons appeared before him at last. Angus stood fast, the full force of their sudden presence surging through every blood vessel and tingling nerve that lay beneath his skin.

Each was as different from the other as the storm prophets they had come from. There was a flare of red, a dazzling swoop of yellow, a flash of burnished green, and a blaze of brilliant orange. His own fire dragon was still nowhere to be seen. But he was no longer alone. He stood with the ghosts of four storm prophets beside him, each as determined as he was to destroy Dankhart and his monsoon mongrels forever. The burning creatures filled the sky above, waiting for his silent command.

"Four fire dragons?" Dankhart's voice broke over the roof in a wave of fury. "The boy has already used the blue scales, Swarfe!"

"Even so, you cannot hope to win, Angus!" Swarfe shouted above the howling wind. "We will snuff out their existence like a single spark of fire."

Whoosh!

Angus sent the dragons zooming low across the weather machines, forcing Swarfe and Dankhart to dive for cover. A sudden surge of adrenaline shot through his bloodstream. The dragons were powerful, much stronger and more agile than his own. The creatures turned, twisting and looping around one another, with flickers of burnished green and dazzling yellow, with flares of red and brilliant blazes of orange as they shot straight up into the cloud.

"Oh!"

Angus staggered, struggling to keep his balance on top of the fallen storm vacuum. The unnatural forces of the storm had hit the dragons head-on. Hurricane winds howled from every direction. Sinister black clouds roiled as flashes of lightning danced around like giant electrified spiders, and Angus understood. All the terrifying weather that he and Indigo had seen in the storm nurseries at Castle Dankhart had been unleashed over Perilous at once. The dragons fought and thrashed and twisted, flung about the skies like tiny insects caught in a deadly whirlwind.

Whoosh!

He sensed the glimmer of dark scales before he saw them. Dankhart and Swarfe had sent their huge dragons down from above, falling from the skies with the force of two deadly meteors.

Smash!

The red dragon had been hit. The black creatures ripped at it viciously, tearing with talons, gouging scales from its fiery body. The heat of the attack burned through every part of Angus, scorching his muscles and bones.

Whoosh!

The green and yellow dragons smashed into black scales. Flames and talons locked together in a fearful fight. A fire dragon storm blazed through the skies above Perilous once again. Fire dragon plunged after fire dragon as they chased across the skies with the heat of a volcano until it was almost impossible to tell the creatures apart.

But the black dragons were relentless. Stronger and faster, they struck again and again with brutal force. Angus tried to outwit the sinister creatures, pushing his dragons through fantastic loops and turns. But slowly, slowly, he could feel the flames of all four dragons starting to flicker and fade. Dankhart and Swarfe were going to defeat him. The end would come just as it had so many times in his dreams, with four fire dragons beaten this time, flames extinguished, plummeting toward the ground.

"No! Uncle Scabious, wait!"

Indigo had broken free of Dark-Angel. She shot across the roof toward her uncle and set the mini projectogram box she'd taken from the testing tunnel down onto the roof.

"Scabious wasn't interested in the weather as a boy." The sound of her mum's voice echoed suddenly through the night, blending with the sounds of the storm, her grainy image distorted by the wind. "I believe he hated living at the castle almost as much as I did."

"E-Etheldra?" Dankhart hesitated, a look of disbelief crossing his face. His fire dragon stalled. Angus took his chance. He sent the four creatures swiftly away, into the upper reaches of the cloud, the vessels in his heart almost bursting with the effort as the dragons fought against the howling winds.

He crouched on his knees, fighting for breath, trying

to gather his scattered senses. Indigo was playing for time. But what if the fight was already lost? The black fire dragons were too strong, the storm too fierce. Wouldn't it be easier just to turn and run?

"Everything your uncle Greville told you about the storm prophets was a lie!" Indigo was speaking again. She faced her uncle defiantly as her mum's voice filled the air around them.

"We have no time for such ridiculous distractions, Scabious," Swarfe said, sounding furious. "We must take these children and destroy Perilous."

"But Indigo's telling the truth!" Bravely, Dougal had joined Indigo. "We've all seen the projectogram, and you've been tricked." Dankhart flinched. "Fitch, Twinge, and Blacktin fled from Perilous after they deliberately unleashed the never-ending storm, and then *they* attacked the Exploratorium. And your mum and dad were killed in a stupid weather accident at Castle Dankhart. It had nothing to do with the lightning catchers."

"You've got to believe us, Uncle Scabious. You're making a terrible mistake!"

"Enough!" Dankhart roared. He kicked the projectogram

box and smashed it to pieces. The image of his sister faded. Indigo recoiled from her uncle. "Etheldra betrayed me long ago. I will not listen to any more of her lies!"

His fire dragon swooped low, skimming the underbelly of the cloud. The creature dived straight toward Indigo, dragging a long wisp of storm on its wings. Lightning lashed out.

Crash! Crash! Crash!

Angus twisted his head away, forced to shield his eyes from the blinding glare. But Indigo's screams echoed above the wind. When he turned back, her lifeless-looking body lay broken on the ground.

"All is not lost, Angus." Swarfe's voice rose above the storm. "We will spare the life of the Dewsnap boy if you surrender now! I will extract the essence of the four dragons from your blood, and we will be victorious."

"Stay away from me!" Angus yelled. Anger burned inside him with a new fire. It glowed and roared and screamed at the dreadful sight of Indigo's body. Familiar fire and flame suddenly stirred. He clutched his chest.

Bang!

After months of hibernation his golden fire dragon had

finally awoken. Its wings scorched the dark night with molten fire. It felt bigger and stronger, more powerful than ever before.

Angus didn't hesitate. He sent it racing up into the heart of the storm. The black creatures were already waiting, eager for victory, arrogance surrounding them like an extra layer of scales. Angus's own fire dragon twisted high and dove like a comet, forcing the two black creatures to separate. Red, green, yellow, and orange flew down from the top of the cloud and hounded the smaller of the two dark dragons across the skies until it could take no more. Angus watched as the fire died behind its startled eyes. It plummeted toward the ground, its wings drooping, its flames suddenly extinguished with a final roar of rage that seemed to come from Adrik Swarfe himself.

The monsoon mongrel turned tail and fled, his great coat flapping behind him like the blackened wings of his defeated dragon.

"Swarfe!" Dankhart bellowed after him. "Abandon me at your peril! I will send all the storms of the deadly seven to find you!"

But Dankhart's chief monsoon mongrel disappeared

swiftly through the trapdoor and down into the depths of Perilous. Indigo's uncle now stood alone.

The creatures turned as one and dived with lightning speed toward Dankhart's dragon, dragging the storm with them, herding fracture lightning with each flap of their vast wings.

"No!" Dankhart's screams of rage pierced the wail of the mighty storm as Angus's dragon grabbed the black creature by its wing. It pulled the black dragon toward the ground, forcing them both into a deadly spiral.

Swoop!

Angus suddenly released the creature, pulling his own fire dragon up, hard and fast, as Dankhart's dragon crashed into the roof. With a final blaze of angry flames it vanished, leaving a blackened pit behind. Dankhart staggered toward the weather station as the lightning continued to strike.

But the fracture storm hadn't finished with Perilous yet. With no one to control it, it was now ripping at walls, tearing through solid rock and stone.

Angus sent the five dragons up into the cloud once again. They twisted high above him, swooping and diving through every wisp and strand of tempest, forcing storm particles and fracture lightning to smash together, to tussle for space in the skies above until he could see nothing but flickers of flame.

Boooom!

A huge shock wave blasted him off his feet and sent him smashing painfully into the roof. And darkness fell.

19
THROUGH THE MIST

It sounded like the swish of a dragon's tail. Somewhere close by, Angus could hear it flicking and scraping its hard scales across the floor in a slow, soothing rhythm. If he just opened one eye, he was sure he'd be able to see its fiery body.

"Angus?"

The swishing stopped abruptly. There was a shuffle of hurried footsteps, and a familiar face suddenly loomed over him with a wide grin.

"Germ?" Angus said. His throat felt dry and croaky. He struggled to prop himself up onto his elbows. "What's happening?"

"Don't panic," Germ said. "You're in the sanatorium. You've got a few bruised ribs and a broken toe, you've had a bang to the head, and we've been treating some minor lightning burns on your arms and legs, but it's nothing much to worry about," he told Angus cheerfully. "A few hours of sleep and some of your uncle Max's special chicken and maple syrup soup and you'll be ready to sneak into Valentine Vellum's room with some more storm fluff. I happen to know where you can get your hands on another jar, no questions asked."

"H-how do you know about the storm fluff?" Angus asked.

"Good news travels fast. You are now as legendary as the great Rollo Rawlings, who once buried an entire team of lightning catchers in a humongous pile of yeti poop."

Angus stared around the sanatorium, confused. All the other beds were empty. The swishing sound had been made by Germ, who'd clearly been sweeping the floor close to his bed. But there had been dragons, lots of them, he was sure of it.

"Indigo and Dougal!" He suddenly remembered Dankhart, Swarfe, and the furious fire dragon battle that had taken place on the roof. “Are they okay? What happened? Where is everyone?”

“There’s no need to get your rubber boots in a twist. Dougal had no injuries except a few bruises on his arms and legs.”

“But Indigo got struck by the fracture lightning. I saw her b-body.” Angus searched the rest of the sanatorium once again. Indigo was nowhere to be seen.

“Most of her lightning burns were superficial, but she’s got a bad case of lightning shock. Doctor Fleagal says she’ll be fine,” Germ said, although his usual happy smile slipped slightly as he said it. “He says she’ll still be the same annoying sister when she eventually wakes up.”

“But I’ve got to see her.” Angus tried to push the covers off his legs.

“Not a chance,” Germ said, easing him back into bed. “Doctor Fleagal will have me scraping out vomit buckets for weeks if I let you go wandering off by yourself. Stay here, I’ll go and get Dark-Angel,” he added, making a face. “She wanted to see you as soon as you woke up.”

Angus slumped back against his pillows; every part of

his body was now aching, as if he'd been sucked through a series of storm vacuums. His ribs gave him a sharp stab of pain every time he took a deep breath, and his head was starting to throb. He could no longer feel any of the fire dragons, including his own, burning inside his chest. He closed his eyes, trying to block out the light fissures overhead, but terrible images of Indigo being struck by fracture lightning filled his thoughts instead. He opened his eyes again swiftly.

He still had no idea if Perilous was in one piece, or if Jeremius, Rogwood, and Gudgeon had flown safely back to the Exploratorium in the weather station. Or if his mum and dad . . .

"McFangus!" Dark-Angel was marching across the sanatorium toward him with a look of deep concern on her face. Rogwood, Gudgeon, and Jeremius followed close behind. Gudgeon had some nasty-looking cuts on one side of his face. Jeremius had his left arm in a sling. Rogwood's beard had been badly singed and was now several inches shorter than it had been.

"What happened?" Angus asked, desperate for news. "Was Castle Dankhart destroyed? What about my mum and dad? Are they alive? Have they come back to Perilous?"

"Calm yourself," Jeremius said as they reached his bed. "We will tell you everything, but you mustn't get overexcited or Doctor Fleagal will throw us out of the sanatorium. You've been unconscious for several days. You gave us all quite a fright."

"D-days?" Angus said, shocked. The events on the roof felt as if they'd happened just moments before, as if he could race back up through the trapdoor and find the smell of a thousand lightning strikes still lingering in the air, the imprint of the fire dragons still burning across the night sky. He took as deep a breath as his bruised ribs would allow and rested back against his pillows.

"We've pieced together most of what happened, thanks to Principal Dark-Angel and Dougal," Jeremius explained as he, Rogwood, and Dark-Angel arranged themselves in the chairs beside his bed. Gudgeon remained standing.

"Young Mr. Dewsnap has become quite the hero of the hour in the kitchens," Rogwood added, his amber eyes twinkling.

"So, does everyone know about my fire dragon now?"

Gudgeon shook his head. "Dewsnap's been telling everyone you three toppled Dankhart with some storm globes. Every time he tells the tale it gets longer and even more far-fetched. They'll be calling him the Bard of Perilous soon."

Angus nodded, grateful that his secret was safe for now. But the thought of telling some of his friends the truth about his strange weather-wrangling skills no longer brought him out in a clammy sweat. Perhaps one day soon he might even give Germ, Nicholas Grubb, and his favorite fellow second years a quick demonstration.

"Perilous survived the attack," Rogwood said, "but there has been a lot of damage to the roof. The forecasting department was badly burned by some stray fracture lightning, and I'm afraid the Rotundra and the storm hollow have been completely destroyed."

"We were lucky the whole place didn't burn to the ground," Gudgeon added with a grunt.

"Nobody at Perilous was seriously hurt," Jeremius said. "We've all had a very lucky escape thanks to you, Dougal, and Indigo."

"Your storm prophet skills have surpassed those of even

the great Moray McFangus," Rogwood added, smiling through his beard. "He would have been proud of your courage and determination to protect your friends and save Perilous. It takes a storm prophet with a great deal of skill and character to control five fire dragons in the face of such a vicious attack."

Angus swallowed hard and stared down at his hands, which were resting on top of his bed covers. There had been unbearable moments when he'd been sure that Dankhart would defeat him and that Perilous would fall, when his courage had almost deserted him and it would have been easier to turn and run.

"Although the fact that you, Indigo, and Dougal have also broken about a hundred promises you made about staying out of trouble and not tackling Dankhart on your own has not gone unnoticed," Jeremius said, folding his arms across his chest and suddenly sounding stern.

"But what happened to the lightning tower?" Angus asked, keen to move the conversation on. "Dankhart said the storms you made weren't strong enough to destroy anything."

"That's certainly what we wanted Dankhart to believe," Jeremius said. "We've been feeding him false information for weeks now about failed experiments and explosions in the Lightnarium and serious problems with our lightning accelerators."

Angus stared at his uncle, flabbergasted. "But the explosions were real. I felt the walls shake."

"I will admit some of our difficulties were genuine, but the rest were created deliberately so the news of our failures would reach Dankhart and lull him into a false sense of security."

"He had no idea that our work with the accelerators was so advanced," Rogwood said, "and they performed perfectly on the day."

"They cut through that stinking lightning tower like a hot knife through butter," Gudgeon said proudly.

"Although when the tower was destroyed, it had an unexpected side effect. A small residue of confused weather particles have since drifted across the island and settled inside this Exploratorium." Rogwood turned to look at an odd patch of dense mist that was hovering at the far end of the sanatorium. "We've also had three hailstorms in the kitchens and a torrential downpour of newts in the experimental division."

Jeremius smiled at the surprised look on Angus's face as he stared at the strange mist. "We kept the truth from Delphinia, of course, believing as we did at the time that she would betray our real plans to Dankhart."

Dark-Angel nodded gravely but said nothing, allowing Jeremius to complete his story.

"Mrs. Stobbs heard all about our failures, which she then passed on to Dankhart, and the plan worked beautifully."

"Even if we were aiming our deception at the wrong person," Rogwood added.

"If I'd known about your hunt for the blue scales, I would have told you of our plans in the strictest of confidence," Jeremius said, shaking his head sadly. "I had no idea you were planning to tackle the lightning storm by yourself. I have failed to keep you safe at every turn, Angus. I am truly sorry. I have been a very poor uncle."

"The blame is all mine," Dark-Angel said, finally breaking her silence, her usual steely voice sounding extremely shaken. "I was the one who enrolled McFangus, Dewsnap, and Midnight in my plan to find the dragon scales, and I knowingly placed them in great peril. I selfishly encouraged McFangus to train his storm prophet skills in the testing tunnels, in the hope they could be used to save this Exploratorium and my brother. And by doing so, I forced him into the path of mortal danger. It was only when I saw the true power of the storm that was about to destroy Perilous that I realized what a grave and dreadful mistake I had made. I knew then that I had placed an intolerable burden upon three young and fearless lightning cubs when I should have sought the help of those faithful lightning catchers around me."

Gudgeon grunted. "Those three would have got themselves into trouble whether you tried to stop them or not. I've never known any lightning cubs so determined to get themselves struck by lightning or sucked up by a fognado."

Angus smiled at the gruff lightning catcher, but he was suddenly glad that Dark-Angel had driven him so hard, had encouraged him to take risks and discover exactly what he was capable of.

"You were only trying to save your brother, miss," he said.

Dark-Angel shook her head and stared down at her hands, ashamed. But Angus could sympathize completely.

He would have done almost anything to save his mum and dad.

"And I never would have been ready to face the other fire dragons if you'd kept me locked up inside the library."

"Thank you for being so understanding, Angus, but it does not change the facts. I have not acted in the manner that a senior lightning catcher should toward her lightning cubs, and for that I can never apologize enough." She stood up abruptly. "Now, if you will excuse me, I will leave Jeremius to tell you everything else. I have an important meeting with Trevelyan Tempest."

"Trevelyan and a team of experts from London have already drawn up some interesting plans for a series of ice caves that could be built under a new Canadian Exploratorium," Rogwood explained, seeing Angus's puzzled expression.

"He's also got some ridiculous notion about rebuilding the Icelandic Exploratorium up in the clouds," Gudgeon said, looking less impressed. "Somebody needs to tell him he's losing his marbles before he starts muttering about weather stations at the center of the earth."

Dark-Angel, Rogwood, and Gudgeon departed a

moment later, leaving Jeremius alone with Angus and the strange drifting mist.

Jeremius sat back in his chair and studied Angus carefully. "I should probably let you get some rest."

"But you can't go yet. There're loads of things you haven't told me! What happened to Dankhart and Swarfe?" Angus asked hastily before Jeremius could leave, too.

Jeremius sighed. "We believe Swarfe may have fled through the tunnels beneath Perilous. In the confusion of the attack it would have been easy for him to slip away unnoticed, and I'm afraid he hasn't been seen since. Dankhart made his escape on his weather station, taking the rest of his monsoon mongrels and Mrs. Stobbs with him."

"S-so they could come back and do it all again," Angus said, suddenly feeling his anxiety levels rise. "Swarfe and Dankhart could meet up somewhere and start making rancid rain and lightning storms and threaten to destroy Perilous all over again."

But Jeremius was shaking his head. "Swarfe failed Dankhart utterly. That happy little partnership ended when you destroyed their storm prophet powers in the duel. Swarfe will stay well clear of Scabious if he values his life as much as he appears to. And as for Dankhart, there's nothing left for him to come back to. He lost everything when the lightning tower was destroyed. Hundreds of years of weather engineering are now lying in ruins. Dankhart won't be causing us any more problems."

Angus leaned back against his pillows once again, his head throbbing.

"What about Dark-Angel's brother?" he asked. "I mean, everyone thought he was dead."

"Including Delphinia," Jeremius said, nodding. "Dankhart contacted her some months before you first arrived at Perilous. He told her that her brother was still alive, that instead of being buried by a huge explosion in the testing tunnels, he'd been kidnapped by Swarfe when he'd fled from the Exploratorium. He promised she could secure her brother's freedom by agreeing to help the monsoon mongrels.

"Dankhart is an expert schemer. He waited until he needed Delphinia's help and then put her in an impossible position. She could never betray the lightning catchers or Perilous, but she also felt compelled to rescue her brother if she could. At the same time she knew there was someone at Perilous who was feeding very important information back to Dankhart, so she decided to use it to her advantage."

"But how?" Angus asked, gripped by the tale.

"Delphinia agreed to Dankhart's plan," Jeremius said. "She then hatched a very clever scheme of her own, making it appear as if she'd broken into the tomb of Moray McFangus and stolen some of his fire dragon scales. In the end, of course, she gave him scales from Silas Sevenstar instead, which were entirely ineffective when added to storm particles. It was a brilliantly conceived plan. I feel somewhat ashamed that I ever doubted her loyalty, but when you and Indigo saw her handing over the dragon scales in the bone merchant's, there seemed to be little doubt that she had betrayed everyone." Jeremius still looked taken aback. "She has already taken me, Rogwood, Gudgeon, and Catcher Sparks down to the crypt to inspect the tomb of Moray McFangus. The only scales missing are the ones taken in 1777 for the original experiments, which we checked against documents written at the time. There can be no doubt. Delphinia is telling the truth. It will please many people that her brother has now returned safely to Perilous, where he belongs, and I hope that he will remain here for years to come."

There was only one difficult question that now remained unanswered.

"What happened to Castle Dankhart?" Angus finally asked, fearing what the answer would mean for his parents.

"Castle Dankhart has been reduced to rubble," Jeremius said. "Dankhart's experimental chambers, storm nurseries, and large stockpile of vicious storms have all been completely destroyed."

"But what about my mum and dad?" Angus asked. "Did you rescue them? Are they all right?"

He swallowed hard, searching his uncle's face for any sign that his mum and dad had survived. Or was Jeremius preparing him for bad news, for the worst possible news?

"I think it might be best if somebody else explains what happened next." Jeremius checked over his shoulder as the door opened at the far end of the sanatorium, causing a disturbance in the swirling mist.

Angus held his breath, his heart beginning to thump wildly inside his battered rib cage. Time seemed to slow down deliberately. The seconds ticked by at an Imbur snail's pace as he stared hard at the edge of the churning haze, then . . .

"M-mum? Dad?"

Two figures finally appeared, thin and pale, their hair limp, their smiles as broad and loving as Angus remembered. He clambered out of bed with difficulty, clutching his ribs, and hobbled across the sanatorium on his broken toe to meet them, his heart suddenly swelling with a long-forgotten feeling of joy.

The next few days passed in a heady blur of happiness and relief. Angus found it extremely difficult to stop smiling, and it took him some time to tell his mum and dad about everything that had happened since they'd been kidnapped on the Imbur marshes. He told them long, detailed tales of his adventures with Dougal and Indigo in the lightning vaults, the Rotundra, and the bone merchant's in Little Frog's Bottom. In return, his mum and dad told him of the daring rescue that Jeremius had mounted, releasing them from the dungeons just moments before Castle Dankhart was destroyed.

Jeremius joined them as often as he could, and for the first time in two years, Angus felt his family was complete. He soon started to feel cooped up inside the sanatorium, however, and he couldn't wait to see Indigo, Dougal, and the rest of Perilous with his own eyes.

Doctor Fleagal finally allowed him to leave a few days later when his mum and dad went to meet with Miss DeWinkle to learn details of the new fogs that had been discovered by Catcher Hornbuckle. He headed swiftly down the marbled stairs and into the main entrance hall, where stone pillars and walls still bore the scars of the recent troubles. Now that the danger had passed, most of the other lightning cubs had returned, and the kitchens were bustling with life.

"There he is! Hey, Angus!" Nicholas Grubb shouted from the far side of the kitchens as Angus poked his head around the doors. "Come and tell us how you beat Dankhart and the monsoon mongrels."

Edmund Croxley, Jonathon Hake, and Violet Quinn were all beckoning him over to their tables.

Angus waved back and smiled. "I'll tell you later, okay? There's something I want to do first."

He hurried down the spiral stairs that led to the lightning cubs' living quarters, immensely glad to find his bedroom had survived the ordeal intact. He raced into the Pigsty, where Dougal, who had clearly got wind of his release from the sanatorium, was already waiting with steaming mugs of hot chocolate. And sitting in a chair next to the fire . . .

"Indigo!"

Her face looked pale and tired. Her arm was in a cast, and the lightning burns on her neck had only just started to heal. They would leave a permanent scar, he realized, an everlasting reminder of her amazing bravery and loyal friendship.

"When did Doctor Fleagal let you out?" Angus asked, feeling extremely pleased to see her at last. "Are you all right? How do you feel?"

Indigo nodded. "I'm fine. I wanted to come and see you, but Doctor Fleagal wouldn't let me out of my room."

"She only turned up here ten minutes ago, so we waited," Dougal said, handing him a mug. "You've both missed loads of stuff while you've been up in the sanatorium," he told them excitedly as they settled themselves before the cozy fire. "Dark-Angel's announced that she's retiring, for a start."

"You're kidding!" Angus almost choked on his hot chocolate.

"She says she wants to spend more time with her brother, but I reckon she's just had enough of Theodore Twill and Nicholas Grubb and all the food fights in the kitchens. Plus, I think she feels bad about almost getting you and your fire dragon killed. Rogwood's taking over, so things are definitely looking up around here."

Angus grinned.

"The weather's still doing strange things," Dougal said. "There was a snowstorm in the boys' bathrooms yesterday evening. We were having a brilliant snowball fight until Catcher Mint came storming in and broke it all up."

"Storming?" Angus said, grinning at Dougal's choice of words.

"Oh, and I almost forgot, the best news of all!" Dougal paused for dramatic effect. "Valentine Vellum is being transferred to a tiny Exploratorium in Belgium for three years. Turns out he's been blackmailing Dark-Angel for ages."

Angus stared at Dougal in shock.

"But how do you know?" Indigo asked.

"I heard Jeremius telling Rogwood in the kitchens. Apparently, Vellum accidentally found out that Dark-Angel had been meeting with monsoon mongrels and had some connection with your dear old uncle Scabby. He's been threatening to tell everyone else unless Dark-Angel let him attend all the important meetings at Perilous and put him in charge of the Lightnarium."

"That explains why he always knew what was going on," Indigo said.

"Yeah." Dougal nodded. "And then he told Pixie and Percival everything."

"Are those two gargoyles being transferred, too?" Angus asked hopefully.

But Dougal shook his head. "Dark-Angel's letting them stay on. I think she's hoping to discover some hidden brains somewhere. It's a hopeless task, if you ask me. I'm amazed she didn't sack Vellum, though, for being such a jerk."

"What about Castle Dankhart?" Indigo asked, shivering as she said it. "Doctor Fleagal wouldn't let anyone talk about it in the sanatorium, in case it upset me."

Dougal leaned over the side of his chair and grabbed a copy of the *Weathervane*. "The latest edition came out this morning. You won't believe what the castle looks like now."

On the front cover was a graphic picture of the dark castle. The total destruction of the lightning tower had also caused most of the building to collapse. It now looked like a crumbling ruin that might have been standing empty and abandoned for hundreds of years. Only a thin column of rising smoke and some twisted scraps of tower gave its violent fate away.

"Most of the monsoon mongrels have already fled from the island, but Jeremius says Dark-Angel's promised to hunt them down and make them pay for everything they've done," Dougal explained.

"So, what happens now?" Angus asked, sipping his hot chocolate thoughtfully.

"It's business as usual, of course," Dougal said, grinning. "There's a big feature in the *Weathervane* about sudden spontaneous snow swamps in Yorkshire. Just because Dankhart's gone it doesn't mean the weather's going to start behaving itself. And Catcher Sparks is sending us to the Lightnarium for lightning identification classes next week, so we'd better get reading up on strike patterns and stuff. I reckon we could teach her a thing or two about lightning after everything we've been through. That's if you still want to stay at Perilous." Dougal suddenly looked uncertain. "I mean, nobody would blame you if you never wanted to see another lightning storm again."

For the first time ever, Angus considered the possibility of a life without Perilous. He could attend a normal school on the mainland, where nobody would try to make him clean out storm drains. Lessons in math, English, and geography would replace hazardous classes in cold weather survival, dodging the deadly seven, and iceberg hopping. His fire dragon could sleep peacefully inside his chest without ever being called on to save his friends from lethal storms full of lightning tarantulatis. . . . And life would be duller than a whole year's worth of lectures on vapor sickness with Miss DeWinkle.

"So?" asked Dougal, watching him anxiously, his mug suspended halfway to his mouth. "Are you staying at Perilous, or what?"

Indigo smiled and nodded once. Angus grinned at his two best friends. It was impossible to imagine life without staring at the wonders of ancient rain or discussing the latest explosions in the experimental division with Jeremius, Gudgeon, and Rogwood. And now that his mum and dad had returned safely to Perilous where they belonged . . .

"Of course I'm staying," Angus said, plumping his cushion and settling himself down into his armchair. "Germ's just told me where we can get our hands on another jar of storm fluff."